Charleston's Lonely Heart Hotel

Charleston's Lonely Heart Hotel

Steve Brown

CHICK SPRINGS
PUBLISHING™
SOUTH CAROLINA

Copyright Steve Brown 2011

Cover design by Heineman Design
Copyright Steve Brown 2011

First published in the USA in 2011 by
Chick Springs Publishing
PO Box 1130, Taylors, SC 29687
E-mail: ChickSprgs@aol.com
Web Site: www.chicksprings.com

Library of Congress Control Number: 2011916523
Library of Congress Data Available

ISBN: 978-0-9839824-0-1

10   9   8   7   6   5   4   3   2   1

Author's Note

This is a work of fiction. Names, characters, places, and incidents are products of the author's imagination or are used fictitiously. Any resemblance to actual events, specific locales, organizations, or persons, living or dead, is entirely coincidental and beyond the intent of either the author or the publisher.

Acknowledgments

For their assistance in preparing this story, I would like to thank Julie Bailey, Hank Brown, Mark Brown, Sonya Caldwell, Sharon Gilstrap, Sally Heineman, Missy Johnson, Stacey King, Kate Lehman, Stacey Randall, Susan Snowden, Helen Turnage, Ellis Vidler, Dwight Watt, and, of course, Mary Ella.

For
Jason Annan and
Pamela Gabriel
Keeping alive the memory of the
Cooper River Bridge
(1928–1929)

THE GIRLS:

Hartleigh Randolph	Daughter of Elizabeth
Elizabeth Randolph	Mother of Hartleigh and Mary Anne
Rachel Belle	Franklin Belle's sister
Sue Ellen Stuart	James Stuart's sister
Laurens Rutledge	Lawrence's pregnant wife
Polly Blount	Engaged to Prescott Mitchell
Abigail Mullins	Engaged to Nicholas Eaton

THE ENGINEERS:

James Stuart	West Point
Franklin Belle	Citadel
Nicholas Eaton	MIT
Lawrence Rutledge	Clemson
Edmund Hall	NC State
Prescott Mitchell	Georgia Tech
Christian Andersen	University of Chicago

OTHERS:

John Patrick Grace	Bridge promoter
John Jacob Boozer	YMCA director
Jeb Stuart	James Stuart's father
Nicholas Eaton, Sr.	Nick's father
Susan Chase	Baker's daughter
Artie Moultrie	Sandhog
Alexander	Randolphs' servant
Pearl	Alexander's wife
Molly	Pearl's sister
Dory	Runaway

"The business of women is families."

—Rachel Belle

ONE

"I'm moving in with your girlfriend," said James Stuart.

"What?" asked Franklin Belle, bringing along his drink and his walking stick and following his friend across the crowded floor of the speakeasy. They were headed for a back room where card games were usually played. "What'd you say?"

The two young men were in a "blind tiger," one of many speakeasies in Charleston. It was December of 1927, and with Prohibition being the law of the land, blind tigers were doing a land-office business. And it wasn't just liquor. Any blind tiger worth its salt provided a decent jazz combo, a tiny dance floor, and a buffet. And when you patronized a "blind tiger," you were paying for the opportunity to see a nonexistent animal, not the complimentary drinks or the food on the buffet.

James stuck his cigarette in the corner of his mouth and twisted the doorknob. "You won't marry her, so you have no claim on her, nor can you object to her future living arrangements."

Franklin glanced around to see if anyone might've overheard. James had just returned from living up north and wasn't as protective as he should have been of the girl next door.

It didn't appear anyone had heard, but once they were in the back room, Franklin intended to remind James not to allow the looseness of their surroundings to influence him; those at any blind tiger acted like they were eager to blow the roof off the joint. Or perhaps it was all the newcomers in town. These days, Franklin could go anywhere in the city of his birth, a place he had lived all his life, and never see a familiar face.

In the back room a large black man was wiping off the poker table and a buffet had been laid out. Among the trays of food were champagne bottles in ice buckets, glass pitchers full of martinis, and several small silver trays filled with cigarettes. The sound of the band followed them through the door until Franklin closed it.

"If it makes you feel any better," said James, "I won't be the only guy living with Hartleigh. I've signed up four others, and another's bringing along his wife."

Franklin didn't know what to say, and he certainly wasn't going to argue in front of the help.

"Evening, Mister Belle," said the black man, tossing the cloth over his shoulder. He wore the white jacket of the servant class.

"Evening, Alexander."

The Negro picked up a green tablecloth from one of the chairs, unfolded it, and snapped out the cloth, allowing the fabric to float down over the table. Once the cloth was smoothed to his satisfaction, Alexander took a stack of heavy glass ashtrays and placed them around the table.

"I put these out, and you're all set." Inclining his head toward the opposite wall, Alexander added, "Extra folding chairs against the wall and a couple of card tables if you need them, but I should be able to collect all their coats as they come through the door."

James nodded approvingly. "Bring them back as they arrive. No stops at the bar." He put down his martini glass on the far side of the table and snubbed out his cigarette in one of the large ashtrays. Looking up, he asked, "Will you recognize them?"

"James," said Alexander with a small laugh, "I met most of them at the train station when they arrived."

Another trait of his friend's that concerned Franklin Belle: James's familiarity with the servants. Yes, James had grown up with Alexander, but still . . .

Before he left, Alexander placed a single ashtray and several packs of matches on each of two tall tables at the end of the buffet. At these tables people could stand, chat, and whine about their losses at the poker table.

Once the door closed, quieting the jazz band again, Franklin leaned his cane against a chair, put down his glass on the cloth-covered table, and took a seat opposite James.

He took out a pipe and began to fill it from a pouch. "This is more than a simple welcome-to-Charleston party, isn't it?"

"Yes, it is. The newcomers need to know the lay of the land. You only get put in jail for public drunkenness, propositioning a girl on a street corner, or shooting craps in some dark alleyway, and the engineers need to know that. John Patrick went to a lot of trouble getting us these jobs. We can't afford to disappoint him."

"It's his bridge. He can do whatever he wishes."

"Within six million dollars, he can."

Franklin stopped tamping his pipe. "But if the company comes up short, the state and county will certainly make up the difference."

"This is a toll bridge, Franklin, built by people who want to sell lots on the Isle of Palms. It has to pay its way." Leaning back in his chair, James took his empty martini glass by the stem and twisted the glass one way, then another.

"Is there any possibility of federal money? The navy built that huge shipyard here." Franklin picked up a book of matches, tore one from the pack, and closed the pack.

"Federal, state, and county—they don't do anything but create headaches." James looked up from twisting the stem of the martini glass. "There's not to be any low-level structure with mechanical spans that have to be raised or lowered when ships enter or depart the harbor; no swing bridges like the ones beginning to dot the Intracoastal Waterway."

Franklin lit his pipe and sucked on it until he got it going. He let out a smoke-filled breath. "You know, James, we'll be one of the last generations to remember the river without a bridge."

The two young men had grown up along the Battery. They had played together as children, chased the Randolph twins through Battery Park on bicycles, and double-dated when they finally realized they would like to catch one of those girls. Well, at least James had wanted to catch one.

James stuck his little finger in the vest pocket of his suit and fingered out a diamond ring. "Franklin, are you planning on asking for Hartleigh's hand?"

"What? What did you say?"

James repeated the question.

"I'm not sure that's any of your business." Franklin leaned back in his chair and drew on his pipe.

"I could help you with this." He leaned over and placed the ring in the middle of the table.

Franklin peered at the stone. It sparkled in the light. "Is that an engagement ring?"

"You've lived down the street from her all your life and you still don't know if you care about Hartleigh or not."

"James, what's your interest in this?"

His friend pushed back from the table. "I don't want to see you lose Hartleigh as I did Mary Anne."

"Even if you do have my best interests at heart, you simply don't rush things like this. Perhaps you've been away too long."

"True, but we turn thirty next year. Maybe we should take a wife before Charleston's overrun by all these out-of-towners."

Franklin said nothing, only puffed on his pipe. Franklin Belle was a true bon vivant, living the good life with plenty of family money to smooth out the bumps in the road. If Franklin Belle thought a wife could assist him in that journey, then he could cast his line into the pool of young women living south of Broad and the chosen one would consider it her birthright. Any girl living north of Broad would consider his proposal a great honor.

The Belles were Huguenots, driven out of France over two hundred years ago; James Stuart's lineage rested on more questionable grounds. The first Stuart had arrived in Charleston as a pirate, then became a pirate hunter, and later started what would become the largest shipping line in the American South.

Yet, despite the Stuarts' success as blockade runners, most of their ships had been destroyed by the Union navy, just as the Belles' rice plantation had been laid to waste by the Union's army. Fortunately for both families, Charleston never had much of a tradition when it came to hometown banking, so a good amount of the families' fortunes had been in banks up north or some offshore island. This allowed both families to land on their feet after war, reconstruction, and a multitude of financial panics.

Now these two young men could pick and choose, not only among the beauties of Charleston, but from careers outside the realm of the mercantile. Both young men had chosen to become civil engineers, and up to a few weeks ago, Franklin had been working in his father's architectural firm while James had finished work on the Carquinez Bridge in California, the largest bridge west of the Mississippi. And the girls, well, they were doing what Charleston ladies had done for centuries: waiting to be chosen.

But almost overnight the boy-girl equation had been upended by the sheer number of young men flowing into town. Now there was no reason to accept the first proposal that came along. If they chose to, and many did, the young ladies of Charleston could break off their engagements and go dancing for the next couple of years.

James picked up his glass, left the diamond ring on the table, and went to the buffet where he poured another drink. With his back to Franklin, he asked, "Remember the ferry that went down several years ago in the harbor?"

"Of course I do. I was here."

"Mary Anne, her father, and her brother were on that ferry. Hartleigh and her mother only escaped because they were at home down with the flu."

"Truly a tragedy."

James faced his friend. "If I hadn't gone to West Point, Mary Anne Randolph would be alive today."

"And what could you've done? How would you have known to even be on that particular ferry?"

James returned to his chair. "I'd do anything to help Hartleigh and her mother, but I don't want to run over you in the process."

Franklin had returned his pipe to his mouth. Now he removed it. "Oh, please, don't be so melodramatic."

James leaned back in his chair, thinking, considering, and wondering. "Mary Anne and I were lovers, in every sense of the word. Whenever I returned to Charleston, we'd find places where we could shuck our clothing and get down to business."

Franklin wasn't sure he'd heard correctly.

"I never told you because it wasn't any of *your* business."

"You and Mary Anne Randolph—really?"

"First time it happened," said James, staring at the ring, "I wanted to go to her father and ask for her hand, but Mary Anne pointed out that I couldn't finish at West Point if I was married. We agreed I should finish my schooling, and during summer leave we'd be engaged, then marry after graduation.

But the ferry went down at Easter."

Twisting the stem of his glass again, James added, "I might not've been able to save her whole family, but if I'd attended the Citadel instead of West Point, I would've been in Charleston."

"James, I don't think I follow."

"You really think I would've allowed my girl to go to Sullivan's Island without me? Boys would've been all over her."

Franklin couldn't believe what he was hearing. Was it possible that his friend had seduced one of the neighborhood girls? That wasn't how things were done. If you want to hustle a dame, you pick one living west of the Ashley.

Gesturing at the ring, James added, "And with all the engineers descending on Charleston to begin the surveying, you still think you can take your own sweet time courting Hartleigh."

Once, when he and Mary Anne had lain in each other's arms, Mary Anne had suggested a double wedding, if Franklin would only propose to her twin. James had laughed and told her Franklin wasn't that bold. It might be years before Franklin felt the stars were properly aligned.

"Besides," he had whispered in Mary Anne's ear, "I'm not slowing down for Franklin to catch up. And I'm certainly not backing up."

James picked up the ring, tossed it into the air, and caught it. "Like many businessmen, Hartleigh's father was overextended. Creditors seized his business, and they would've taken the house, but the court frowns on widows and their children being thrown into the street."

Franklin puffed on his pipe as he watched the

ring being put away. "I'll have to take issue with you about their plight. The Randolphs appear to be renovating. I saw new commodes being delivered just the other day."

"That's my doing, under the auspices of the Cooper River Bridge Company."

"Your doing? Why would you be installing commodes in the Randolphs' house?"

"For the engineers. They can't all use the downstairs half-bath, and Mrs. Randolph certainly isn't going to allow them upstairs where she and Hartleigh live."

Franklin laid his pipe in an ashtray. "Are the Randolphs serious about turning their home into a boarding house?"

"Franklin, have you not considered the number of young men required to build this bridge?"

"Of course, but the Randolphs live south of Broad. What will the neighbors think? What will your family think? What will my family think?"

James leaned into the table. "Franklin, listen to me. You need to ask for Hartleigh's hand before those out-of-towners realize she's up for grabs. If I learned anything living up north, it was that Yankees might not be all that polite, but they are damn efficient."

"I don't know. I can't imagine my family agreeing to a union under such circumstances."

There was a knock at the door, and the sounds of jazz followed Alexander and a young couple into the room. Prescott Mitchell, a graduate of Georgia Tech, was accompanied by his fiancée, Polly Blount. But before introductions could be made, another young man came through the door right behind them: a short, stocky fellow with wiry blond hair.

The stocky young man looked from one man to the other as the two men at the table rose to their feet. "James Stuart?"

"That would be me," said James, coming around the table and offering his hand.

"Nicholas Eaton." Names and handshakes were exchanged, with Nicholas adding, "Nice to meet you" to Polly.

Hearing the newcomer's accent, Prescott asked, "Yankee, are you?"

"Yeah," said Nicholas, giving Prescott the eye. "My father said I might have trouble with you Rebs."

Prescott pulled out a chair. "Bound to happen."

"Well," said Polly, settling into the chair, "I'm from Missouri and we're used to dealing with Rebs. They're thick as thieves in the lower part of the state." Polly was a plain girl with no distinguishing features, but she did have a lovely smile. "I attended Randolph Macon with Prescott's sister." She turned that smile on James. "So you're the one I have to thank for this job?"

"What she means," said Prescott, "is that I was ready to take a steamer to Australia when I received your telegram. I was going to spend the next few years building bridges in Australia."

"He promised to send for me," said Polly.

"Well, of course," reassured her fiancé.

Polly didn't appear all that reassured. She wore no engagement ring.

Nicholas clapped his hands and rubbed them together. "You really believe we can bring this project in under six million dollars?"

"Have to," said James. "It's all the money John Patrick could raise."

"You sent him a copy of the plans?" asked Franklin.

"Well, I didn't think anyone from MIT was coming south unless I showed him the goods. Eaton's top in his class."

Franklin studied the Yankee. "Where are you from, if I might ask?"

"Lowell, Massachusetts. Family's lived there since the first textile mills came to town. Now that the mills have expanded into the South, that's another reason I'm here." Nicholas grinned. "You'll probably need a bunch of new mills after I finish with this bridge, and this way I get a leg up on the competition."

He turned his attention to Polly Blount. "There must be some dames you could introduce me to while I'm down here." Yes, thought Nicholas, a replacement for the one who wouldn't move south and live among a bunch of bumpkins.

"Sorry," said Polly, returning his smile, "but this is my first visit to South Carolina."

"My grandmother was originally from Lowell," said Franklin.

"Then how'd she get down here?" asked Nicholas. "That must've been about the time of the Civil War."

"The War Between the States," said Prescott from the buffet, "if you want to keep your teeth." He was filling a plate for his fiancée.

Heads turned as Alexander opened the door again and escorted a young woman into the room to the sounds of more jazz. Everyone stared at this girl, who had the same coloration as Franklin: coal black hair, bright blue eyes, and pale skin. She was gorgeous, and it wasn't only men who realized it.

As a member of an old-line Charleston family,

Rachel Belle was haughty and imperious; still, with the number of cute engineers her brother had brought home for dinner lately, Rachel was having second thoughts about being considered stuck up.

She was followed by Lawrence Rutledge and his pregnant wife, Laurens. When Lawrence had married Laurens Pinckney, he'd connected two of the oldest and most prominent families in South Carolina.

This, however, did not put off Franklin. "James, I thought you only wanted the best."

"You watch out, Franklin," cautioned Lawrence. "Clemson may have lost to the Citadel, but we beat Erskine, Wofford, and Carolina."

"Football?" demanded a boyish young woman who followed the last couple through the door. She was James's sister, Sue Ellen, and one of the girls who had broken off her engagement when all these young men had begun to descend on Charleston. Growing up, her friends knew that Sue Ellen would be the first in line for any game, the first to kiss a boy, the first to allow a boy to get to second base, or go all the way. They just hoped she would share the details. "I was promised dancing, not football."

"That goes for me, too," said the attractive young lady accompanying her.

Hartleigh Randolph's temperament paired up nicely with the vivacious Sue Ellen Stuart, as she was the quiet twin of the deceased Mary Anne. But in an age that put a premium on boyish figures, including winding strips of cloth around their chests to flatten their bosoms, the Randolph twins had been a throwback to the era of the Gibson Girl with ample bosom, hips, and bottom.

But all these young ladies were au courant when

it came to fashion, dressing more to reveal than to conceal. For this reason, they had checked their coats at the door to better display their knee-length, high-waisted, sleeveless chemise dresses, which allowed more freedom of movement on the dance floor; cloche hats kept their bobbed hair in place. Their young men wore three-piece suits, ties tucked into vests, and baggy trousers. Only Franklin had arrived in a tux, one with shortened tails, and had also checked his coat and top hat at the door.

When Sue Ellen saw her brother was incapable of introducing Hartleigh to the rest of the group, she performed the task, warning the engineers that her friend would rule their household with an iron fist. It was enough to cause the poor girl to blush. Hartleigh was nothing like that, closer to being a wallflower.

The last engineer, Edmund Hall, of North Carolina State, joined them. Once introductions were made, Rachel, Sue Ellen, and Hartleigh joined Polly and Laurens at the table. More than one inquired about the baby, especially the due date. Right there and then, Sue Ellen volunteered for "babysitting duty," and Hartleigh offered to pour a drink and fetch a cigarette from the buffet.

Laurens accepted the babysitting offer but refused the drink and cigarettes, saying she had given up liquor and smokes "until I deliver this baby." And as Rachel Belle listened to the conversation, she realized these girls planned to move into the Randolphs' boarding house and live on the second floor.

It was the most outlandish idea Rachel had ever heard. What must these girls be thinking? What must their parents have been thinking to agree to such a proposal? And why hadn't she been invited?

Soon the room was filled with smoke and laughter and the glasses filled with martinis. Even Nicholas Eaton of Massachusetts felt right at home. He thought Franklin's sister, Rachel, particularly attractive and sufficient reason to forget any girl back home. Then, after cracking the door to allow the sound of the jazz band into the room, Sue Ellen Stuart took Nicholas's hand and pulled him into an empty corner.

She grinned at him. "I have to evaluate your skills, Nicholas, not as an engineer but as a dancer."

Edmund Hall had had his eye on Sue Ellen, but now she was taken, or had she chosen Nicholas Eaton? It was hard to tell.

Rachel Belle was led into another corner by Lawrence Rutledge at the encouragement of his wife, who began to tap her foot in rhythm to the music through the cracked door. Lawrence and Rachel were quickly followed to the dance floor by Prescott Mitchell and Polly Blount, and unaware of the furtive looks given James Stuart by Hartleigh Randolph, Edmund Hall took the girl's hand and pulled her onto the crowded dance floor.

At first, Hartleigh resisted, but Edmund said, "No, no, kiddo. It's your job to welcome me to Charleston."

Hartleigh smiled, then enthusiastically began dancing the Charleston.

Everyone was sipping martinis and eating finger food, or discussing the stock market or last season's football results, when a balding middle-aged man entered the smoke-filled room and closed the door behind him.

"Ladies and gentlemen, I am John Patrick Grace— the reason you're all here in Charleston."

TWO

A whistle sounded at six the following morning, and a thin, short, middle-aged man entered the engineers' sleeping quarters on the ground floor of the Randolphs' house. There, he blew the whistle a second time. Some of the men merely sat up, some swung their feet over the side of their bed; others groaned and rose up on their elbows; one of them didn't remember where he was, examining the oddly elegant bunk room that had once been a reception hall. Most of the engineers wore pajamas, though Edmund Hall wore a sleeping gown and cap he would soon discard. Radiators kept the room toasty warm on a chilly day.

"Good morning, gentlemen," said the short, thin man, after rolling the pocket doors back into the walls. The whistle-blowing intruder stood in the wide doorway leading in from the hall, his feet apart, whistle on a lanyard, and parlor behind him. He wore a lightweight sweater, knickers, long stockings, and sneakers.

"What time is it?" muttered a couple of the engineers.

"When I blow the whistle, you are to immediately dress and, after a visit to the toilet, line up on the walkway in front of the house. This should not be all that difficult since most of you attended military schools."

When two of the young men fell back in their beds, he blew the whistle again. Upstairs, a woman shrieked; downstairs, the men hustled out of bed.

"At the end of your bed, on the trunk, is a pile of clothing for your exercise routine: a light sweater, knickers, long socks, and a pair of sneakers. This clothing has been provided by the Charleston YMCA. Treat it as if it were your very own, gentlemen. You will not receive another set."

"Just who the hell are you?"

Another blow of the whistle and several of the engineers stuck their fingers in their ears. Again, a woman shrieked upstairs.

"There will be no cursing or profanity in this house, and I assume Captain Stuart told you: no drinking or smoking."

Everyone looked at James, who was busily pulling on his knickers.

"Smoking is frowned upon but allowed outside. Drinking is not allowed on the premises unless sanctioned by Mrs. Randolph. As for me, I am John Jacob Boozer. My ancestors arrived on the *Eagle* in 1736 and settled along the Congaree River. I have been assigned to the Cooper River Bridge Company for the next two years to make it easier for you to sit for hours at a desk and work for long hours during a long, hot Charleston summer. We will follow this schedule six days a week, and it goes without saying that everyone will attend church on Sunday. The week between Christmas and New Year's, you will have off."

Pointing down the row of wooden-framed beds dominating the former reception room, Boozer added, "The last bed is mine. If you have messages for me, or if you decide to move to other quarters, leave that information and your exercise clothing there. Beyond that far set of pocket doors, you'll find armoires, dresser drawers, and your footlockers and suitcases."

He watched the young men hustle into their clothing or lace up their sneakers. "There is no mail call. You will find letters, telegrams, or packages left on your bed. If there is no mail, then you did not receive any, despite how often that old flame of yours promised to write while you were away."

A nervous laugh ran through the room.

"Outgoing mail can be left on the table near the door in the foyer. Breakfast is at seven sharp, lunch at noon, supper at six. This is a schedule running about an hour or so earlier than the locals, but you have a bridge to build, so for the next couple of years this house shall run on what I call 'fast time.'"

Most everyone was dressed now.

"No food or drink is allowed in this room or we'll be inundated with all manner of creatures that make Charleston their home. And the radio"—he pointed at an Emerson console model across the hallway in the parlor—"is to be turned off at ten sharp."

As the engineers filed out of the room and headed toward the rear of the house, Boozer finished with, "These pocket doors are always to be pulled together—

they roll out of the walls like this—whenever any of you disrobes. You are also obligated to pull the curtains on all windows, if they are ever left open. You are living in Charleston and the rules of decorum shall be strictly observed. It goes without saying that men are not allowed on the second floor, the only exception being workmen, priests, or preachers, and they will be escorted by either Mrs. Randolph or her daughter."

And the priests and preachers came, many for a good meal, or, in most cases, to examine the first house they had ever been admitted to along Charleston's famed Battery.

The engineers filed through the screened door of the back porch, down the steps, and across the backyard. To the left, they saw Alexander sitting on the second-floor porch of the carriage house, drinking a cup of coffee. There was no motor car or carriage parked underneath; extra furniture had been stored there for the duration. The building the young men were headed for dated back to a day when kitchens were required by law to be built of brick and housed in separate buildings at least ten feet away from the main structure. Inside the former kitchen were showers, sinks, and commodes. When finished with their toilet, the engineers formed up at the front of the house, then crossed the street and entered Battery Park, a chilly wind off the harbor welcoming them to Charleston.

There they went through a series of calisthenics, including jumping jacks, squat thrusts, and duck-walks—to the great amusement of men heading to work. The catcalls and jeers were enough to make the engineers wonder if there was actually a shortage of quarters in Charleston; that is, until a University of Chicago and a Carnegie-Mellon engineer asked if they could join them. They even participated in the mile run, though they had already hiked the entire length of the Battery wall.

After the run, one of the young men asked, "Mind if we join you tomorrow, you know, beginning with the calisthenics?"

Nicholas Eaton, bent over, forearms on knees, and puffing, looked up. "You want to do this again?"

"I don't want to do any of this, but my father's a lifelong engineer and from all the sitting over the years, he can't walk down the street to the corner grocery."

"Then we'll see you in the morning," said James.

"Where you guys bunking?" asked Carnegie-Mellon.

James gestured at the Randolph house.

"With girls?" asked the Chicago grad.

Through the trees, James saw two girls leaning against the railing of the second-story porch and waving to the returning engineers. If he wasn't mistaken, one of them was his sister.

"What is that place?" asked the Carnegie-Mellon grad. "Some high-class bordello?"

"Hardly," said James, trying to keep an even tone in his voice. "Men are forbidden upstairs."

The Chicago grad, a fellow with thick, blond hair and good cheek bones, waved to the girls. "Oh, I'm sure you are, and for good reason."

"Well," said the engineer from Carnegie-Mellon, "see you in the morning."

His companion smiled as the breeze tossed his blonde hair around. "Perhaps even sooner."

THREE

A message waited for James on a pad at the telephone in the hallway. John Patrick Grace expected to see him at his law office at eight sharp and to bring along one of his fellow engineers. So, after showering and shaving, James dropped by the dining room. The girls had decided to join the engineers for breakfast and were seated around a table that would seat eighteen.

John Jacob Boozer chided James for missing grace, then returned to a conversation with Hartleigh Randolph about the stock market. John Jacob was having a hard time making up his mind as to whether it was too late to get in or not.

Through a swinging door leading to the kitchen, Hartleigh's mother brought a coffee pot. Elizabeth Randolph was followed by a little black boy and his sister; he carrying a plate of biscuits, she a silver cup filled with cream, both of which they placed in the middle of the long table.

Alexander's wife, Pearl, came through the swinging door, grabbed the two children, and dragged them back into the kitchen. "What you children doing out here?"

"We want to work," said the boy, indignantly.

"Your work is at school today."

"I want a job," said the boy, disappearing behind the swinging door. "I want to make some money."

At the far end of the table, Sue Ellen was in an animated conversation with the engineer from MIT. The chair beside Hartleigh was open and she asked James to join them. He didn't appear to hear her as he headed around the table to his sister.

Sue Ellen smiled up at her brother. "Good morning, James."

"Nicholas," said James, "I don't want to interrupt your breakfast—"

"Then don't," said Sue Ellen, continuing to smile.

James saw Hartleigh gesturing at the empty chair beside her. "Oh, good morning, Hartleigh."

"Good morning, James."

Hartleigh's mother gave her a severe look, and when Hartleigh saw this, she returned her attention to John Jacob. "I can't see girls performing calisthenics. We get all the exercise we need on the dance floor."

At the other end of the table, Sue Ellen turned up her cheek. "Morning kiss, James?"

"What?" He glanced around the table. Other than the Yankee, none of the men appeared to be watching, so he bent down and gave his sister a peck on the cheek. Jeez, he had to get his sister out of here.

"I'm heading over to John Patrick's office. Would you like to come along?"

When his sister frowned at the suggestion, James quickly added, "He asked me to bring along another engineer and you expressed an interest in our budgetary constraints. I believe some of the out-of-town investors will be there."

"You're not sure?" asked his sister.

"What?" asked James. What business was it of hers?

"Oh, come on, James. Nick doesn't have to report for work until tomorrow. Let him enjoy the day."

Nick?

Sue Ellen gestured at the seat on the other side of her. "Sit down and enjoy your breakfast. I'm sure Mister Grace can wait."

"But can those out-of-town investors?"

"You're not even sure they'll be there."

James hadn't eaten since last night and those buttermilk biscuits looked pretty good. "Well, maybe a biscuit with honey."

Sue Ellen pulled the plate over and reached for the honey. With practiced ease, she slit open the biscuit and slathered it with honey.

She held out her empty hand. "Handkerchief, please."

Nicholas realized that Sue Ellen wanted *his* handkerchief. He jerked it from an inside pocket.

Sue Ellen reached for the handkerchief then stopped. "Oh, how silly of me." She pulled a lace handkerchief from inside her bosom. "I have one of my own." And before her brother could object, she had wrapped Nicholas's biscuit in her handkerchief and handed it to him.

Nicholas thanked her, pushed back his chair, and stood up.

"Don't forget to return it," said Sue Ellen, smiling impishly. "It was a gift from my mother and I wouldn't want to have to tell her that I lost it to a Yankee."

"Oh, yes, yes, I will—the very next time I see you."

"That would be lunch," said Sue Ellen, still smiling. She looked at her brother. "Isn't that so, James?"

"We may eat downtown," said James, a flatness in his voice.

"Not with all these new people in town you won't. Nick, you're paying for three meals a day, and I insist you receive your money's worth. Supper is oxtail soup, pork, boiled potatoes, steamed asparagus, and salad. Lunch will be much more ordinary fare, but there's pie."

"Then I'll make sure I'm here." Nicholas glanced at the biscuit wrapped in the girl's handkerchief. "Aren't you preparing one for your brother?"

"It's not necessary. James has been fixing biscuits all his life."

And James pulled Nicholas from the room, where, in the hallway, they ran into Franklin Belle with his sister on his arm.

"Where you two headed?" asked Franklin.

James explained.

Franklin glanced at his sister.

"Oh, do run along, brother dear," said Rachel, patting his arm. She saw the handkerchief. "Mister Eaton, what in the world are you doing with a lady's handkerchief?"

"James's sister prepared this biscuit for me." Nicholas made to peel back the handkerchief, but Rachel held up her hand.

"I've seen biscuits before," said the Belle of

Charleston before disappearing in the dining room.

On the way out the front door, everyone picked up their hats; Franklin grabbed his walking stick and Nicholas took a letter from inside his coat pocket and laid it on the table. The letter was to the girl back home, relating how easily he was adjusting to life south of the Mason-Dixon Line. The Rebs had gone out of their way to make him feel at home, especially the young ladies.

On the front porch Edmund Hall was snubbing out a cigarette and Alexander was walking around the postage-stamp-size front yard, picking up butts. The large Negro reached over the railing and offered his bucket to the young man from NC State. Edmund looked at the butt smeared across the deck, bent over, and picked it up. He dropped the butt into the metal bucket, and Alexander thanked him and returned to patrolling the yard.

"Where you going?" Edmund asked the three engineers.

"Have to run an errand," said James.

Edmund grinned. "You did leave some breakfast, I hope."

"And all the girls," said Nicholas.

Edmund pulled up short at the front door. "The girls are eating with the engineers?"

"Yes," said James, "and some of them have their own agenda." He went down the steps and into the breeze off the harbor. Not enough for an overcoat but still chilly.

Coming up the sidewalk were the engineers from the University of Chicago and Carnegie-Mellon.

"What are you two doing here?"

"Didn't you say this was a boarding house?"

James glanced over his shoulder. "Er...yes. I guess so."

"Well, any food's better than what they're serving at the Francis Marion."

Alexander laughed, and in a low voice no one could hear, said, "And here we go."

James glanced at his wristwatch. "Alexander, would you take these gentlemen inside and introduce them to Mrs. Randolph?"

"Yes, sir." The Negro gestured for the two white men to precede him up the stairs and into the house. "I'll tell Miss Elizabeth that they are more of your special friends."

Nicholas and Franklin caught up with James outside the wrought-iron gate where James had run into two young women strolling the sidewalk, parasols in a position to keep the wind off.

"Oh, hello, James," said a blonde, twirling the handle of her parasol, "we heard you were back in town."

James didn't know what to say. He'd never seen these two up before noon.

Franklin introduced Nicholas, adding, "He's from up north."

"Nice to meet you," said the blonde, returning Nick's smile.

The brunette frowned. "I never did understand how you're going to cross the main shipping channel without any supports."

"Oh," said Nicholas, "I'd be happy to explain the concept of the cantilevered truss."

"Why are you two up so early?" demanded James.

The brunette smiled at Nicholas. "We stopped by to welcome this Yankee to Charleston. Neither wind, nor cold, nor gloom of night shall prevent a Charlestonian from being cordial."

"Yes," said the blonde, laughing. "We certainly don't want to be as inhospitable as our grandparents were."

James shook his head and stomped off down the street. Had everyone living south of Broad suddenly gone mad?

"So nice to meet you, ladies," said Nicholas. "I was afraid you gals wouldn't even speak to me."

"Well, we will," giggled the blonde, "if we can understand what you're saying."

"Please call me 'Nick.'"

"We certainly will," said the brunette, demurely, "if you won't think us too forward."

"I never could think that of such charming..."

Franklin tipped his hat. "Ladies..." He took Nicholas's arm and pulled him down the street.

The girls watched them go, Nicholas looking over his shoulder, smiling, and tipping his derby.

Glancing at the Randolphs' house, the blonde asked, "Should we speak to Hartleigh?"

"The least we can do is to leave a card."

"And warm up. It's freezing out here."

The two women headed up the walkway.

"I do believe Sue Ellen spent the night."

"Really?" gasped the blonde. "What will people think?"

"No more than they think of her now, I suppose."

On their way up the steps, the blonde asked, "Don't Yankees talk funny?"

The brunette glanced down the street. "He didn't sound all that funny to me. He sounded kind of cute."

Christian Andersen could do nothing but stare. The most stunning creature sat at the breakfast table: black hair, skin the color of marble, and the clearest blue eyes.

"Chris?" asked his fellow engineer from Carnegie-Mellon.

Andersen did not reply.

"Christian!"

Christian's head snapped around. His friend had already seated himself.

"You here to eat or not?" asked the Carnegie-Mellon engineer.

Evidently, he was here to turn beet red. Good thing he'd been out in the sun lately.

The stunning-looking woman continued to smile as Christian pulled out a chair and took a seat.

"Sorry," said the gorgeous gal, continuing her smile, "but it's boy, girl, boy, girl."

Christian glanced left and right. On one side sat his new buddy from Carnegie-Mellon, on the other a guy with a pregnant wife. Christian knew the guy with the pregnant wife. He had an excellent touch. Almost as good as Franklin Belle, the acknowledged master of the pen and pencil set.

Christian pushed back his chair and got to his feet. When he looked at the gorgeous girl again, she was gesturing to the open chair next to her.

"This seat is open, Mister . . ."

"Christian Andersen. People call me 'Chris.'"

"Please sit here. I'm Rachel Belle."

Christian did, and five minutes later the blue-eyed, blond young man from Wisconsin had told the raven-haired beauty with skin like porcelain everything she wished to know about him.

Four

With her two children in tow, Pearl hurried out of the house, down the steps, and through the gate. A block down the street she caught up with James, Franklin, and Nicholas. The three young men had been joined by the wife of someone with whom Franklin and James had attended the all-male High School of Charleston.

"With all the strangers in town," said the young mother, "I'll have to start taking them to school, and that won't go over well with my husband. Doctors have to make house calls."

"Trolleys?" inquired Franklin.

"Trolleys either make you too early or too late."

"Sounds like you need a school bus," suggested James.

The young mother laughed. "Well, I'm not holding my breath for that."

All four adults and the three children turned around as Pearl thumped to a halt behind them.

"Mister James . . ." Pearl paused to catch her breath. "You've got to take these children...with you. Alexander and I've got too much to do...with all these guests...and Mrs. Randolph said you were going right by the school."

"I don't want to go to school," said the little black boy. "I want to go to work."

Pearl bent down and got in his face. "You listen here, Benjamin, you'll go to school and you'll like it."

"Oh, he'll be just fine," said James, hoisting the boy to his shoulders to straddle his head. "We'll take yours, too, Claire. No reason for you to have to walk home all by yourself."

"Are you sure?" The young mother looked at Franklin and Nicholas. "I thought you had a bridge to build."

"Nothing to worry about," said James. "We don't start surveying until next month. All this is organizational work."

"Yes," said Nicholas, grinning, "but the early bird catches the worm, meaning the best assignment."

Everyone looked at him.

"Sorry," apologized Nicholas, "isn't that something you say down here?"

"We're just surprised to hear you say it down here." Franklin swung Chloe up to his shoulders. "Watch my hat there, girl."

"Thank you, James," said the young mother. To her three, she said, "You children do as Mister Stuart and Mister Belle say."

"And you, too," Pearl ordered her two kids.

"And you, Chloe," asked Franklin as the group set off, "your brother wants a job. What is it you want?"

"I want to be a princess."

Franklin laughed. "Well, that sounds about right."

"I want to be a princess, too," said the little white girl to Nicholas Eaton. "Will you carry me?"

"Of course." Nicholas picked her up, and careful not to knock off his bowler or drop the handkerchief with the biscuit, he placed her on his shoulders. "Every princess should have her own carriage."

The little white girl looked around. "Then where's mine?"

"It's a figure of speech."

"You talk funny."

"Put me down!" said Benjamin, fighting to have James lower him to the sidewalk. "I'm old enough to walk."

The boy knocked the derby from James's head, and the breeze caught it, sending James running down the sidewalk.

"I only go to school because Mama makes me."

"If I was a real princess," said Chloe from Franklin's shoulders, "I wouldn't have to go to school."

"Maybe I could work on the bridge," suggested Benjamin. "Daddy says they're hiring."

"I think you have to be a little older," said Franklin.

"I'm nine years old. There must be something I could do."

"Yes. Stay in school and get your education."

"You don't understand. The bridge is a good opportunity for colored folks."

All three men looked at the boy. James had caught his hat and waited for them to catch up.

"Daddy says even black folks make money in good times, and these are good times."

Neither Nicholas nor James knew what to say.

Franklin did. "You like peanut butter, don't you?"

"For sure."

"George Washington Carver, didn't he invent peanut butter?"

Benjamin viewed him suspiciously. "Is this true or are you making this up?"

"I'm just saying that George Washington Carver needed an education to invent peanut butter and you should get one, too."

"I don't know about that. Peanut butter tastes too good for anyone to need an education. Carver probably mixed it up right in his kitchen."

All three young men laughed.

"It's apparent that this child spends entirely too much time around adults," said Franklin. "Benjamin, when was the last time you went gigging for frogs?"

"Frog gigging? That's for children. I want a job."

Back down the street Pearl and Claire watched the young men and their wards turn north and proceed inland.

"Franklin and James still available?" asked Claire, pulling tight her coat as the breeze off the harbor hit her.

"Yes, ma'am, they are," said Pearl, arms crossing her chest in an attempt to keep warm.

"Well, I know Franklin's a mama's boy, but where's James been hiding all this time?"

"Mister Grace keeps him pretty busy."

"Too busy to attend church Sundays?"

"I believe Mister James catches up on his sleep Sundays."

"So, you can usually find James at home?"

"No, ma'am. The only time Mister James goes home is for Sunday supper when nobody in the family is allowed to discuss the bridge."

Very quickly Claire took the conversation in another direction. "Girls south of Broad—that's all they've been talking about: young men coming to live on the Battery. We're looking at more than one wedding once the bridge is completed."

"Even Mister Nick, the Yankee?" asked Pearl.

"Oh, him most of all. How can any Yankee resist a belle's charms?"

At the offices of Logan and Grace, a group of men expected someone to bring them up to date before the surveying began. These men represented investors in Chicago. The original investors had backed out, so John Patrick Grace had to sweet talk this new group of men into backing a bridge that had doubled in cost before the first piling had been driven. These out-of-towners were in town to see if everyone was singing off the same page of the choir book.

Grace's partner, Turner Logan, took James aside. Logan was a blueblood who had partnered with the working man's hero, John Patrick Grace. A former congressman, Logan knew the Stuarts from his yacht racing days when James's father regularly whipped him with his reckless style of racing. Logan had watched James grow into a formidable competitor, replacing his father on the yachting scene, and it was rumored that when James began to beat Logan, as his father had done before him, that was the source of Senator "Pitchfork Bill" Tillman's recommendation of James Stuart to the military academy at West Point.

Now James was employed as the eyes and ears of the Cooper River Bridge Company, not only because he was an engineer, but because he had access to more than one boat at a time when the only means of crossing the Cooper River was by water.

"Did you have a good breakfast?" asked Logan.

James shook his head. "No time."

"Well, you can't do this on an empty stomach." Logan snapped his fingers and his secretary crossed the room.

"Hattie, would you get this boy a ham biscuit and coffee?"

The secretary nodded and disappeared into the rear of the building. Hattie had come prepared, getting up early this morning and baking biscuits for more than just her family.

Logan gestured at those shaking hands with Franklin Belle and Nicholas Eaton. "They're expecting you to make the presentation."

"Me?" asked James. "But I've never—"

"Spoken to a group of investors?"

"I've explained projects to other engineers and spoken in front of my classmates, but I've never made a speech to important people before."

"So pretend they're engineers."

"For that, Mister Logan, I'd need a blackboard and chalk."

"Good, good." And Logan clapped James on the shoulder. "That'll take a moment to set up. Now you go into my office and eat that biscuit and drink some coffee before you pass out in the middle of your presentation."

FIVE

It took some time for Elizabeth Randolph to corner her daughter, and when she finally found Hartleigh in an upstairs bedroom, she took her daughter's hand and led her onto the second-floor porch, closing the door behind them. The girls in the bedroom watched, then found something else to do. All but Sue Ellen who went to stand at a window that had been raised to allow in some fresh air.

Once outside, Elizabeth did not let go of her daughter's hand but tugged her over to the railing. "Trying to catch the eye of James Stuart? Do you know how that looks?"

"I was just making him feel at home. James hasn't been here for quite some time."

"Then look me in the eye and deny that you weren't flirting with him."

"I just wanted him to have the open chair."

"There were other chairs available."

"Are you saying I can't make the smallest gesture

of kindness toward James? He's setting the proper example for the other engineers by lodging here when he could live on his boat. Don't we owe him something?"

"Others don't see your kindness. They see some sort of perversion."

Hartleigh didn't know what to say.

Her mother left her at the railing, but before she returned through the bedroom door, she said, "Just remember, any favors done for this family by James Stuart are being done for the memory of your sister, not you, so don't make a fool of yourself."

When Sue Ellen heard the door open, she turned away from the window and bent over a suitcase. It wasn't her suitcase, but she didn't think Elizabeth Randolph would know that. Once Mrs. Randolph had left the room, Sue Ellen went out on the second-story porch.

"Are you all right?"

Hartleigh dabbed at her eyes with her handkerchief. "Yes, yes. I'm fine."

This porch was Hartleigh's favorite spot in the whole house. From here, you could overlook the harbor and up and down the street. At one time Hartleigh had considered moving chairs and tables out here, but her mother had nixed that idea. It would be much too common to sit anywhere people could actually see them.

Sue Ellen joined Hartleigh at the railing and put a hand on her shoulder. "I'll help you with James. I've told you that before."

"It's not your brother I have a problem with. It's my mother."

"Hartleigh, I was listening at the window."

Her friend stepped back and the hand fell from her shoulder. "How could you do that?"

"I'm your friend."

"But listening at keyholes...some families have secrets they'd rather not have overheard."

"You're just overly sensitive about taking in boarders, but widows have been doing that ever since the war. The only thing that's different is that you live on the Battery and have a higher class of neighbors to look down their noses at you. But they're really not your friends if they hold this against you, and it's best you learn that now."

Then, in a low voice, Sue Ellen added, "It's not going to be easy, but together we can do this."

"It'll never work," said Hartleigh, looking over South Battery. "People will always talk."

"Oh, come on, do you really think James will remain in Charleston after what happened to your sister? If he wasn't building this bridge, he'd be anywhere but here."

"And here we are, discussing my sister once again." Again she dabbed at her eyes with her handkerchief.

"Hartleigh, you're the only one who can make my brother happy. He needs you."

"Because I favor Mary Anne."

"No. Because my brother's head is all wrapped up in this bridge. It's all he ever talks about. Besides, Mary Anne wasn't right for James."

Hartleigh faced her. "What are you saying? You've never said anything like this before."

"Because you don't care for anyone to talk about your sister."

A pack of cigarettes appeared in her hand. Sue Ellen shook one out and offered it to Hartleigh. Hartleigh waved it off, and Sue Ellen tapped the cigarette against the back of her left hand, inserted the cigarette into her mouth, and scratched a kitchen match across the porch railing. With it, she lit the cigarette, then waved out the match and tossed it into the yard below. Sue Ellen was one of many young women who had been seduced by Lucky Strike's slogan: Reach for a Lucky instead of a sweet.

"Besides, James wasn't returning to Charleston, so why speculate?" After letting out a smoke-filled breath, Sue Ellen looked toward the harbor. "Mary Anne was bold, and she used that boldness to get her hooks into my brother but good."

"What are you insinuating? You don't mean—"

"I don't know what I mean, but James was head over heels."

"That doesn't mean—"

"Oh, come on. You can't say the thought never crossed your mind. It's the mid-nineteen twenties. Women can smoke, drink, be seen in public without an escort—do anything they wish."

"What . . . what are you saying?"

"That if you want my brother for your husband, then we're going to have to have a plan." She drew again from her cigarette and released the smoke through her nose. "We must make James realize you're desirable in your own right, and with all these engineers living here—"

"I won't play the tease."

"Even if Rachel Belle moves in?"

"I'm . . . I'm not sure there's enough room."

"Oh, Hartleigh, your mother would sleep on the

sofa to acquire a guest who'd distract my brother from you, and believe me, Rachel Belle can do that in spades."

"Still," mused Hartleigh, "it would be good for the house to have a Belle living here."

"Oh, my goodness! Must you always be thinking of others?" Sue Ellen glanced at the door leading to the bedroom and took another drag off her cigarette. "Listen to me, Hartleigh. All you have to do is make your guests comfortable—that in itself brings out qualities Mary Anne lacked. Your sister only thought of herself. All four of us, including Rachel, spent years at Ashley Hall and the College of Charleston, and it's never once occurred to you why you and I grew closer and Rachel and Mary Anne grew away. Rachel and Mary Anne were peas in a pod but never the same pod. What you need to understand is that James was too dazzled by Mary Anne to see what a swell girl you are, but you must make the effort."

"Mother won't like this."

"Your mother sees you and my brother remaining in Charleston and raising a family in front of everyone who knew of his previous courtship of your sister. Your mother hasn't realized that my brother can take a job anywhere. Lord knows, I've heard James tell Daddy that on more than one occasion, and it breaks my mother's heart."

Hartleigh faced the harbor. The wind picked at her bangs. "I hate talking about my sister like this. I feel I'm betraying her."

Sue Ellen studied her friend. "Hartleigh, may I ask you a question?"

Her friend laughed. "I'm surprised you asked my permission."

"Have I ever betrayed a confidence of yours?"

"No," said Hartleigh, facing her again, "but you're willing to conspire with me against your brother."

Sue Ellen had inhaled, now she coughed, and Hartleigh had to pound on her back to help Sue Ellen catch her breath.

"You all right?"

Tears formed in Sue Ellen's eyes. She flipped the butt over the railing before dabbing them away. "Yes, yes...I'm okay." She cleared her throat. "I'm not betraying my brother, nor are you betraying the memory of your sister. I'm fixing him up with the one girl who's right for him."

Hartleigh considered this. What could she say? She had had a crush on this girl's brother for as long as she could remember. "What was it you wished to ask me?"

Sue Ellen had to think. "Oh, yes. Do you really think Mary Anne would have wanted James to remain single for the rest of his life, you know, pining away for her?"

"Of course not."

"Well, I know for a fact that my mother hopes and prays that James falls for a local girl. Remember, James didn't have to return to Charleston after working on that bridge in California. He had plenty of offers. So, why's my brother back in town? Is it possible he has unfinished business in Charleston and that you are that unfinished business?"

Six

"The main stumbling block for the project came about when the engineers in the War Department rejected raising and lowering any portion of the bridge, or creating a swing bridge."

One of the moneymen held up a sheet of paper. "Aren't you one of those engineers, Captain Stuart? This short biography furnished by Turner and Logan makes note of your graduating from West Point."

"Harry has a point there," said another man, who directed his comment to John Patrick Grace.

John Patrick rose to the occasion, but his partner pulled him back down in his chair. "They didn't come here to hear your opinion," said Turner Logan. "They already know that."

The eight men sat around a mahogany table in a conference room, its walls decorated with black-and-white photographs of politicians, generals, and athletes, mostly former generals of the Confederate States of America. James Stuart stood before a blackboard set up in the corner; diagonally across the room sat the secretary, Hattie, ready to refill anyone's empty coffee cup.

"So, who do you work for, Captain Stuart?"

"The Cooper River Bridge Company. And you don't have to address me by my former rank. I resigned my commission."

"You're not a spy for the Army Corps of Engineers?"

"What Harry means, young man, is where do your loyalties lie, with us or with the Corps?"

"The Cooper River Bridge Company signs my paycheck."

"Which is as noncommittal as you could be. I still wonder if you're here to monitor this project for the War Department."

"What do you want from the boy?" asked John Patrick from across the table. "A blood oath?"

From there the meeting descended into bickering between Grace and Logan on one side and the moneymen from Chicago on the other. At the far end of the table Nicholas and Franklin shifted around in their chairs as if caught in the middle of a family quarrel.

John Patrick Grace was a self-made man who, during his two terms as mayor, had secured funding for the Memorial Bridge across the Ashley River. His current responsibilities were, as a member of the South Carolina Highway Commission, to develop Highway 40 from Charleston to Georgetown. As a partner in the Cooper River Bridge Company, Grace was also interested in developing the Isle of Palms, which would be enhanced by a bridge over the Cooper River.

As the bickering continued, Nicholas Eaton rose

from his chair. "If I might point out . . . ."

He was ignored.

Nicholas tried again.

He was ignored again.

Finally, Franklin thumped his walking stick on the floor.

Everyone looked down the table.

"Please give Mister Eaton an opportunity to make his point," said Franklin. "We don't want to ignore the boy simply because he's a Yankee."

"We're all Yankees," said one side of the table.

"Even more reason for you to show him the proper courtesy."

One of the moneymen shook his head. "You people never stop fighting that war."

"I just wanted to say . . ." Nicholas cleared his throat. "I just wanted to say that I had other job offers, but I was intrigued by the ceiling of six million dollars. The Cooper River Bridge project will go down in history as one of the few bridges completely erected with private funds, not a dime of city, county, or state money. This bridge will be the talk of the engineering world, not for the audacity of the project but for the audacity of the madmen who thought they could pull this off for as little as six million dollars."

"Madmen?" shouted men on both sides of the table.

At the blackboard, James could not suppress a smile. This Yankee was going to be all right. Franklin Belle gulped and leaned away. He was sitting next to a madman.

"Please, Hattie," said Turner Logan with a laugh, "would you refill everyone's coffee cup?"

She did, and while she moved around the room,

the men from Chicago leaned over to each other, creating an impromptu huddle.

"Oh, please," said John Patrick, "we've agreed on the companies who will build the various sections of the bridge. The bids have been accepted. There can be no secrets at this late date."

One of the Chicago men cleared his throat. "We were just wondering if Mister Eaton might brief us on the project."

"Oh," said John Patrick, sneering, "one of your own? I find that to be extremely discourteous to Captain Stuart."

"Well . . ." said the man from Chicago, opening his hands.

"Surrender," counseled Turner Logan, slapping his partner on the back. "If Robert E. Lee were here today, they'd still prefer that George Meade deliver this briefing." The meaning was clear to everyone around the table. Robert E. Lee was considered the most effective tactician of the Civil War, George Meade a ditherer.

"Nicholas," said Turner Logan from his side of the table, "I know it won't bother Captain Stuart for you to replace him at the blackboard, but I do have one question."

Nicholas had sat back down. Now he stood back up. "Sir?"

"Did you have a good breakfast this morning?"

SEVEN

Elizabeth Randolph sat on the end of her bed and stared at the bedroom door. As she heard Pearl gathering the girls in the next room, she braced herself. She had to go into that room and be someone she'd never been. The world was very much with her, and Elizabeth realized that she might not be up to the task.

When she had come to live in this house, there had been no radio, no telephone, or magazines. She and her husband didn't even subscribe to the local paper, with the exception of the Sunday edition, which kept them up to date with births, marriages, and deaths. And her book club studied the classics, as much for the pleasure of reading as for enforcing the rules of decorum. Elizabeth had never been to a moving picture, nor had any desire to go, or owned a motor car, or driven one. She and her husband had lived quite comfortably, their sole concern the impetuous Mary Anne.

Elizabeth was not against progress per se. She agreed with the laws making it illegal to dispose of human waste in the streets and requiring that the low areas be sprayed regularly for mosquitoes. It was change for change's sake Elizabeth didn't care for, such as this bridge crossing the Cooper River when Charleston had a perfectly good ferry service.

Curiously, Elizabeth bore no ill will against the ferry company, but took the deaths of her husband, daughter, and son as a matter of course. She had, after all, grown up in a city buffeted by storms, rising tides, and hurricanes. Not to mention that disease had left her the matriarch of the Randolph family. Her mother and mother-in-law had succumbed to the Spanish flu; her father and father-in-law had died in the Great War. All were buried in Magnolia Cemetery where their plots were lovingly attended by Elizabeth—until she buried her husband, son, and one of her twin daughters there. After that, tending to the gravesite was assigned to Alexander.

Pearl had gathered all the girls in an upstairs bedroom, even the blonde and brunette from down the street, and everyone had taken a seat on one of two double beds. This included Rachel Belle, who had remained behind after breakfast. Rachel had other responsibilities, such as the long overdue renovation of the Dock Street Theater and the changes her generation insisted on for Charleston's Orphan House; still, she could not resist such goings-on. The concept of a two-year house party was a bit too much to take in at once, but the longer Rachel hung around, well, this just might be fun, like Ashley Hall and the College of Charleston. Those years had been some of the best times of her life.

Besides, Rachel was sick and tired of being nagged to choose between her beaus, especially with all the cute young men moving to Charleston. Her stepmother was old school, literally from another century when women married much younger! But this was 1927, and if you were lucky enough to be alive in this day and age, it made sense to wait a year or two before taking on the challenges of whipping a husband and a family into shape.

Herbert Hoover was running for president with promises of a chicken in every pot and a car in every backyard. Everyone had telephones and boys could call anytime. Any boy could call. He didn't have to leave his card or declare his intentions. He just picked up the phone. Besides, it wasn't like she wasn't ever going to marry. She was, after all, a Belle of Charleston, and eleventh generation Charlestonians weren't anything to sneeze at.

"All right, ladies," said Pearl, "my sister, Molly, is going to clean the downstairs, but who is going to take care of this part of the house?"

No one said anything. No one moved. Many held their breath. What in the world was this Negro talking about?

"For the next few years this house will be run as a boarding house and either you work or you get out."

That did not please these young ladies. This Negro was getting above her place. The room broke into a hubbub of conversation until Elizabeth Randolph stepped in with a small board with a clip attaching papers to it.

"Young ladies, if I might have your attention."

The side conversations quickly wound down, and

anyone who was standing took a seat on one of the double beds.

"Thank you, Pearl." Then to the girls, Elizabeth said, "You and I know each other from a world that disappeared in a wind that blew through the harbor, taking the life of my husband, daughter, and son. Before that mishap, I was Mary Anne and Hartleigh's mother, a person who entertained you, and later your young gentlemen."

The girls shifted around on the beds. One or two began holding hands.

"You remember me as the one who made you turn out the lights and go to sleep when you spent the night, or the one who reminded you to mind the manners your mothers had taught you, or the one who remained out of sight when you came to my daughters, usually Hartleigh, to discuss your latest beau, break up, or engagement."

Rachel stared at Hartleigh on the other bed. Girls went to that girl for advice? What did she know? Ridiculous, but, of course, Hartleigh had always been her mother's favorite.

Elizabeth flattened the board across her bosom as she wrapped her arms across her chest. "Of course, my own girls only chatted about their beaus with Pearl."

Behind Elizabeth, Pearl nodded. The young women chuckled and smiled. Many of them had sought out the sympathetic ear of some black woman. Black servants were not known to talk back or to encourage you to make tough decisions.

"But that world, that house, the person I was, are gone...gone with that wind."

Pearl put a hand on her shoulder and squeezed

it. Elizabeth sniffed, nodded, and cleared her throat. She and her daughter's eyes met. Hartleigh was openly crying. Sue Ellen put an arm around her.

"This house entered a new day when John Patrick Grace asked if I would take in the overflow of engineers coming to our fair city. Mister Grace thought I might enjoy the company of these young men and I gladly agreed." She smiled at the girl from northern Missouri. "And while I've just met Polly Blount, I'm looking forward to being more than just an acquaintance as Polly is certainly welcome to remain here instead of moving into a hotel."

Polly smiled from where she sat. "Thank you," she mouthed.

"A few rules are nonnegotiable, and keep in mind these are the sorts of rules your own mother would apply if she found herself in my circumstances. If you must smoke, it will be done on the back porch. Second, you are not to be seen on any of the porches in your housecoats or any incomplete state of dress, nor are you to wave at those passing by. And thirdly, you may wear dancing attire, but only at dinner. In other words, no sleeveless dresses or hems above the ankle during the day. And don't be surprised if a preacher appears at the table and engages you in conversation or invites you to his church. He may even bring along his wife to take a peek upstairs. Please make them feel at home. We have nothing to hide."

Elizabeth glanced at her notes. "We must discuss this new gadget, the telephone. I know how this new technology has been embraced by your generation, but there could be fifteen or more people in this house, and with one telephone, well, that person could tie up a whole party line."

"We can't talk on the phone?" asked more than one of the girls, looking around at those sitting on the bed and asking their companions the same question.

Elizabeth could only shake her head. "You can...you can take calls...return calls...there will be a pad by the telephone."

"Well, I'm not living here," muttered the brunette.

"But where do we socialize?" asked her blond friend.

"The parlor," said Elizabeth, after clearing her throat and moving on to more solid ground. "The parlor is open to receiving guests after dinner, and the porches are always available, as is strolling in Battery Park, but all young ladies must be inside by dark, unless they're properly chaperoned. And we follow the same standards your parents would hold you to if a young man paid a call: Both feet on the floor at all times!"

Everyone laughed, even the brunette.

Her blond friend leaned over to her. "It's your choice: waiting for some boy to call or entertaining several in the parlor."

Elizabeth held out the board with the paperwork held to it by a clip. "I don't know how many of you are familiar with one of these, but this is called a clipboard." She turned the device so the young women could see how the clip held the papers to the board. "If this were my home as it was in the past, I would have no need for this. Pearl and I would establish a routine with minor adjustments here and there, but we have become what must be called an 'extended family,' including not only the engineers downstairs, but those of you who care to spend time here. There must be assignments or we shall be overwhelmed by the sheer number of people living in this house. On the clipboard you will find sheets to fill in, such as who is sleeping with whom—and choose your partner carefully, my dears, because some of you are quite untidy."

More nervous laughter.

"Pearl's sister, Molly, will make the beds, change linen, and clean downstairs once the men have left for the day. Molly will also be responsible for the upstairs bathroom. She will vacuum and dust the foyer, stairs, and upstairs hallway. Then she will leave the vacuum cleaner upstairs for anyone who cares to vacuum her room. Yes, I said for those who care to vacuum their rooms."

A look of panic filled the young faces in the room. "Ladies, I do not plan to host a sorority party for the next two or three years—that would be beyond my capacity. So, sheets must be filled out, such as who will assist in the kitchen, serve food, or perform simple chores. These chores you'll probably want to rotate, if you choose to live here." Elizabeth held up a finger to make a point. "But I warn you, these young men you find so fascinating will be, in a matter of weeks, so demanding that you'll wonder why you ever considered them Prince Charmings."

Everyone sitting on the edge of the beds laughed.

"Which brings me to Laurens' delicate condition." Elizabeth turned her attention to the pregnant girl. "Laurens can either pitch in and help out or return home and live with her mother."

"No! No!" shouted Laurens from where she lay on the bed. "I'll never go home. You're stuck with me, and my condition."

More giggling.

Elizabeth handed the clipboard to Sue Ellen. "Here you are, my dear. You have a reputation for being bossy."

Sue Ellen flushed as she took the clipboard, but she didn't have it long before Rachel Belle slid off the other bed, stepped over, and took the clipboard from her.

Addressing their hostess, Rachel said, "Mrs. Randolph, everything you have said is true and necessary for the good order of this house, but there's one thing that needs to be corrected."

"And that would be?" asked Elizabeth.

"I know just about everyone in this room and I can guarantee that I'm the bossiest girl living south of Broad. Actually, Belle women are notorious for that particular trait."

EIGHT

Later, in her mother's bedroom, Hartleigh said, "I've never heard you speak to my friends in such a manner."

"Be careful of your tone, young lady. I'm still your mother."

Elizabeth was bent over at the vanity mirror working on a renegade strand of hair. Hartleigh paused long enough before replying that it drew a look from her mother. Still, her mother said nothing, only reworked the flyaway hair.

Hartleigh loved this room, even more than the one she and Mary Anne had shared down the hall. Her mother's bedroom had the usual four-poster bed and vanity, but because houses built almost a hundred years ago had no closets, against the walls were a chest of drawers, an armoire, and a couple of steamer trunks. At the foot of the bed, her mother's hope chest, awarded to her sister because Mary Anne seemed sure to marry first, remained locked, the key still in the possession of her mother.

In this room she and Mary Anne had weathered chicken pox, bouts of flu, or simply lain on the bed and watched their mother dress for a night on the town.

Hartleigh said, "You're all I have, Mother. I'm all you have."

"My dear, what you think of my social skills now that my home has been turned into a boarding house is of little concern to me. As for that 'we only have each other' argument, well, that's not true. You have friends living here and I have work to do."

Satisfied with her hair, Elizabeth straightened up, adjusted the placket of her dress, and faced her daughter. "I would rather have you working alongside me, but if you prefer, you may take a full-time job in the kitchen with Pearl. If you haven't noticed, we must have three meals a day on the table for these young men, and from what I remember of your brother, who was only a bit younger, he had a hollow leg."

Elizabeth realized who she'd just referred to, blanched, and took a seat on the stool in front of the mirror. Hartleigh went to her, but Elizabeth held up a hand. "No! I'm all right!"

"I'm here for you, Mother."

"No. I don't believe you are." She dabbed a handkerchief at her eyes. "I believe the moment you step out of this bedroom, you will be caught up in the excitement of having all your friends living here and forget all about me."

"Mother, how could you say such a thing? I would not!"

"If you believe that, you're still a child."

"Mother, I'm twenty-three."

"And involved with young women who should be married." Elizabeth returned to her feet. "Every one of those girls should be married and pregnant like Laurens Rutledge. Matter of fact, all of you should be tending to families, not gallivanting around."

"Mother, times have changed."

"Oh, yes. I remember using that argument on my mother. I told her that it was a new century, if she hadn't noticed."

Curious, Hartleigh asked, "And what did she say?"

"She said men like your father didn't come along every day." Again Elizabeth faltered and returned to the stool. This time she put her head in her hands. "And they don't." She began to weep.

Hartleigh went to her, putting her hands on her mother's shoulders. "Contrary to what you believe, Mother, I won't desert you. I was simply startled by what you said to Sue Ellen. I've rarely heard you speak like that to someone other than the help."

Elizabeth sat up and dabbed at her eyes. Her cheeks glowed. "I don't have the time to sugarcoat everything. I have a boarding house to run, and if it's true what John Patrick Grace told me, it was at the suggestion of your boyfriend."

"James is not my boyfriend."

"You say that now, but in a short time you'll come to me, telling me that James Stuart is the one." Elizabeth looked over her shoulder at her daughter. "Don't waste your time on this young man. I do not approve of him now and I won't approve of him in the future."

"Why do you have this hostility toward James? He certainly was good enough for Mary Anne."

"I've told you before, Hartleigh. I'm not going to speak of your sister, nor your brother or your father. It's much too painful. Besides, I have plenty of friends who never stop inquiring every time I run into them."

"Those people care about you, Mother."

"Those people are pleased such a tragedy befell me and not their family."

Hartleigh's hands came off her mother's shoulders and she stepped back. "What a horrid thing to say!"

"As I said before, I don't have time for anything but the unvarnished truth. Pearl and I have never run a boarding house so we have a lot to learn. I've already quit my bridge club, I shop more at grocery stores than I do on King Street, and I spend more time picking a laundry than I spent choosing my last dress."

"So will you speak to James about moving out or shall I?"

"Move out? Why should he move out?"

"Because he reminds you of Mary Anne."

"I did not say that."

"Of course you did...in a fashion."

Elizabeth dabbed at her eyes, then returned to her feet. "Hartleigh, I don't have time for this."

"Mother, if we're to be more efficient because of the number of people in this house, then issues must be resolved and resolved quickly. Should I be the one to tell James he'll have to go? Though I have no idea why you wish to drive him away."

"That's because you haven't read your sister's diary!"

"What?" Hartleigh's hand rose to her mouth.

"James Stuart is a seducer of young women. He almost got kicked out of West Point for his many dalliances."

Hartleigh reached for a bedpost to steady herself. Not only had she never heard her mother speak so bluntly, she could not believe what she had just heard. "You read Mary Anne's diary?"

"And it detailed every step of her seduction."

Hartleigh eased herself down on the bed. Breathless, she asked, "What did it say?"

"Nothing I care to repeat."

"May . . . may I read it?"

"Absolutely not!"

"Mother, this is not fair. I want to know what he did to my sister."

"I will not allow the seduction of one of my daughters to become the entertainment for another. How James Stuart led your sister on was wrong, and him setting his sights on you is perverse."

Elizabeth went to the door where she faced her daughter once again. "And if you're thinking what a financial hardship it would be if James chose to move out, think again. Only this morning I was approached by the young man from the University of Chicago. He was willing to give up his room at the Francis Marion for room and board here."

Mrs. Andersen had the phone in her hand when she turned to her husband, who was reading the morning paper at the kitchen table. He had come into the house for lunch.

"It's Christian. He wants to know who our people are."

From behind the newspaper, Christian's father asked, "What kind of fool question is that?"

Mrs. Andersen turned her husband's question on her son.

From Charleston, Christian tried to explain, then his mother tried to explain to her husband.

Mr. Andersen lowered the newspaper. "Is he paying long distance charges for this foolishness?"

"Well," asked his wife, "where does your family come from? Mine are from Copenhagen."

"Everyone in Denmark is from Copenhagen."

"Well?"

"Odense." Her husband shook out his paper and held it up again.

She reported this information to her son.

"Do you know if anyone was anybody?" asked her son over the long distance line.

"Anybody?"

"Yes, Mom, like in famous."

"I . . . I don't know. I'll have to ask your father."

"Please do. It's important."

"Are we related to anyone famous?" she asked her husband.

The newspaper came down again. "What?"

"Are we related to anyone famous?"

"Oh, my Lord. Why would Christian care what anyone thinks of him in Charleston, South Carolina?"

His wife put a hand over the mouthpiece. "Think about it, Erik."

Her husband did but drew a blank.

"It's a girl, Erik. It must be a girl."

NINE

"That went well," said Franklin as the three engineers left the law office and strode in the direction of the Randolphs' for lunch. Broad Street was filled with attorneys, languidly strolling to their next appointment despite the chilliness of the day. Trolley cars, filled with women and children, passed them with impunity.

"Yes, quite well," agreed Nicholas, rubbing his hands together. "I guess it's not so bad to have a Yankee on your team from time to time."

"It's almost as if you planned for this contingency," said Franklin.

James only smiled.

Nicholas took note of James's grin. "Oh, no! It was a setup, wasn't it?"

James continued to smile.

Nicholas stopped, causing the other two engineers to stop. "I ought to punch you in the face."

"You can try." James stepped back and spread his feet.

Franklin moved between the two men. "Come on, Nicholas. You're not looking at this properly."

Nicholas glared at James but asked Franklin, "And that would be?"

"Rachel thinks you're cute."

"Well, that settles it," said James.

Nicholas turned on him. "Settles what?"

"Sue Ellen also thinks you're cute. I don't see the attraction myself, and that accent of yours, well, it leaves a lot to be desired."

"What shall we do with him?" asked Franklin, turning his back on the young man from up north. "Now that Nicholas has completed his part in our little charade?"

James shrugged. "I guess one of the girls marries him."

"Hey," said Nicholas, "I'm standing right here. I can hear everything you're saying."

Franklin took a coin from his pocket. "Flip for him, is that it?"

James nodded in agreement. "A matter of this importance can't be left to girls."

"Yes, yes," said Franklin. "One of them might come to their senses and realize Nick isn't all that handsome."

"And her brother would be stuck with him as a brother-in-law for the rest of his life."

"And the poor fellow would've had absolutely no say in the matter."

"Yes, yes. This must be settled now."

"What we decide here can be used as a foundation on which to build a solid marriage for one of our sisters."

Nicholas stood there fuming, even more so when

James and Franklin got into an argument over who should flip the coin.

"I don't like the results when you flip," complained James.

"Are you calling me a cheater? Remember, Senator Sumner, I'm the one with the cane and liable to beat you to within an inch of your life."

"You can try."

Nicholas was shaking his head in disgust, actually had turned away when a shriek came from farther up Broad Street.

"James? Is that you? Is it really you?"

And the reddish-blond girl ran down the street, dropped the basket she was carrying, and leaped into his arms.

The force of the blow pushed James back, and it was several steps before he could steady himself. When he did, the girl said, "Oh, it is you!" And she covered his face with kisses.

Around them people gawked, as did Nicholas Eaton. This Reb knew more damn women, and they were all cute as the devil.

James succeeded in freeing himself from the young woman's grasp, standing her up, and holding her out where he could see her. "This can't be . . ."

"It is," said the girl, whirling around in a circle and making the cloak she wore fly. "I'm all grown up, yes, I am." She wagged a finger at him. "And you promised to marry me. You said we would sail away and be pirates, just like our ancestors."

James took the girl's hand and turned to Nicholas. "Nick, may I present Miss Susannah Chase. I fell head over heels in love with her, but, alas, she was much too young at the time."

"My father would've shot you."

"Yes, he had done that before so it was no idle threat."

Susannah stood in front of them, legs apart, hands on hips, and cloak thrown back. "Well, I'm no longer young—as you can plainly see."

"Oh, yes," said James, grinning, "just ripe for the plucking."

Her hands came off her hips. "Don't be vulgar, James." She pulled the cloak around her. "My father still has his eyesight and his shotgun."

"Then my apologies. How is your mother?"

"Still matchmaking, but I told her I would have no other but you."

"Well," said James, looking at the other two young men, "it would appear you should get along to lunch while I'm destined to lunch with my future in-laws."

TEN

"What is this place?" asked Susannah as she and James walked down Lee Street to the shoreline. The occasional motor car or truck passed by on America Street and the passengers didn't hesitate to whistle or to call out. Susannah pulled tight her cloak and ignored them.

"This is where the bridge will begin. It will cross Town Creek and use Drum Island for some of its foundations."

Susannah sheltered her eyes. "I didn't even know there was an island out there. I thought it was just another sandbar."

James walked over to a huge sign featuring a rendering of the bridge. "This was done by Franklin. Impressive, isn't it?"

Susannah nodded. "Franklin drew a picture of me. I still have it on my wall."

"Then you'll be proud to know that many of Franklin's drawings were incorporated by Shortridge

Hardesty in his design of the bridge. Mister Hardesty, the chief engineer, will move on to new projects once this one is completed, but the bridge spanning the Cooper will be a member of the welcoming committee for those approaching Charleston in the future, especially from up north."

Susannah held down her cloak as it fluttered in the wind. Susannah had a fine figure, complimented by strong arms and legs she had developed over years of carrying sacks of flour and cans of shortening. And, as there was a Franklin Belle in every generation of the Belle family and a James Stuart in every branch of the Stuarts, there was a Susannah Chase in every generation of the family owning the bakery on Market Street. And since Susannah's mother bore the same name, the younger Susannah had always been called "Susie," but now, since turning eighteen, Susie insisted on being addressed by her more formal name. She was now "Susan Chase," and she informed James of this at lunch in the rear of the family bakery.

Everyone in Charleston knew the Chase family. They had been a fixture in the city for over two hundred years, but most importantly the Chase bakery specialized in cinnamon cookies, buns, and cakes. The smell drew people from all over, and James and Franklin had discovered the bakery as children when their parents took them there for a treat. Later, James, Franklin, Mary Anne, and Hartleigh had ridden their bikes over to the bakery and spent whatever change they had on something made with cinnamon.

At the time, Susan was no more than a baby. It would be several years before she announced that James Stuart was to marry her when she grew up. This sounded silly to James, but the Randolph twins thought it rather cute, and when the twins went to bed that night Mary Anne chose James, and Franklin was assigned to her sister Hartleigh. They couldn't let some little kid get ahead of them in the most important competition of life.

"You don't see that many Yankees in Charleston."

"You will in the future. Henry Ford put America on wheels. Unfortunately, Charleston's on a peninsula, and where that made Charleston important in the past, it now works against her. People have to go out of their way to come here, but with the new Ashley River Bridge and the one we're going to build across the Cooper, Yankees can pass right through downtown."

Again Susan raised a hand to shade her eyes. She looked toward the mouth of the harbor where a freighter passed through. "All the talk was about how the bridge would begin in the market, and now, well, that's almost a mile from here."

"The War Department nixed that idea. They required a thousand feet of horizontal clearance, and it's a good thing they did. When you consider all the trestles and viaducts required, it would've ruined the atmosphere of the market."

"Daddy said we'd get rich if the bridge began at the market."

"He's thinking of a simple trestle bridge that would've extended from Market Street across the river to East Cooper. A bridge like that, with drawbridges, could've been built for a couple of million dollars, but it would've ruined the harbor's ambiance."

"James, how long have you been back in town?"

James only stared at the river, plotting the path of the bridge. Surveying didn't begin until the next year, but he could see it all in his mind's eye.

"James?"

"Sorry." He looked back at her. "What was the question?"

"How long have you been back in town?"

Staring at the river again, James said, "Oh, I don't know, a few weeks, perhaps a month."

"James, that girl who used to ride bikes with you when you came into the bakery, she was your girlfriend, wasn't she?"

"Er...yes, she was."

"I'm sorry about what happened to her."

He shrugged.

"Were you in love with her?"

Now James looked at her again. "Yes, I was, Susie."

"Susan."

He smiled. "Susan."

"But you don't have a girlfriend now?"

James considered this. "I did have one girl in mind."

"Would that girl have been me?"

He smiled. "How could it have been any other?"

"James, I hate to tell you, but I don't want to be any boy's second pick."

"Pardon?"

"I think you heard what I said."

"Wait a minute. You didn't wait for me like you promised?" It was difficult for James not to smile.

"I have a boyfriend."

"Is it serious?"

"I'm afraid so." She looked down the river toward Fort Sumter. "I couldn't wait forever. Besides, what kind of boyfriend would be in Charleston for so long and never come calling?"

"I have been busy."

Susan's hands went to her hips. The hem of her cloak fluttered around. "Well, I hope the next girl you choose, you don't wait so long to declare your intentions."

"So, when do I get to meet the lucky guy?"

"You're not going to fight over me, are you?"

James appeared confused.

"I want your word that you and Arthur won't fight."

"Then you have my word. I'll try to be friends with...Arthur."

"He's been hired as a sandhog. I don't know what that is, and I was kind of scared to ask, but it pays good money. Er...James, what will Arthur be doing? I can ask you, can't I?"

"Of course." James gestured toward the river. "The bridge must have foundations, or piers, but first we have to get rid of the water so we can dig into the bottom."

"All of the water in the Cooper?"

James laughed. "Not at all. We build a caisson and pump out the water. A caisson is a round, wooden structure that sits in the water around the spot where you want to dig. That's when the people like Arthur come into play. When the water is pumped out, they go in and dig down to where the foundation will be laid."

"You can't just put the foundation on the river bottom?"

"The bottom must be solid. Arthur and the other sandhogs will keep digging until they reach bedrock and then dig even deeper. It's very important work."

Dangerous, too, thought James.

"Everyone calls him 'Artie,' but his name is Arthur Moultrie."

"Well, there's a name that goes back a few years."

"Yes, the fort on Sullivan's Island is named for his ancestor. I'm going to be a Moultrie when we marry."

"Well, best wishes. Am I to be invited to the wedding?"

"I'll...I'll have to check with Artie."

"You do that." He took her hand and led her back up Lee Street. "But first, you and I are going to see Hartleigh and Franklin. We must share your good news with them."

ELEVEN

On the other side of the swinging door that led into the kitchen, the matriarch of the Randolph family cowered while one of her neighbors—a child at that!—took control of her house.

Elizabeth bit her lip. In what other ways would she betray her home? And all for a few pieces of silver.

She saw Molly and Pearl staring at her. "Well?" snapped Elizabeth. "Do you want us to do all the work?"

In the dining room, Rachel stood behind an upholstered chair at the head of the table, the only one with armrests. Without instruction, each girl had taken a position behind one of the chairs, leaving open chairs on either side. Outside the dining area, in the hallway, stood John Jacob Boozer, eavesdropping.

He overheard Rachel Belle say: "My grandmother always said that the business of women is families, and, as Mrs. Randolph pointed out, we are a rather large one. But if we are to be judged a success and not become some object of curiosity, what should happen at twelve sharp is that every man should be seated with a meal in front of him, and with a coordinated effort, we should be able to join them.

"On that note, one of us should be responsible for the day's centerpiece. Men will not notice unless the centerpiece is *not* changed occasionally, but a new centerpiece will remind us to make that day special for all of those living in this house."

She pointed at a small silver bell at the head of the table. "That's to summon Molly or Pearl, but I will take it as a personal affront if this many young ladies cannot get a table properly set and their guests properly served. At a glance any of you should be able to see if the proper silverware, napkins, and accessories are all here: salt and pepper, sugar, milk, butter, rolls, etcetera.

"Remember, whoever is in charge of a meal—me for today's lunch—must always remember to ask our guests if there is anything they need before being seated herself, and the seat at the head of the table will be held for the hostess. Traditionally, this chair has been reserved for a male, but it sends a much clearer signal if one of us sits here. It reminds these young men that they are dependent on us to make this house run smoothly, and that can only be done with their cooperation.

"And just as the chores are being rotated among us, saying grace shall rotate among the men. There should be a list—the men must understand that they are required to be here whenever it's their turn—and one of us, probably Laurens because she has such a beautiful script, will write out blessings for those who are not as devout but required to say grace. From our experience at breakfast, we know there will be Yankees among us."

The girl from northern Missouri spoke up. "As the resident Yankee," said Polly, "I must remind you that Yankees can be as devout as any Southerner."

Rachel smiled cordially. "Then you're willing to allow the men to speak off the cuff?"

"Oh, no, I wouldn't go that far."

"Then may we proceed with my proposal?"

"Certainly, Rachel, I meant no disrespect."

"None taken," said the Belle of Charleston.

Down the hallway the phone rang, and it rang until John Jacob walked down and answered it. "No, she will not call you back." And he hung up. Posted on the wall was a beautifully hand-lettered sign that read: No men allowed upstairs without an escort.

Going out the front door, John Jacob ran into a preacher coming up the steps for a walk-through inspection, and probably a free meal to boot.

Although everything had been planned for a lunch of cold chicken, new potatoes, and salad, there were still glitches.

Nicholas Eaton gagged on his iced tea, coughed, and cleared his throat. He held the glass out where everyone could see. "Why is there so much sugar in this tea?"

"That's how we mix it," said Rachel from the hostess chair. "With sugar."

Lawrence Rutledge smiled all around. "That's why our gals are so sweet."

Sitting beside him, his pregnant wife beamed.

Nicholas noticed all eyes on him. *Oh, no, this had*

to be one of those Southern things. "Perhaps I could mix my own?"

"We're forgetting our history," said Franklin Belle who had joined the group for lunch. "People from Massachusetts haven't enjoyed a good cup of tea since the Boston Tea Party."

Laughter broke out all around, and his sister cocked her head in the direction of the kitchen door. Hartleigh got up before either young man beside her could pull out her chair and went into the kitchen where she asked Pearl to brew a cup of tea with no sugar.

Pearl and Molly stared at the white girl.

"You heard me. No sugar."

From where she stood cutting wedges of chocolate pie for dessert, her mother appeared exhausted, and she was. This was like cooking for Thanksgiving or Christmas, and they had to cook these meals three times a day!

"Does he prefer his tea hot or cold?" asked her mother.

Hartleigh stuck her head through the swinging door. "Hot or cold tea?" she asked Nicholas.

"Cold."

Hartleigh passed along the information about the tea and returned to her chair while Nicholas braved a storm of comments about next year's summer.

Rachel had already considered next year's summer. Usually the Belle family decamped for their home in Newport, Rhode Island, but as she looked around the table, aware that the brunette and the blonde had shown up for not only breakfast but lunch, and their names had been added to several of the chore lists, she wondered if she could be away for as long as a whole month.

"And the humidity," complained Prescott Mitchell, shaking his head.

"Keep more than one handkerchief handy," said Lawrence.

Beside him, his wife nodded.

"And sunglasses," argued the engineer from the University of Chicago, pulling a pair from his coat pocket. "You need sunglasses for the glare off the Cooper."

"Fat chance of finding sunglasses in Charleston with all the folks who've recently arrived," said Lawrence.

"Fat chance of finding sunglasses period," said the engineer from Carnegie-Mellon. "There are no sunglasses in the South. I know. I checked every train station from here to my hometown."

Sue Ellen chimed in. "My brother has a pair. He picked them up at Coney Island last year."

"Where's James?" asked Edmund Hall of NC State. "Whenever I need anything, I ask James. He's a first-class scrounger."

The girls didn't know what "scrounger" meant, and it didn't sound like anything a young lady should inquire about.

"That's not all James can come up with." And Nicholas related the story of the girl who had leaped into James's arms.

Hartleigh gaped at him, then stared at Sue Ellen.

"That rogue!" muttered Rachel. "He gives those living south of Broad a bad name."

Sue Ellen felt the heat rush up the sides of her neck. Furtive glances were shot at her and also at Franklin, who in no way disputed Nicholas's claim.

She stared at her plate. Her appetite had completely left her.

How could James have done this? How could he do this to their family? How could he have embarrassed her? But that wasn't the worst. If she remained in this house, she had to work beside these girls, all of whom knew much too much about her brother, the seducer.

Someone must uphold the family's honor; certainly a job for a male, but James was the transgressor. Sue Ellen choked down a few bites of her meal, hardly hearing anything said.

She'd be waiting when James returned. She'd be waiting on the front porch. She could not bear to be in this house one moment longer if her brother intended to seduce every woman living here.

Twelve

"James?" called a woman from the pier.

She stood in the light of a bulb hanging from a pole. A second woman stood beside her. The second woman called to James, but couldn't be heard over the revelry. Along the waterfront people were in a celebratory mood. Lights flickered here and there and water lapped against boats. Several boats plowed through the harbor, running lights on, horns blaring. Fireworks exploded over the harbor. The bells of Saint Michael's rang joyously.

A man walked down the dock behind them, taking careful steps because of the young woman in his arms. "It's the new year," he announced, "time to kiss someone."

The second young woman put one foot on the yacht, leaned over, and hammered her fist against the bulkhead. "*James!*"

A few moments later, a hatch slid back and a head appeared. "Who is it?"

"Hartleigh," said the first woman.

James came up on deck and looked around. "You can't be out here. It's too late."

"It's all right," said the woman who had hammered on the side of the boat. "I'm with her."

"Rachel?"

"And Franklin and Nicholas," added a man with a cane.

"Okay, so you have escorts. Now go away."

"Can't do that," said Nicholas. "We've kidnapped your sister."

When Nicholas came into the light, James could see that he held Sue Ellen in his arms.

James rushed to the side of his boat. "What's wrong?"

"She's drunk," said Rachel, coming aboard.

"I think you have to ask permission," said Hartleigh.

"Permission, hell. James is why we have this problem."

James didn't know what that meant, nor did he care. He wanted to know what was wrong with his sister.

"Let me bring her aboard," said Nicholas.

Franklin Belle was at the stern, casting off a line.

James saw this. "What the devil are you doing?"

"I want to see the Christmas lights from the harbor one last time. Next year there'll be the beginnings of a bridge out there."

"But I don't want you onboard."

"James," said Franklin, walking to the bow line. "You need to crank the engine and move *Rising Market* away from the pier." He cast off the bow line. "You're free," he said unnecessarily.

Franklin gave Hartleigh a hand, then stepped aboard.

"Where do I put her?" asked Nicholas.

"Downstairs," said Rachel. "I'll show you where."

"Listen, people . . ."

The sound of old tires rubbing against the side of the yacht could be heard over the lapping of water. This caused James to step lively to the controls, crank the engine, and man the wheel.

Hartleigh passed him on the way to the hatch. "Sorry about this, James."

Without looking at her, he guided *Rising Market* out of its slip at the city marina and into the harbor. "Would someone mind telling me what you people are doing?"

Franklin locked his cane into a rack and motioned for James to step aside.

"No, no," said James. "Only I take her out to sea."

"I've done this before," said Franklin. "Go down and check on Sue Ellen."

On the way below, James ran into Nicholas coming up from the main cabin. In his hands were several bottles of liquor.

"What are you doing?" demanded James.

"Rachel said to throw all the liquor over the side. Hell of a way to spend New Year's, if you ask me."

"Don't throw it overboard. With Prohibition, it's hard enough to get good whiskey." James took a key from his pocket. "Lock it in the cabinet and keep the key."

"I can do that."

Down the passageway, James found the door to his cabin closed. He knocked.

"Give me a minute," said Rachel. "I want to get

her out of her clothes. It'll be another way to slow her down. Does Sue Ellen have anything onboard to sleep in?"

"Check the footlocker under the porthole."

In a moment, Hartleigh said, "Got it." And a few minutes later, the two young women emerged from the cabin.

"Is she okay?" asked James.

"We just don't want her to have any more liquor," said Hartleigh.

"But it's New Year's Eve."

"For heaven's sake," said Rachel, "don't tell her that."

"Don't tell Sue Ellen what?" asked James.

"That it's New Year's Eve."

"Rachel, what in the hell is going on?"

"Don't use such language."

"You do."

"Only for shock effect. I'm a lady. Different rules apply."

Hartleigh said, "Let's have a seat in the lounge and consider your sister's predicament."

After checking on his sister, James joined Rachel and Hartleigh in the lounge. Once Rachel was helped out of her coat by Nicholas, she shooed him out of the lounge. "I need to talk to James."

James followed Nicholas toward the stairs. "I'll just check on the boat."

"Oh, sit down, James. Franklin's done all this before."

"And so have I," said Nicholas, gripping both railings to pull him up the stairs. "Off Cape Cod. I may take a turn at the helm."

"In the dark?"

"I can do amazing things in the dark."

"Nicholas!" said Rachel, who had moved into the galley. "Don't be fresh!"

Smiling, the New Englander pulled himself up the stairs by the railings.

Hartleigh had taken a seat on a padded bench. Behind her were a series of portholes, and draped around her, her coat.

Hartleigh gestured at the opposite padded area with its accompanying portholes. "Please sit down, James."

Instead, he remained standing. "What's going on?"

"Your kitchen's a mess," said Rachel, wandering in from the galley.

James almost corrected her, but Hartleigh shook her head.

"Dishes stacked up six ways from Sunday, and your bedroom's no different. Ants have made a home in your sink and your bedroom reeks of muck. I'll send someone over from my house, not Hartleigh's, with specific instructions. I can imagine the state of your toilet."

"Head," corrected James, finally revealing his exasperation.

"What?" Rachel waved off the correction. "Oh, give it a rest, James. I know that Stuarts love the sea, but the Belles are landlubbers, and when in Rome—"

"We're not in Rome."

"My point exactly. You're in Charleston, and you will act accordingly."

James tried to object, but again Hartleigh held up a hand, silencing him.

Rachel took a seat beside Hartleigh. "You and Sue

Ellen must make up. It's silly for such an episode to keep you apart. Besides, things have changed at the Randolphs'. While you've been living aboard *Rising Market*, I've been short a girl around the house. I'm actually short two if you count Laurens moving home—some complication with her pregnancy. And Polly Blount returned to Missouri. It would appear that she and Prescott were never engaged. It was all wishful thinking on Polly's part, and when she didn't receive a ring for Christmas, she packed up and went home. I can't handle all this work by myself."

Again, from Hartleigh: "James, would you please sit down?"

Reluctantly, he did, across the cabin from them.

"So," continued Rachel, "I'm down two girls, and when you moved out, the engineer from the University of Chicago and the engineer from Carnegie-Mellon moved in. One took your bed, the other took John Jacob's, at least while John Jacob's gone for the holidays. And those two expect to be waited on hand and foot."

"So call the police and have them kicked out."

In unison, the two women said, "*James!*"

"Look, this is not my problem."

"You're just being selfish."

"I don't need a mother, Rachel. I already have one."

"And too much pride to forgive Sue Ellen for slapping you when she thought you were leading on the Chase girl. She had no idea you were funning Nicholas."

"I didn't want to hurt Susan's feelings."

"Well, you've hurt your sister's."

"She hit me, Rachel!"

"My grandmother always said—"

"Rachel," cut in Hartleigh, "let me handle this."

The raven-haired woman looked at her companion like she didn't quite believe what she'd just heard.

"Give us a moment," said Hartleigh. "Please."

Rachel looked to James and back to Hartleigh. "Leave you two alone down here?"

"Don't worry," said Hartleigh, without smiling. "We'll keep both feet on the floor."

"Deck," said James.

Hartleigh glanced at him. "Deck."

"Well, then, very well." Rachel got to her feet and headed for the stairs. "I'll be right upstairs."

"Topside," corrected James.

"Yes, well, I'm not closing this hatch."

"Just go, Rachel," said Hartleigh. "Please."

James smiled. Few had the nerve to order about a Belle of Charleston. The Belles were originally from Paris, and if you didn't respect their ancestry, the Belles would remind you by speaking French exclusively at your next gathering.

Once Rachel had disappeared topside, James said, "You know, Hartleigh, I really don't have much interest—"

"James, hush up!"

He did.

"James, you must keep your sister out of that house."

"Your house?"

"Don't play dumb. This is serious. It's been weeks since Sue Ellen slapped you—"

"In front of God and everyone along the Battery." James leaned forward, elbows on knees. "And every damned chair on the porch had a guy sitting in it and watching the show."

Hartleigh closed her eyes. When she opened them again, she let out a long sigh. "Anyway, Sue Ellen's been living at home because she's too embarrassed to move back in." Hartleigh glanced at the hatch, then got to her feet, went to the stairs, and up them far enough to slide the hatch shut. She locked it.

"Hey!" shouted Rachel, but her voice was muffled.

Hartleigh returned to her seat. "You may think you can live on this boat without a care in the world, but once this bridge is finished, your long days of work will stop running together and you'll have to face the future."

James, too, knew that day was coming, the day he would leave Charleston forever. In that scenario, his sister would remain behind, happily married, and raising a family.

"Sue Ellen's not as tough as you think. Both of your parents drink beyond getting tight and so does Sue Ellen. It's like some disease and Sue Ellen has inherited it. You may not believe it, but she's been drunk since Christmas."

Hartleigh tossed her hand. "Oh, it's only a little sherry, she says, but that little sherry is enough that she can't stand on her feet. And your parents, not that they would notice the end of the world this time of year, don't care that your sister locks herself in her bedroom with a bottle every afternoon. Seriously, James, if you don't move back in, we could lose Sue Ellen forever."

When James didn't reply, only stared at her, Hartleigh shifted around on her padded seat. "Anyway, the four of us just performed what we call a 'disconnection.'"

"A what?"

"You disconnect the vacuum or radio or sewing machine from electricity and they can't function. We decided to disconnect Sue Ellen from liquor, and that's why we brought her to the marina, threw all the liquor overboard, and sailed into the harbor."

That reminded James of Nicholas Eaton. "Why didn't Nick go home for the holidays? He had a whole week off. Plenty of time to take a train north and return to Charleston."

Hartleigh glanced at the stairs. "Nick is sweet on Rachel."

"What? I thought—"

"That he was sweet on your sister?"

"Well, I thought Sue Ellen was sweet on him."

"When Rachel Belle sets her sights on a man, he doesn't have a chance, and neither does any other woman. Of course, it doesn't help when your father threatens to kick Nicholas's butt—pardon my French—to sour any young man on such a future father-in-law."

James sat up. "When did this happen?"

"A couple of nights ago, a week ago." Hartleigh tossed her hand in a careless fashion. "We've all been busy with the holidays and parties every night.

"So, James, you must convince Sue Ellen that there are no hard feelings. If you do, Rachel and I will go over tomorrow while your parents are sleeping off their latest toot, pack some clothes, and move her back into my house. I'm counting on you to make sure Sue Ellen's safe."

"Safe? Wait a minute, there's more?"

"No more than when you got tired of watching your father knock your mother around. A couple of times Sue Ellen stepped in between them. It wasn't a pretty sight."

James was on his feet. "I think I'll pay a visit to my house."

"Oh, sit down, James. Why do you think we left the marina? We don't need you going off half-cocked."

"I can control myself."

Topside, Rachel rapped on the hatch. "Hartleigh! James!"

"Come on, James, do you really think you could drag your folks away from the mayor's New Year's Eve party? And if you do hit your father, your mother will remain behind to tend to his injuries, and tell everyone it was her fault. Just be thankful we got Sue Ellen out of there. Now, let's keep her out even if she has to live at my house the rest of her life."

James began to pace back and forth across the lounge.

"James, please sit down."

"I can't."

"You'll only work yourself up."

"I am worked up! It's not fair you telling me this at sea."

"Another public row," said Hartleigh, shaking her head. "Just what Sue Ellen needs."

James stopped his pacing. "Would this be the reason why your mother doesn't like me?"

"No. That is an entirely different matter."

"What did I ever do to your mother?"

Hartleigh stared at the deck. "You seduced my sister."

A long silence, then, "Really?"

Topside, Rachel thumped again. "Hey, you two! Open up down there!"

James stepped closer to Hartleigh, the spitting image of Mary Anne. "If that were true, how would your mother know?"

Hartleigh didn't look up. "She read Mary Anne's diary."

"Mary Anne had a diary. What did it say?"

"I don't know. Mother wouldn't let me read it."

"That hardly seems fair."

Hartleigh's head snapped up. "James, don't go chasing rabbits." She got to her feet, shoved him out of the way, and headed for the stairs. "The reason we're here is to make sure you do whatever it takes to keep Sue Ellen safe, even if you have to stash her on this boat." At the stairs, she faced him again. "So take some responsibility for your family and be the big brother Sue Ellen has always thought you were."

James gestured helplessly from the middle of the lounge. "But what can I do?"

Hartleigh considered the question. "Well, there's not a girl alive who doesn't love to go dancing."

"Take my sister dancing?" James was incredulous.

"No, you ninny, not you. Fix Sue Ellen up, even if you have to go on a double date."

"A double date? What's that?"

Hartleigh had to keep herself from laughing. "It's when two couples go out together, you know, for dinner, then dancing."

"I don't like dancing."

"I'm sure everyone knows that by now, but our concern here is Sue Ellen, not you. You're the one who has the ear of John Patrick Grace, and that has to be rather intimidating to your fellow engineers, not to mention that your father has a reputation for knocking people on their derrieres."

Stunned James could only stand there. He'd never considered that he might be the cause of his sister's plight. He, too, had put a few men on their butt, and well before Sue Ellen had ever slapped him.

"James," asked Hartleigh, "do you really not remember what you did to make my sister fall in love with you?"

"I did anything Mary Anne asked me to do."

Hartleigh smiled before reaching up and unlocking the hatch. "Well, that would be a good start."

Thirteen

The morning of the ground-breaking, Saturday, May 19th, James returned to the house after being up all night. He was tired and cranky and needed some sleep. Rolling back the doors, he ran into John Jacob, who gave him a severe look.

"Business first," said James, "then the whistle."

John Jacob walked down the hall, passing the phone, which had been left off the hook overnight. He hung up the phone, and it instantly rang. He answered it and told the party on the other end to call back later. He, then, left the phone off the hook. John Jacob felt no compunction about leaving the phone off the hook. A dedicated line had recently been installed at the insistence of others on the party line, who complained they weren't receiving any calls.

Most engineers were sitting on their beds, trying to wake up. The whistle had been abandoned after the engineers chipped in for an alarm clock. Christian Andersen was putting on his slippers.

James stepped over to Christian's bed. "You went upstairs."

Andersen touched his head where a knot had risen. "And paid for it, too."

"They want you out of here."

Hearing this, the other engineers grabbed their ditty bags and headed for the showers; all but Edmund Hall, who continued to snore away.

"This coming from you or the women?"

"Does it matter?"

"No. I guess not." Christian got to his feet. "I thought the rule about men going upstairs was a joke."

"It might've been anywhere else but Charleston. They take the rules of decorum very seriously in this town."

"What if I object?"

"Well, we are at the point where we don't need as many engineers now that the surveying is finished."

"Yeah. There's that."

"Look, you and I can go round and round, but in the end you're leaving, and we both know it."

"Yeah, but I might want the satisfaction of knocking someone on their butt before I go."

"You can try," said James, spreading his feet. These days James wore workmen's clothing with a slouch hat and boots. A handkerchief hung around his neck. His shirt was always red and sweat stained.

Christian looked him over, clearly considering his chances.

"Come on, Christian. Do you really want a police record?"

"You'd do that?"

"Mrs. Randolph would do that. I'm the one who

would make sure the report was made available to your next employer."

"You are a jerk. No wonder your sister popped you."

"Yeah, well, if you aren't going to take a poke at me, I've got a ceremony to attend." James turned to go. "Just make sure you leave within the hour."

"For the record, I didn't see anything. I don't even remember Rachel hitting me over the head. I was that drunk."

James smiled from the doorway. "Oh, another guy who got popped by a girl."

"Actually, Rachel is, well, I've never met a woman with—"

"Such a sense of superiority."

"Yeah. I guess I wanted to take her down a peg or two." He rubbed his unshaven chin. "These Charlestonians...they're different."

"And where are your people from?"

"Dairyland, Wisconsin."

"Oh, yeah," said James, laughing. "I'd say there's a difference. The Belle family has been on this peninsula for over two hundred years."

"That doesn't make them better than the rest of us."

"And what were your ancestors doing two hundred years ago?"

"I have no idea." Christian made a mental note to call his mother.

"The Belles know what their ancestors were doing all the way back to Charlemagne, or so they say." James clapped him on the shoulder. "Well, if you need a room, let me know."

"Can you give me more than an hour to clear out of here?"

"To find a room? Sure."

"No. To pay a call on Rachel Belle. I wonder if she has an escort for the ground-breaking ceremony. Many a pretty girl has stayed home because guys are too intimidated to ask them out."

Hundreds of Charlestonians gathered at the corner of America and Lee streets where a platform had been decorated with red, white, and blue bunting and a microphone amplified the event. Paramount had even sent down a unit from New York. Signs of encouragement were mounted on the rear of the platform, but not large enough to block the view of the river, the undeveloped East Cooper, and the seafood capital of South Carolina, Shem Creek.

A table had been set up by Alexander, who snapped open a tablecloth. The girls opened picnic baskets and covered the table with food. A couple of gallon glass jars had brewed tea in the sun, and James, Edmund, Nicholas, and Lawrence hauled in coolers filled with pop, illegal beer, and overflowing with ice. A haze of dust hung over everything.

It was the last year this river would shape the destiny of Charleston and many wished to be here for the changing of the guard. Charleston would finally have a route north; still, the harbor would never be the same, and there were those who regretted it.

James's parents could be counted in that group. The Stuarts had fought the good preservationist fight right up until Jeb and his wife began to dip into their private stock of liquor. After that, the Stuart family was never taken seriously as the Progressives seized control of the city and dragged Charleston kicking and screaming into the twentieth century.

John Patrick Grace spoke that day, as did Shortridge Hardesty, the chief engineer who was having a devil of a time overcoming the impression that John Grace was the driving force behind the bridge. Both men knew history would be the judge and lobbied hard for their names to be attached to the project.

The mayor spoke, a state senator spoke, the congressional representative spoke, and both United States senators. The shortest speech was the invocation given by a preacher. Bands played, food and soft drinks were sold, kisses were stolen, and even a couple of fistfights broke out. Despite the length of the speeches and the rising temperature, couples and groups formed and mingled, then broke up and reformed elsewhere along the shoreline or among the heavy equipment, stacks of timbers, and piles of gravel and sand. Monday morning, crews would start on opposite sides of the river with plans to meet in the middle. The whole project should take about eighteen months to complete.

James and Sue Ellen strolled along, arm in arm, a parasol in Sue Ellen's hand, the other busy with her fan. It was, after all, springtime in Charleston.

"I didn't know you were such a good dancer."

"I try not to let on." In fact, James was as surprised as his sister. At West Point, he had done whatever it took not to dance, one time feigning a twisted ankle so he wouldn't have to participate in ballroom dancing.

"James, what do we do when the bridge is

finished? I don't fancy living on a boat the rest of my life."

He patted his sister's arm. "We'll cross that bridge—"

"James, please!"

"Well," said her brother, puffing up and speaking sonorously, "like any other male in the family, it's my duty to marry you off to the first fellow who comes along."

"In that case, I might choose to live on a boat."

Susan Moultrie, née Chase, saw the Stuarts coming and steered her husband toward the street. Sue Ellen saw the maneuver and swung her brother in the same direction, cutting off the Moultries before they could reach America Street.

"Susan!" shouted Sue Ellen.

People turned and stared. Charleston ladies never shouted but used bells to summon their offspring. Or their help.

The Moultries waited for the Stuarts to catch up. Susan's husband wore a black suit and she wore a sunbonnet instead of carrying a parasol. In her hand was a lace handkerchief.

"James says you're pregnant."

"Five months." Susan glanced at James.

"Congratulations."

Sue Ellen congratulated the husband and startled him by shaking his hand. Arthur Moultrie was a small, wiry young man, about his wife's height.

"Boy or girl?" asked Sue Ellen.

Susan smiled at her husband. "Artie wants a boy."

"Oh, yes, what man doesn't?"

"I told my sister most sandhogs come from other

bridge projects," said James, "but you snared one of those high-paying jobs all on your own. How'd you do it, Artie?"

"Well, Captain Stuart, there's plenty of chimneys in Charleston, and I cleaned my fair share in my youth. Then the city hired me to repair the sewers, so when the foundation company called, they knew I could stand odors and tight spots. You might say I'm not afraid of getting my hands dirty."

Susan wrinkled her nose. "Or the rest of you."

"She makes me pull off my clothes before—"

"Artie," snapped his wife, "these people don't need to hear our business." Instead, Susan aired one of her own concerns: "I still don't understand how these cofferdams work."

Everyone looked at James, even Artie.

"Give it a try, Captain Stuart. Maybe it's repetition the girl needs."

"Hey," said Sue Ellen, "don't belittle the poor girl. There's men's work and there's women's work, and explaining bridge building is definitely my brother's line of work."

Susan Moultrie laughed. Like others, she'd heard James go on and on about the bridge.

"Hey," asked James, "you want me to explain this or not?"

"Oh, yes," said Sue Ellen, squeezing her brother's arm. "I can't wait to hear more about the bridge."

"Captain Stuart, don't let the twittering of a couple of women put you off your stride. Explain both the cofferdam *and* the pneumatic caissons."

"Well, if you're sure you want to hear this."

When no one objected, James explained that a circular wooden wall would be built around the location of a proposed foundation and all the water pumped out. Clam-mouthed cranes, mounted on barges, would then be brought in to excavate the river bottom so the concrete foundations could be poured.

Susan turned to Artie. "That doesn't sound like anything you've had experience doing."

"That's the cofferdam, hon. I won't work in there."

"Then what?" asked Susan of James.

"The anchor foundations and cantilevered piers require not only the complete removal of the muck covering the river bottom, but a hundred feet below the river's surface where the foundation will be poured."

"This is where I come into the picture, hon."

"The pneumatic caissons are structures like cofferdams but built on shore and towed to their locations. Now this is going to sound like something out of a Jules Verne novel, but pneumatic caissons have steel cutting edges on their bottom side. We literally pound them into the river bottom. That's where Artie's work begins, in a watertight chamber continually excavating its own bottom."

Artie grinned. "That's why they need scrawny little men like me, hon. I'll go down a set of narrow stairs and shovel out that mud and sand and send it topside through special lifts."

James nodded. "The foundation company has no other way to remove all that soil unless men like Artie go in and dig it out. Remember, this could be a hundred feet below the river's surface where the water pressure would collapse any cofferdam."

"Then they pour in the cement," said Artie.

"*Pour in the cement?*" asked the two young women.

"Right on top of the roof."

"I don't know if I like this," said Susan. She began to twist the handkerchief.

"There's nothing to worry about," said James. "As the sandhogs send up their mud and sand, an equal amount of concrete will be poured on the roof of their watertight chamber, forcing the caisson, with its steel cutting edges, into the river bottom."

"You pour cement right on top of him?" asked Sue Ellen.

"On the roof of the caisson, Miss Stuart."

Susan was absolutely speechless. The handkerchief fell from her hand.

"Until Artie reaches the proper depth. Then he surfaces and the chamber he's been working in will also be filled with cement."

"I told you about the bends, honey. That's all I have to worry about. Coming up too fast."

"The bends?" asked Sue Ellen. "You mean what divers get when they dive too deep."

"Come up too fast," corrected her brother.

"I can only come up thirty feet per minute, Miss Stuart. If I follow that rule, I won't get the bends."

"Well," said his wife, "as long as you'll be safe." Susan rubbed her stomach. "You have a child to consider."

"Artie will be just fine." James bent over and gathered up the handkerchief. "Why don't you take a look. One of the caissons is already completed." James pointed down the shoreline. "And just waiting to be towed out to its position."

Susan looked at her husband.

"If you're up to it, hon."

"Well, I am a little tired."

"Then we'll catch it another day."

James returned the handkerchief to Susan. "This'll be hard work, so make sure Artie eats a hearty breakfast and brings plenty of lunch because he'll work two very intense three-hour shifts."

"Well," said his sister, as they strolled away from the expectant parents, "I have to admit that none of the dignitaries' speeches was quite as exciting."

"So I can drone on and on about the bridge anytime."

"I wouldn't go that far." She gripped his arm. "I can't wait until I'm pregnant. I want a baby so bad."

"What're you talking about? You said you and I make a pretty good family, just the two of us."

"Well," said Sue Ellen, elevating her nose, "I'm certainly not having *your* baby despite how well you've learned to dance."

"Oh, yeah, well look at what you're turning down. I'm prime, grade A male on the hoof. Just ask any Charleston girl."

"And all those girls will be pretty well picked over before you and Franklin ever get around to asking for someone's hand. Anyway, I prefer Citadel boys, not some traitor who went north for his education."

"That eliminates not only me but Nicholas Eaton, who you flirted with right up to the moment his fiancée arrived."

"Who would've thought some Yankee girl would travel all this way south to claim *him*. Well, she's welcome to him—engaged and not telling a soul!"

They walked in silence until Sue Ellen tugged on his arm, slowing them down. After glancing behind her, she said, "I want to be serious, James."

"Certainly."

With her parasol spinning over her shoulder, Sue Ellen asked, "That building Artie goes down in, you know, to dig out the river bottom."

"The pneumatic caisson."

"I don't care what it's called." Her parasol stopped spinning. "James, there's only you and me now."

"Uh-huh."

"Well, I don't like the idea of concrete being poured on top of those sandhogs. You don't have to go down there, do you?"

"Sue Ellen, I wasn't hired to dig holes in the river bottom."

"Good." She started them along the shoreline again, her parasol spinning. "I don't think I could stand to lose you. Where would I go? What would I do?"

FOURTEEN

All along the shoreline, couples strolled, or stood and stared at the river flooding the harbor—a combination of high tide and early spring runoff. One of the couples was Elizabeth Randolph and John Jacob Boozer. John Jacob had escorted Elizabeth to the ground-breaking ceremony, and now they observed an intimate conversation being held between Hartleigh and James.

Hartleigh and James had ended up together after Edmund said he wanted to buy a Coke float for Sue Ellen. This made sense to Lawrence and Laurens Rutledge. The Rutledges wanted to get their baby out of the sun, so the two couples set off to find a taxi, confident they could catch a ride since they had a baby with them.

James and Hartleigh were left where a causeway would soon rise over a series of staggered-height concrete piers. A tug boat passed and tooted, a ferry disembarked cars at a wharf down the way, and *Rising Market* stood offshore, flags flying; the rigging flags were miniature university flags of the participating engineers.

"James," asked Hartleigh, "would it be heresy to ask why anyone would care to spend the day on the Isle of Palms? There's no trolley service, its only hotel burned down years ago, and mothers do not care to take their children to a beach where there are no bathhouses."

James remained silent, staring as though he could see the preparations being made on the far side of the river. Barges with clam-mouthed drills were moored on both sides of the river.

"James?"

Still silent.

"James!"

"Sorry." He turned to her. "What's the question?"

Hartleigh gripped his arm and leaned into his shoulder. "You were always going to build this bridge, weren't you?"

"I'd hoped so. It also gave me a chance to return to Charleston."

Her head came off his shoulder. "You missed Charleston?"

"Well, my mother kicked up a fuss when I stayed so long in California." He grinned. "And I'm certainly going to miss all those meals you whip up once I move out."

"There's no reason for you to move out once the bridge is finished."

He faced the river again. "I don't know what you mean."

"It'll be near impossible for us to keep the house unless we continue to take in boarders. Why couldn't you be one of those boarders?"

"Oh," said James with a laugh, "I'll defer that answer to your mother." He paused. "You do love that house, don't you?"

"It's the only home I've ever known"—again, she gripped his arm and leaned into his shoulder—"and there were plenty of cute boys living down the street."

"How much can you sell it for?"

"James, we don't want to sell."

"I didn't ask that. I asked: how much is your house worth?"

Again her head came off his shoulder. "I have no idea."

"Perhaps you should ask the bank."

"That would be up to Mama. I've never been inside a bank."

"Well, then," he said with a smile, "marry a rich fellow, you know, like Franklin Belle. He lives just down the street."

"Maybe I should marry someone who knows how to play the stock market." Her gloved fingers took his rough ones in hers. "*Rising Market* isn't any slouch when it comes to boats."

Behind them, Elizabeth and John Jacob took note of this intimacy and headed in the couple's direction.

James cleared his throat only to say something inane. "The way engineering terms roll off your tongue, you'd be a natural at playing the market."

"Oh, hardly."

"Oh, Hartleigh, yes!"

She chuckled, gripped his arm, and leaned into his shoulder. She remembered the play on words from their youth when her name could become the catalyst of a dare.

"I purchased *Rising Market* on credit," said James, "just like all the stocks I own. It's called buying on the margin."

"We don't purchase anything on credit."

"Your mother has a good number of rules."

"Our house would descend into chaos without those rules."

"Listen, Hartleigh," said James, putting some distance between them, yet not enough to lose her touch, "I don't know how many meals I'll be able to eat during the construction."

"Don't talk like that, James. It doesn't make you sound like good husband material. Wives expect husbands to be home at night for those meals we whip up. Remember: love, honor, and obey?"

A look of puzzlement crossed his face. "I thought those were vows for the bride."

Hartleigh convulsed with laughter, holding onto his arm to remain on her feet. When she could speak again, she said, "That's why we make you fall in love with us. We don't want to enforce the obeying. It puts a damper on the romantic aspect of marriage."

Hearing the word "romantic," Elizabeth Randolph knew she had arrived just in time. She slid a hand between the couple. "Let me take my daughter off your hands, Captain Stuart."

Startled, the couple quickly separated.

"You're not getting enough rest," added John Jacob. "You're burning the candle at both ends."

"And the middle," said Elizabeth, pulling her daughter away.

John Jacob gestured at *Rising Market*, riding the incoming tide. "Instead of staying out tonight, why don't you get a good night's sleep? Tomorrow's services will be as long as anything you've endured this afternoon."

"Bye, James," said Hartleigh, but she was not smiling as she was led down Lee Street toward a taxi stand.

And as Hartleigh walked away, James experienced such a sense of loss that it astonished him. It felt like losing Mary Anne all over again.

Oh, don't be such a fool! Any feeling you have for Hartleigh is a residual of your attraction to Mary Anne, and that isn't fair to Hartleigh.

Before ducking into the backseat of the cab, Hartleigh looked back and saw James looking forlorn.

Did James even know what he needed, or was he too caught up in the building of this bridge? And if he did remain distracted, what could a girl do to catch his eye? Evidently, the occasional double date had not been good enough.

Hartleigh shook her head after taking a seat in the taxi. You practically live with a man, take your meals with him, show an interest in his work. What else could a girl do to catch a boy's eye?

But James wasn't alone long. The young woman who lived down the street, the one with the children James, Nicholas, and Franklin had walked to school, asked James to explain the importance of the bridge to her husband.

"It's such a beautiful harbor," lamented the doctor. "Shame to deface it with some monstrosity."

"But the river's jam-packed with traffic, not to mention the twice-a-day tides that complicate the situation. Besides car ferries, merchant ships, fishing boats, barges, and ships of the line, there's all sorts of recreational watercraft. People will happily pay a toll to load up their cars at home and drive across a bridge to the beach."

"I hear they'll want fifty cents, and the ferry's only a dime."

"It's not about the money."

"It's always about the money," grumbled the husband.

"No, darling," said his wife, "what James means is that minutes after we finish packing we'll be spreading our blankets on the beach."

"And you won't waste time waiting for the ferry on a busy Sunday afternoon," added James. "Or wait for a return ride on the other side."

"It's probably the same amount of time," said the husband.

"Actually . . ." said James, but he was stopped by the wife, who put her hand on his arm.

Claire took her husband's arm as they walked away, trying to make her husband understand the difference between fussy children stuck on ferries and excited ones crossing a bridge and arriving shortly at the beach.

Abigail Mullins stood with her fiancé in front of the huge panoramic sign bearing a rendering of the proposed bridge. Sue Ellen had recommended Abigail bring along a fan and parasol for the ceremonies, and Abigail was pleased that she had done so. Charleston in springtime was nothing like New England.

"According to this rendering, the bridge zigzags across the harbor." Abigail was a short, plump girl who already dressed as though she was middle-aged. No flapper clothing for her.

"Actually," explained Nicholas, "it'll sweep in an arc to buttress the piers against the current, causing a severe turn over Drum Island." He looked down at her. "I didn't know you cared that much about my work."

Abigail laughed. "You talk of nothing else, and I have nothing to do but read newspapers and write letters explaining the bridge to those back in Lowell. But you'll never see me encouraging you to go on and on. I'm no belle."

"This must be awfully dull for you."

"Actually, it's the girls who're driving me crazy. I do believe they're the biggest bunch of phonies gathered under one roof. I daresay no one could have that much interest in my family tree or the church I attend, but those are the only questions I get from the women of Charleston."

Trying to lift her spirits, Nicholas said, "They have a saying down here: In Charleston they ask who your grandfather was, in Atlanta they ask what kind of work you do, and in Savannah they ask what you're drinking."

Abigail didn't smile, didn't even acknowledge his attempt at humor. "These belles are so inept. They don't know how to clean a lick. I give them pointers, and they're gracious enough whenever I'm critical, but really, I don't believe any of them has ever lifted a hand to pick up after themselves. They all have servants."

"But Mrs. Randolph won't allow other servants in the house, even though the girls' families have offered to pay."

"I do believe that's why Rachel Belle—the queen bee—left, and also poor Polly Blount. Yes, yes, everyone believes Prescott Mitchell wouldn't pop the question so that's why she returned to Missouri, but I truly believe it was the constant picking up after Rachel Belle that forced Polly to leave. She was sharing a room with Rachel, wasn't she?"

"I don't know. I've never inquired into the girls' sleeping arrangements."

Abigail spread her fan below her eyes. With an exaggerated Southern accent, she said, "Oh, sir, you've never climbed a tree and crawled into the window of some winsome young lady?"

"Well," said Nicholas, grinning at her, "if I did, it definitely wouldn't be the window of some girl. It would be someone special, and we wouldn't bundle all night like our ancestors."

Alexander found James surrounded by men who wanted the latest news about the stock market. The big Negro was accompanied by his son, who had spent the afternoon selling fried chicken to those who had forgotten to bring along picnic baskets to the ceremony.

Pockets jingling with coins, Benjamin strutted up to Stuart and asked, "Mister James, this where you got stuck in the mud?"

James looked at him. "No. The other side of the river."

Around him, the crowd fell away. Who wanted a tip from some stick-in-the-mud?

"You should've had my daddy with you. He would've pulled you right out of that mud."

"Boy," said Alexander, "why don't you go find some rocks to skip. You skip one five times and I'm buying you ice cream."

Benjamin thought that a fine idea and raced to the water's edge where he started scouring the riverbank.

"You really couldn't get out?" asked Alexander.

"I was up to my hips in muck."

"How'd you finish the survey?"

"We built platforms for the tripods, but we still had to go down almost twenty feet before we hit solid ground."

After a long moment, Alexander asked, "Are we invested in this bridge, James?"

"No one in Charleston has any money in this project—it's all from Chicago. If the principals won't stick a toe in the water, why should we?"

They stood there watching the boats disperse, most returning to the wharfs along the harbor or heading to Shem Creek for dinner or the dances on Sullivan's Island. Music floated over the water, a product of Saturday night combos on car ferries.

"James, how will you know when it's time to sell?"

The white man turned to the black one. "You know all those people you hear talking about the market?"

Alexander smiled. "You know I don't run in the same circles as you."

"Well, when you hear the average Joe touting a particular stock, not speculating about how high the market will go, you tell me and we'll cash out. The average Joe cannot pick stocks."

The music from the jazz bands could be heard on *Rising Market*, even in the lounge where Rachel Belle was flanked by the blonde and brunette, who had been invited along for the groundbreaking ceremonies. Since James had just signaled that he wouldn't be joining them, Franklin was sailing to Sullivan's Island for an evening of dining and dancing.

I do declare, thought Rachel, James Stuart has become as boring as my brother. What is it girls like Hartleigh Randolph find fascinating about men devoted to their work? Life's far more interesting when a man's devoted to his lady. Well, at least that's what her grandmother had always said.

"That span crossing the Cooper," asked the brunette, "are you going to lay a row of steel planks across the channel?"

Prescott laughed. "Not hardly."

Rachel considered Prescott to be a complete and utter ass, so she counterattacked. "From what I've seen of the plans, you're using some sort of truss to support the middle."

Both Prescott Mitchell and Christian Andersen stared at her.

Rachel met their gaze. "I read the newspapers."

After accepting Christian's apology for coming upstairs at the Randolph house, Christian had been invited to watch the ceremonies from James Stuart's yacht. Obviously, he was a pawn in some game being played by Rachel Belle, and Christian could not believe his good fortune.

"A cantilevered truss," explained Prescott, leaning forward to shut Christian out of the conversation. "Think of it as two diving boards facing each other."

"Diving boards are flexible," said Rachel, leaning back where she could see both men. "Is that your point?"

Now he was getting somewhere, thought Prescott.

Evidently, you had to treat these dames like they did have a brain in their heads. "Cantilevered trusses ease the tension so cars can pass over without shaking the bridge to pieces."

"They must be awfully long diving boards," said the blonde.

"So," Rachel asked Christian, "how do you connect the diving boards? Do you weld them together? That would seem to defeat the purpose."

"Hinges and bolts," said Christian. He wasn't about to be left behind. He'd show Rachel Belle her pawn was a knight. "The critical piece of equipment is called a 'shoe,' and it supports the truss. It, too, gives when traffic crosses the bridge."

"The bridge really moves?" asked the blonde. "That sounds pretty scary."

"Actually more like it wiggles," said Christian.

"Still sounds scary."

"How high will that be?" asked the brunette. "You know, where cars pass over the channel?"

"One hundred fifty feet," said both young men in unison. They glanced at each other.

"And we're expected to drive across it?" asked the blonde.

"Oh, no, my dear," said Prescott, smiling again. "That's what you have boyfriends for."

James Stuart did not take John Jacob's advice about getting a good night's sleep but changed clothing and ranged over both ends of the project, checking to see that everything was at the ready. He returned to the Randolphs' just after midnight.

The sound of the pocket doors being rolled back woke Hartleigh, who had fallen asleep on a settee in the parlor. She hurried across the hallway and found James sitting on his bed and trying to unlace a mud-caked boot. The task seemed beyond him.

"James," she said, taking his arm and pulling him to his feet, "come with me."

With little energy left to protest, James allowed Hartleigh to lead him down the hall toward the rear of the house. At the same time, Prescott Mitchell staggered through the front door and into the former reception room. Without closing the doors, or disrobing, Prescott fell across his bunk and dreamed that one of the girls had taken him upstairs and showered him with her affections.

A few hours later, Prescott, and any other engineer found sleeping in this Sunday morning, was rousted from bed by John Jacob Boozer. A search of the house, the backyard showers, and *Rising Market* turned up no James Stuart. For this reason, James was able to catch up on his sleep in a bed on the second floor of the carriage house as church is an all-day affair in the African-American community.

FIFTEEN

During the long, hot summer of 1928, curious onlookers gathered along the shoreline as a staggered row of pilings grew out of the water in Town Creek and on Drum Island. Between the pilings, temporary scaffolding was installed and the causeway poured as the bridge marched toward another set of matching pilings, scaffolding, and causeway approaching from East Cooper. Cranes, working from barges and the uppermost point of the bridge, along with a miniature railroad, maintained a steady flow of material as workers began to put together the superstructure.

Also moving in were the heat and the humidity. Both remained mired in the nineties, and more workmen would have collapsed if not for a steady breeze off the Atlantic. Still, many workmen simply walked away, not returning to even collect their last paycheck. And at the end of the day, there was always congestion on the Charleston side of the bridge where men ignored the metal stairs leading down from the bridge and simply leaped into the shallows of Town Creek. After a few broken limbs and the loss of a paycheck or two, most fools stopped doing that.

Although the walls of the pneumatic caisson had been painted white and electric lights installed every fifty feet, James almost ran over Artie Moultrie in the semidarkness.

James grabbed the scrawny man before they lost their balance and fell into the muck. The ground floor and the walls were always soiled, and despite how many times you had worked "below," the compressed air took time to get used to; you worked up a sweat that never evaporated, and before your three-hour shift ended, you were ravenously hungry. And you talked funny, your voice rising a couple of octaves.

Once they were sure they would remain upright— you really didn't want to tumble into the muck since many of Charleston's sewers emptied into the river— they let go of each other.

To reach his workplace, Artie took a boat to where he stepped onto the roof of the caisson, crossed the roof, dodging wheelbarrows and piles of shovels, and then went down a service shaft to the ground floor, or river bottom, where a door admitted him to the compressed-air chamber. Then Artie picked up a shovel and went to work, shoveling the river bottom into a wheelbarrow he pushed over to a service shaft and dumped there. And when that door opened, the muck was sucked up the shaft because of the extreme air pressure; topside, it shot out of the tube and piled up in an empty barge. From there, the muck was ferried over to where it could be used as a base for the causeways.

Artie grinned at him. "I swear, Captain Stuart, but I had better light cleaning chimneys."

"Probably so. How's the wife?"

"About to burst."

In the background came the monotonous sound of shovels striking the river bottom. A couple of men pushed wheelbarrows past them. No one wore anything more than britches and boots. Sweat covered them and would do so until they left the caisson. Artie, himself, had a farmer's tan.

"Any problems with the depth?" asked James.

"A couple of men have some paralysis, but they don't take enough time to surface." He smiled again. "Took your advice, Captain Stuart. I'm always the last one out of the decompression chamber. And most men, once they're topside, don't lie down and rest or drink some coffee or tea before heading to the local speak." Artie laughed in a squeaky voice. "They say they've got the solution to the pain in their next beer."

"There are posted signs."

Again Artie gestured at their surroundings. "Signs that can't be read in the dark."

James considered this. "Did pumping more air into the chamber stop your eyes from swelling?"

"Aw, that hydrogen sulfide coming out of the rocks didn't bother me none. It was shutting down the job. We need the money with a baby on the way."

In the corner and under a light, a man gobbled down a sandwich. Nobody interrupted you if you were wolfing down food.

James leaned over. "Don't tell anyone, but they're

going to bump up your pay once you pass sixty feet. It'll be another twenty-five cents an hour."

"Well, that should put a smile on Susan's face."

The following morning, Hartleigh held out the bib of her apron to let in a bit of air, then held out her blouse. The kitchen was hot as the dickens, even with the windows open and fans running. Earlier in the morning Alexander had hauled in fifty pounds of fresh shrimp from Shem Creek, and Molly sat nearby, legs splayed around a large pot.

As she peeled, Molly said, "Now you know why white girls have servants."

Hartleigh couldn't help but laugh. She took a sterling silver dinner knife from a drawer and held the flat side to the back of her neck. Instantly she felt cooler. A person could get used to that.

"Watch your tongue," said Pearl, who sliced tomatoes on a long table in the middle of the kitchen. Scattered on this table were squash, bell peppers, okra, yams, unshucked corn, cucumbers, onions, and heads of lettuce and cabbage.

"I'm only speaking the truth."

"Well," said Pearl, "white people don't want to hear the truth, least of all from colored folks."

Hartleigh picked up a mixing bowl. She had put away the dishes in the dish rack and had moved on to stirring the hush puppy batter. As a child, she had fallen in love with the warmth and smells of the kitchen, and the taller she grew, she had discovered the contents of every single drawer or cabinet. Nowadays, she and the kitchen were not on such amiable terms, practically at war.

"You shouldn't be here," said the black girl peeling shrimp.

"Molly!" Pearl pointed the knife at her younger sister. "Watch your tongue."

"Watch my tongue? Vicky needs a job and we need help or we're never going to get to church on time."

"That's not Miss Hartleigh's concern." To the white girl, she said, "Just for meals. That's what Molly's talking about."

Hartleigh stopped stirring the contents of her mixing bowl. "I don't think I can ask Mama to hire more help. It would be too self-serving."

"All you girls want to stroll along that bridal path where they're building the bridge. We know that."

Molly corrected her sister. "The bridge path."

Pearl shot her a look. "I know what I said." To the white girl: "You're a lady," said Pearl. "You're not cut out for this."

Hartleigh's eyes turned moist. "I've certainly tried. You can't say I haven't."

"And come down with two colds and the flu ever since all those white boys moved in. You're working yourself to death."

Hartleigh looked at Molly, but she said nothing. The conversation was going her way so why mess with it.

"We're having trouble with other folks' help," admitted Pearl. "They don't treat us with the proper respect."

"Who...I'm sorry, but, who do you want my mama to speak to?"

"I don't want her to speak to nobody. I want your

mama to hire Vicky so she can help with all these meals and you can go to the bridge like all your friends."

"I . . . I don't know." Once again, Hartleigh stopped stirring the batter. "Why are the neighbors' servants disrespectful?"

"We ain't rich no more."

Hartleigh mulled this over. Anyone's help took on the status, or lack of status, of their employer, and the Randolphs were simple working people as Hartleigh had overheard more than one person say. And those same people, ones who rarely talked money, would inquire as to the asking price of her home.

"You think Mister James would let you work like this if he were your husband?"

"What?" Hartleigh's head snapped up. "What'd you say?"

"You heard me. I want to send for my sister, Vicky, and I want you to go to the bridge Sunday afternoons."

"No, no, what did you say about James?"

"Oh, honey," said Molly, giggling, "don't you know he's rich?"

Hartleigh returned to stirring the batter. "I hardly think so, not on an engineer's salary."

"He plays the market with his inheritance, and a lot of money he don't have," said Molly, gleefully. "Why even Alexander—"

Again Pearl swung the knife in Molly's direction. "Watch your tongue, girl."

"I was just saying—"

"You just want to strut." Pearl lowered the knife. "My husband knows what kind of money Mister James is making, and that boy's sleeping right across the street from you."

"You're saying James is rich?"

"That's why he told his father to go jump."

"He what?"

Pearl would not repeat what she'd said, but her sister did. "Told Mister Jeb to go jump."

"That sounds rude." And not at all like James.

"Oh, honey, you don't know what rude is. That's why the Stuarts can't keep help. Mister Jeb gets downright mean when he starts drinking, and then he goes around picking fights."

Uh-huh, thought Hartleigh. And when Sue Ellen had slapped her brother, it reminded the mothers south of Broad what kind of family their son would marry into if he pursued Sue Ellen Stuart.

And who did new husbands spend Sunday afternoons with? Even before the engagement was announced, beaus knew where they would be each and every Sunday afternoon. And after the couple wed, it would be church services every Sunday and a noon meal with the in-laws. The couple might even move in with the bride's parents to save for—

Down the hall the telephone rang, and Pearl shot her sister a hard look. "Your turn."

Molly sighed, heaved herself off the chair, wiped her hands on a dishrag, and pushed her way through the swinging door.

"Throw the switch!" shouted Pearl.

Molly stuck her head back through the door.

"You heard me. I said throw the switch."

Molly nodded, and then hurried down the hall where she rolled back the doors and stepped into the engineers' sleeping quarters. Edmund Hall had beaten her to it. He flashed a guilty smile.

When Elizabeth Randolph had been out one day,

Prescott Mitchell had spliced a switch between the incoming calls and the phone in the hallway. When the switch in the former reception room was thrown, the phone did not ring, and the engineers could get some much-needed sleep. Most everyone in the house was on to the trick, the exception being their landlady, who appreciated that the phone no longer rang in the middle of the night.

In the kitchen, Pearl returned her attention to Hartleigh. "You don't have to marry Mister James, but you could ask his advice. He might be able to save you some money."

Hartleigh snapped out of her trance. "Sorry, I drifted off." She started stirring the hush puppy batter once again. "But you're wrong about James. He isn't on his boat. At least not this morning. This morning he's taking his sister to the bridge."

Pearl shook her head. "Oh, you poor dear."

Upstairs, Elizabeth sat at the lid of her drop-down desk, her face in her hands. This could not be correct. If these numbers were right, they had even less money at the end of the month than when they'd started.

Her hands came away from her face. She stared at the numbers. What had she done wrong? She must have Hartleigh refigure everything.

That's silly. Hartleigh didn't have the head for figures, and, in truth, neither did she. This whole project was doomed from the start.

The bank! She would ask someone at the bank.

But if these figures were correct...what then?

There would be no other recourse but to go see John Patrick Grace about the amount of money the engineers paid for room and board. Or perhaps it was the girls. Maybe they shouldn't be able to live here scot-free? That was Hartleigh's position.

Elizabeth certainly didn't want to charge the girls for room and board. They were so helpful around the house. And absolutely charming.

Elizabeth uttered a sick little laugh. Why can't you ask them? They're the children of the people who no longer speak to you or invite you into their homes. What do you have to lose if you ask their children to pay their own way?

Sixteen

Lawrence Rutledge ran all the way to his mother-in-law's where he and his wife and baby girl lived. Flinging back the door, he thundered through the house, sailing his derby down the hall, past the grandfather clock and the chairs no one ever sat in.

"I got it! I got it!"

His mother-in-law walked toward him wiping her hands on a dishtowel. She noticed the derby on the carpet runner and picked it up. "Lawrence, don't you know we have a baby in this house?"

His wife appeared at the head of the stairs. "Lawrence, please. You'll wake the baby."

Lawrence hurried to the stairs where his wife soon joined him. Lawrence grabbed her up, whirled her around a couple of times, then took her hands and held her out where he could see her.

"They love my drawings! I never thought we had a chance. I mean, you know, competing with Franklin Belle, but I've been asked to join the firm."

Laurens' voice caught in her throat, but since wives should always be supportive, she said. "Congratulations, my dear."

"It sounds like a great honor, Lawrence." His mother-in-law placed the derby on the narrow table between the door of the parlor and the dining room.

Laurens gave her husband a peck on the cheek. She took his hand and squeezed it. "Now, my dear, you need to explain to Mother what this honor entails."

"An increase in salary!"

"Well," said his mother-in-law, smiling, "you two are on your way now. You have a sweet baby, each other, and now this commercial opportunity."

"My dear," said Laurens, "you must tell Mother everything."

"Well, yes." But Lawrence could not meet his mother-in-law's eyes. "I guess we'll have to move to New York."

His mother-in-law looked to her daughter, then back to her son-in-law, who continued to stare at the floor. "Leave Charleston? Now why in the world would you want to do that?"

Alexander knocked on the door of the room he had found for Christian Andersen when the University of Chicago grad had been kicked out of the Randolph house.

Prescott Mitchell opened the door, saw Alexander, and called over his shoulder, "Christian, it's your bootlegger." He looked over the big Negro. "No. That's not right. You're Alexander."

"Yes, sir, I am."

"What you doing here?"

"Came to see him."

Alexander pointed at the man who had joined them at the door. Christian Andersen held a copy of Emily Post's *Etiquette in Society, in Business, in Politics, and at Home.*

Alexander handed him a small white envelope. "Captain Stuart said for me to hand deliver this."

Puzzled, Christian still remembered to thank the Negro and tip him. After all, he was reading Emily Post.

Once the Negro left and the door closed, Christian opened the envelope and read the scribbling on James Stuart's business card.

Tomorrow Rachel returns to the Randolphs'. I've taken you off the schedule so you'll be free to assist her.

Prescott turned away and coughed into a handkerchief. The two engineers could not be more different. After almost a year of surveying and bridge building, Prescott still treated the project as a well-paying job with plenty of coworkers who would down more than their fair share of drinks during the cocktail hour. Christian, however, had recently been made assistant construction engineer for the East Cooper side. His duties involved getting the right beam to the right location, along with the corresponding nuts and bolts. It was usually dark and lonely when he returned to his apartment. He was paying a high price for his transgression against the girls living on the second floor.

"What's that?" asked Prescott, gesturing at the envelope with a jigger glass he had been about to use to mix another drink.

"I need to go out."

"Well, I'm not feeling so good. I may lie down and catch forty winks."

"Don't know when I'll return." Christian went over to a table and left Emily Post there. "You don't want to be sick here when you've got all those girls to take care of you at the Randolphs'." He smiled. "I know I wouldn't."

A short time later, Christian split off from Prescott to present his card at the Belle house on South Battery.

"Good luck, buddy," said Prescott. "It's the lady or the tiger for you," referring to the short story everyone studied in school.

At the door, the Belle family butler said, "Yes, Mister Andersen, Miss Belle is expecting you."

"I'm just leaving my card."

The Negro stepped back and gestured toward the interior of the house. "Would you please wait in the parlor? I'll check with the upstairs maid and see when Miss Belle can see you."

"Er...okay."

Christian walked into the parlor where, once again, he was surrounded by some of the oldest and most elegant furniture he'd ever seen. Emily Post wasn't going to be enough. He needed a book about furniture making. He knew all he needed to know about houses.

He could read the basic plan of the ground floor with a single glance: a reception room on the right, the parlor where he stood on the left. Beyond that, on the right, the former dining room converted into either a billiards parlor or a library, and directly across the hall from the former dining room, the new dining room, its location dictated by the new kitchen. Behind the new dining room was a modern-day kitchen, which, since the kitchen had been an add-on, chopped off a good bit of the garden in the backyard.

Over the fireplace hung a painting of Pierre Belle, the first of the Belle family to arrive in the New World. In the portrait Belle wore the uniform of a general officer of militia, and it dominated the small room.

Had he heard correctly? Had the butler really said Miss Belle was expecting him? How'd she know he was dropping by? He'd only made up his mind a few minutes ago.

He doubted Rachel wanted him to lift and tote with all the servants her family employed, but he was ready, willing, and able to assist her in her return to the Randolphs'. At least he'd be able to have meals with her again, even if he couldn't live there. James Stuart, the very definition of a sharp customer, was turning out to be one of the strangest friends he'd ever had.

Christian walked over to the bookshelves and studied the titles. Most of the books looked like they hadn't been opened in years, maybe decades. In a corner was a small black-and-white of another Belle who had been photographed with a handsome-looking woman. This Belle wore the railroad tracks of a captain of engineering. Clearly, a West Point man.

The Belles were an odd family, just as were the Stuarts: the younger generation coming down soundly on the side of the bridge, the older generation firmly against it. Franklin Belle had admitted as much, having worked for his father's architectural firm where two partners were for the bridge, two partners dead set against it. And Franklin's father was...

The butler cleared his throat; Christian started, then, as he turned around, jerked a thumb at the portrait of the woman and her husband. "Who's that?"

"Franklin Belle," explained the Negro.

"Seems to be wearing the wrong uniform."

"Well," said the servant, with an easy smile, "that depends on your point of view. On the matter that brought you to the house, Miss Belle invites you for dinner tonight. The senator, the mayor, John Patrick Grace, Turner Logan, and their wives will all be here. Eight o'clock sharp. Black tie. Drinks at seven."

"Where can I rent a tux?"

The butler gave him an address on King Street. "Though you may find purchasing such a garment to be an excellent investment in the future."

Christian walked away in a daze. Fifty feet down the street, he turned and stared at the house, ignoring two old women wearing caps who addressed him as they passed on the sidewalk.

Christian realized he had just caught a glimmer of the powerful shadow government running this city. Everyone at tonight's dinner was in favor of the bridge; still, the bridge supporters were coming to pay homage to an older generation of Belles, continuing to woo them, although the project was past any point where it could be halted.

Hmm, thought Christian, as he continued toward King Street. He needed more than Emily Post or a book on furniture. He needed a book on the social goings-on of Charleston, though he doubted such a book existed. To learn such lessons, you probably bungled through Charleston society like the proverbial bull in a china shop.

At seven-thirty, the butler opened the door and ushered Christian into the reception room where he was introduced to Rachel, who, as usual, was nothing short of stunning in a light blue dress against her pale skin and glistening black hair. The dress matched her eyes.

Rachel stood in an abbreviated reception line beside her stepmother, Georgiana, a plain-looking woman with mousy brown hair. Rachel had once told him that her stepmother was from Georgetown when Georgetown had counted for something.

"And where are your people from?" asked Georgiana Belle when introduced to the engineer.

Franklin Belle, John Patrick Grace, Turner Logan, Rachel's father, the mayor, and the senator, along with their wives, halted their side conversations and listened closely. Georgiana was about to put this Yankee in his place.

Christian had been anticipating the question. "My people are the Andersens of Copenhagen, Mrs. Belle. I'm sure you've heard of them. You have several of my ancestor's books in your parlor."

"We do?" asked Georgiana, incredulous.

"Hans Christian Andersen wrote the fairy tales you read to your children, such as *The Ugly Duckling*, *Thumbelina*, and *The Emperor's New Clothes*."

Beside her stepmother, the gorgeous girl uttered an unladylike snort. From this day forward, Rachel Belle knew her heart would always belong to this young man from Dairyland, Wisconsin.

SEVENTEEN

The girl was sleeping in the farthest stall of the men's bathhouse when Prescott Mitchell jerked back the curtain. The engineer from Georgia Tech had come down with a twenty-four-hour virus, but was now on the road to recovery, just a little weak.

After a day of rest and plenty of liquids, Prescott was ready to shave, shower, and learn if his stomach could stand a drink. Besides, it was high time he rented his own place as Christian Andersen had done. He was sick and tired of communal living, especially since every woman in this house blamed him for Polly's return to Missouri. Having to marry a girl just to make all those women happy; it simply wasn't his style.

Prescott had never seen a shower curtain closed unless he heard water running behind it, and signs on the wall encouraged the curtains to remain open when not in use. No loitering signs had been posted inside and out. If families weren't diligent, hobos would take up residence in your outbuildings.

When Prescott jerked back the curtain, the girl's eyes popped open and she looked up from where she lay on several towels. Startled, Prescott stepped back from the scrawny thing who wore a sleeveless sundress but no shoes. The girl, who looked to be about eleven or twelve, had long brown hair pulled back in a ponytail.

Leaping to her feet, she ran barefoot into Prescott, knocking him out of the way, then out the door of the former kitchen. Losing his balance, Prescott sat down hard on the concrete floor and slammed his head against one of the washbasins. He saw stars before passing out.

From the upstairs porch of the carriage house Benjamin saw the white girl race out of the showers, across the backyard, and then through the side gate. She disappeared down South Battery.

Benjamin raced after her, hustling down the steps and through the gate. Chloe looked up from where she played with her dolls, and seeing her brother gone, burst into tears. Her mother heard the girl's wailing through an open window of the kitchen, and in short order, Hartleigh, Sue Ellen, and Pearl stood on the carriage house porch, examining the girl. About the same time they got Chloe calmed down, her brother had returned from the street. As Pearl was applying the belt, Hartleigh and Sue Ellen headed for the showers, where they shrank back at the door. Neither young woman dared cross the threshold.

From the back porch of the house, Molly called, "A little help in this here kitchen, please."

Finished with waling the daylights out of her son, Pearl came down the stairs and walked over to where the two girls stood at the entrance to the bathhouse.

Once they explained their dilemma, Pearl stepped into the showers, but only after hammering on the door and shouting, "Cleaning lady coming through!"

That was when she saw Prescott lying on the concrete floor, unconscious and wearing only a towel around his waist. "You girls need to come in here."

Tentatively, Hartleigh and Sue Ellen entered the men's bathhouse, but upon seeing Prescott on the floor, they rushed over, knelt beside him, and discovered the bump on the back of his head. Prescott was groggy, but he could tell them what had happened.

"I'll find her," said Hartleigh, standing up.

"Just be thankful that she's gone," said Sue Ellen.

Outside the showers, Hartleigh called to the porch. "Benjamin, where's the girl Mister Prescott's talking about?"

Benjamin came to the railing, tears running down his cheeks. "What's . . ." He cleared his throat. "What's it worth to you?"

Pearl came out of the shower behind her. "I heard that! You tell Miss Hartleigh what she wants to know and right now!"

Benjamin didn't like it, but he told them. It might have had something to do with the belt. "She sleeps there during the day."

"I asked you where she was now."

Benjamin stalled.

Pearl did not. "Tell Miss Hartleigh or I'm coming up there again!"

Hartleigh and Benjamin found the girl in the

backseat of the Stuarts' Cadillac parked just down the street. When Benjamin jerked open the door, the girl tried to slip out the other side, but Hartleigh was waiting for her.

"Oh, no, you don't, young lady!"

The girl used her feet and elbows, and once she slipped from Hartleigh's grasp, she reversed direction and headed out the other side of the car. That's when Hartleigh reached through the window and grabbed the girl's ponytail, making those feet and elbows irrelevant. The girl yelped and fell back on the backseat. With Hartleigh having a hold on her hair, she couldn't even turn over.

"What are you doing on my property?"

No answer.

"I said: what are you doing on my property!"

"None of your business!"

"My property is my business, young lady, and you will tell me why you're sleeping there."

Benjamin leaned into the car from the opposite window. "You best do what Miss Hartleigh sez. She's a woman of her word."

The girl tried to kick him in the face. "Why'd you tell? I gave you a dime. Why'd you tell?"

Hartleigh looked across the backseat at the boy. "Are you renting out my rooms without giving me a commission?"

Benjamin didn't know what to say, and Hartleigh didn't know where that had come from. No wonder her mother bemoaned their fate as operators of a boarding house. It could do nothing but coarsen them.

"Let go my hair!"

"I'll let you go when—"

"You let go of me!"

Hartleigh jerked back on the ponytail, clunking the girl's head into the window frame. The girl cried out, and Hartleigh loosened her grip.

When Hartleigh loosened her grip, the girl broke away, flinging herself over the front seat. She was reaching for the handle on the driver's side door when James Stuart's father, Jeb, rose up, the girl straddling his chest.

"What's going on here?" demanded Jeb, keeping a hand on one of the girl's arms and retrieving his derby from the floorboard with the other.

Eighteen

When James's father sat up from where he'd passed out after coming home for lunch, he gripped the girl's waist so she couldn't slip away. Again arms and elbows flew, but Jeb was having none of that. He rapped the girl upside the head and she went limp.

"Mister Stuart!" Hartleigh scrambled around to the driver's side. "Don't hit her!"

"Why not? She hit me."

Hartleigh opened the door and reached inside, and James's father released the girl so he could climb out. Once he was out of the car, Jeb brushed down his pants, straightened his suit jacket, and placed his derby on his head. He bent down to examine himself in the rearview mirror. Out of the corner of his eye, he saw Hartleigh helping the woozy girl down the sidewalk.

"Hey, you, wait up there!"

Hartleigh didn't wait, and Benjamin ran after her.

"Where are you from?" demanded Hartleigh.

No answer.

"Where do you live?"

Still no answer. The girl remained unsteady on her feet.

Hartleigh glanced at the front porch of her house where several men sat in rockers, then motioned Benjamin to push his way through the wrought-iron gate and hold it open. In the backyard, Prescott staggered out of the showers with the assistance of Sue Ellen and Pearl. Blood ran down the back of his head.

"That's the little brat," sneered Prescott, who had been helped into his bathrobe.

Sue Ellen told him to pipe down, and Prescott did, but only because he was experiencing another wave of nausea.

Sue Ellen and Pearl helped the engineer up the stairs, across the screened-in back porch, and into the house—all to the incessant ringing of the telephone. Once they reached Prescott's bed, they eased him down onto it, then wrapped a towel around his head.

"I'll call Doctor Rose." Pearl went into the hallway, picked up the phone, depressed the bar, then jiggled it for the operator.

Prescott looked up. "My angel."

Sue Ellen laughed. "You sit right there. I'll get some ice."

"Before you do, tell me something."

"What's that?"

"How come you and I don't go out more often?"

"Probably because you're afraid of my brother."

"That must really hamper any possibility of romance."

"What possibility?"

After delivering a towel filled with ice to Prescott, Sue Ellen found Hartleigh showering the girl with cold water and Benjamin watching the show. The girl jumped around, screamed and hollered, and tried to fight her way out of the stall. Hartleigh planted her feet and shoved the girl back under the cold spray.

"What are you doing?" asked Sue Ellen.

"Trying to get some answers, but she won't talk."

"Leave her to me and help Molly and Pearl with lunch. Prescott's lying on an ice pack, and Rose will be here shortly."

The girl took this opportunity to make a break for it, but Hartleigh shoved her back into the stall. Benjamin watched all this, openmouthed. Riled up, Miss Hartleigh was something fierce.

"Benjamin's been extorting money from her to sleep in the showers once the engineers leave for work. He also makes her pay for whatever food he can sneak out of the kitchen."

This caused both women to look at the boy.

"Well, I gots expenses, you know."

The girl was skin and bones under the wet sundress and her hair a tousled mess. She shivered under the spray and wrapped her arms around herself.

"Like I said: Leave her with me," said Sue Ellen. "I'll get her story out of her."

"I don't want you smacking her."

"Just tend to lunch, Hartleigh. The boys will be home soon."

"If you promise not to hit her."

Sue Ellen gritted her teeth. "I promise."

"Then she's all yours."

Once Hartleigh left the building, Sue Ellen reached into the shower and turned off the water. She tossed a towel to the girl.

"Dry yourself."

The girl began to mop her sundress.

"Benjamin, you want to earn some money?"

"Do you have to ask?"

"Go inside and bring out a big bowl of ice cream."

"Before lunch?"

The girl stopped drying herself and looked at Sue Ellen.

"You can't make money standing here yapping."

"Yes, ma'am." And Benjamin raced out of the shower.

Sue Ellen grinned at the wet girl. "When my brother was off at school and my parents were hung over, I ate ice cream every morning. Hung-over parents should be good for something, right?"

Reluctantly, the girl nodded in agreement.

"While Benjamin's gone, strip off your dress and underwear. I'm going to hang them out to dry."

The girl shook her head.

"When that ice cream arrives, young lady, if you're not undressed, I'm dumping it at your feet and you'll eat it off the shower floor."

Reluctantly, the girl slipped out of her dress and her panties. By the time Benjamin returned with a bowl of chocolate ice cream she was completely naked but also dry.

Benjamin glanced at the girl swathed in a towel. "Mama says this here ice cream is for Miss Abigail's birthday."

"Well, ice cream can always be replaced."

Sue Ellen handed the bowl to the girl. The girl grabbed the bowl and she started stuffing ice cream into her mouth.

"Where's your sister, Benjamin?"

"In the kitchen shelling beans with Molly."

"Okay. You know the mother who lives down the street with a daughter about this girl's age? I believe her name is Claire."

"Yes, ma'am, I do. Her husband's a doctor." He watched as chocolate streamed down the girl's chin, dotting the towel.

"Now listen closely because there's a dollar in it if you do exactly as I say."

When Benjamin returned with a clean dress and panties, the girl had finished her ice cream and her hair had been rubbed dry by Sue Ellen. Ordering Benjamin into the house to fetch James and Alexander's lunch, plus a comb, Sue Ellen made the girl change. Once her hair had been combed she was told to hold the picnic basket out in front of her as they marched across the street and down the street to the marina.

"If she gets away, Benjamin, so does your dollar."

Over her shoulder, the girl smiled wickedly.

"Oh, yeah, girl, you just try it. Folks in Charleston take crimes against property real seriously, and that dollar's my property."

At the marina, they boarded a ketch manned by Benjamin's father. The water intimidated the girl and she huddled at the mast.

"Can you swim?" asked Sue Ellen.

The girl shook her head.

"Well, then, don't fall overboard."

Alexander took the basket and told his son to skedaddle. Benjamin raced down the pier and back down the street.

"Going to teach this girl how to sail," announced Sue Ellen.

Alexander studied the girl, who had regained her balance and now stood on deck, arms crossed and jaw jutting out. "She don't look like she cares to learn." Alexander wore pants, a straw hat, and a long-sleeved shirt buttoned up at the neck to avoid windburn.

Sue Ellen cast off the lines and scrambled aboard. "While you're eating, I'll get started."

Sue Ellen took the wheel, and Alexander went to sit in the bow. The girl looked around, unsteady on her feet. She grabbed the mast as the sails filled and the ketch rushed into the harbor.

Sue Ellen shouted across the boat. "If she doesn't show any ability, we'll take her outside the harbor and toss her overboard." She looked hard at the girl. "I really doubt anyone's looking for her."

Nineteen

As they sailed past the series of wharfs dotting the shoreline, the girl looked to the far side of the river, then to where concrete piers in various stages of development grew out of the water. The causeway over Drum Island was taking shape, and on the East Cooper side the other half of the bridge grew toward it. The sky was startlingly blue with only the occasional cloud, but the near horizon was filled with boom derricks, clamshell dredging machines, barges for the fill, car ferries; all manner of watercraft. A fireboat remained on station at all times, and seagulls shadowed everything.

By shading her eyes, Sue Ellen made out her brother on one of the anchor piers and pointed him out. "My brother's the one in the red shirt. James always wears red so Alexander can find him." Sue Ellen gestured at the mast. At the top flew a bright red flag. "Made from the same material. Some kind of family tradition."

"Find him for what?" asked the girl.

"So James can move quickly from place to place."

On the bow, Alexander raised two semaphores, moving his arms up, down, and sometimes across his body. In a moment, the man in the red shirt responded with his own set of black and yellow flags.

"They communicate with flags. There's a telephone line, but it has to be kept open for emergencies so they semaphore."

The girl sheltered her eyes and studied the piers rising out of the water. Only a few yards away, the second pneumatic caisson was being floated into position. Made of wood, the caisson had extremely thick walls, an accompanying roof, and appeared to be the size of a small house. Shafts ran down both sides of the floating structure; wheelbarrows, shovels, and block and tackle cluttered its roof. A pump constantly spit water into the river.

"What are they doing?"

"Ruining a perfectly good harbor."

That made no sense to the girl.

Sue Ellen saw this. "They're building a bridge."

"Why?"

Weaving her way through the cargo haulers, car ferries, and fishing boats, Sue Ellen considered the question. "Ever have the itch to travel and see the world?"

"It's why I left home."

"Well, Charleston wants tourists to come here and spend their money, but no one's willing to drive down the peninsula."

"What's a peninsula?"

Sue Ellen tacked in the wind and sailed through the row of silent sentries waiting for the causeway to be built across them. "Land that sticks out into water."

The wind whistled through the sails and several times the girl had to hold down her dress. "You know," observed the girl, "roads go two ways. Folks in Charleston could leave, too."

Sue Ellen eyed the girl as she maneuvered the ketch toward the anchor pier. "Just how old are you anyway?"

"Twelve."

"You're very astute for a child your age."

"I don't know what that means."

"Clever."

"Oh." Pause, then, "Can you drive a motor car?"

"Of course."

She looked at the boat's wheel. "If I learn how to sail this here boat, would you teach me how to drive a motor car?"

Sue Ellen smiled. "That begs the question: where would you want to go?"

"Anywhere. I just don't want to be here."

When James came aboard, he asked, "Who's this?"

Wolf whistles issued from the pier behind him.

Sue Ellen ignored them. "My new friend."

"What's her name?"

"Don't know."

"Who's her family?"

"Oh, James, don't be so nosy."

More whistles as the bow line dropped away from the pier, and Sue Ellen maneuvered back into the main channel.

"Well," said James, doffing his hat, "Nice to meet you . . ."

"Dory. My name's Dory." She stared at James as he took a sandwich from the picnic basket. "What's those glasses?"

James took them off. "Sunglasses. A friend of mine made them." He put them back on. "Sam Foster."

"I can't see your eyes."

"That's why the Chinese invented them, so you couldn't read their eyes."

"Can I try them?"

James gave the sunglasses to Dory, a sandwich to his sister, and unwrapped his sandwich from the waxed paper. Written on the waxed paper with a grease pencil was: Pride in workmanship means long hours. He smiled at Hartleigh's note, inspired from serving chicken chow mein one evening last week, complete with a fortune cookie. Ever since that meal his sandwiches had come with an accompanying pithy saying. Where the devil Hartleigh had come up with a recipe for chicken chow mein, James had no idea.

Dory turned the sunglasses over, fitted them on, and then snatched them off. She put them on again and looked toward the sun. "They turn down the light."

"That they do."

Dory held out the glasses.

James shook his head. "You keep them. I've got other pairs."

"Well," groused Sue Ellen, "you should share with your sister."

Dory extended the glasses to Sue Ellen.

"No, thank you. I have a birthday coming up. Maybe I'll receive a pair for my birthday."

James harrumphed while Sue Ellen gave her sandwich to the girl. Alexander dug soft drinks from a metal Coca-Cola cooler and passed them around.

"Nothing for you?" James asked his sister, who had used a rubber band to turn her hair into a ponytail.

"I'm on a diet."

"Sure you are." He gestured to where massive cranes worked both sides of the bridge. "Drop me at the Mount Pleasant car ferry unless you want to make a run upriver."

"I always want to make a run upriver."

With her mouth full, Dory said, "Your sister said she'd teach me how to sail."

Sue Ellen chastised the girl for talking with her mouth full.

James gave his sister half a sandwich and ordered her to eat.

"Aye, aye, Captain."

Sue Ellen bit into the ham sandwich, holding it between her teeth as the ketch dodged boats and ships and raced up the Cooper. Muscles bulged in her forearms and neck as Sue Ellen braced her feet and fought the wind. She was remarkably strong for someone so slender.

When she'd put the river's traffic behind her, she asked, "James, what's the story behind the red shirt? I know it's so Alexander can locate you, but how did the tradition begin?"

Alexander heard the question as he returned amidships. "It was so my ancestor could locate your ancestor when the pirate James Stuart was in a sword fight on the deck of an opposing ship. My ancestor, also named Alexander, was the cannoneer and didn't want to blow up his captain."

"You're related to the man who killed Blackbeard?" asked Dory, staring at James. "My family's from Scotland, well, a long time ago."

"Aren't we all?"

Sue Ellen asked the Negro, "Is there an Alexander in every generation of your family like there's a James in ours?"

Alexander used an opener to pop the top off the Coke bottle. "You know about us Charlestonians— we're all about lineage."

"But your son is Benjamin."

"That's his middle name."

Sue Ellen brought the boat around, tacking in the wind. "I wonder what Charleston was like when your ancestor sailed with mine?"

"Don't get him started," groused her brother. "Alexander's a real history buff."

"So what," fired back his sister, "you're a bridge buff." Returning her attention to the Negro, she asked, "What was Charleston like back then?"

Alexander smiled at James. "It was only a few blocks wide and a brick wall ran down the far side of Meeting Street to keep the Indians out. The Yemassee had sworn to drive the colonists into the sea. When Charleston finally defeated the Yemassee, they tore down the wall and began building suburbs. At that time, the peninsula was covered with trees—all but White Point Gardens. It was covered with oyster shells."

Dory remembered that a peninsula stuck out into the water. What else could she learn from these rich folks? And besides the sunglasses, what else could she steal?

James saw the look of avarice on her face and said, "If I remember correctly, there was once a young girl who ran away from home, and when her father found her, he took her sailing, then over to King Street to buy a very expensive—"

"Hairdresser! Don't forget the hairdresser! I never looked so good."

"Pardon me. They went to the hairdresser before dinner at the Francis Marion. Evidently, the father wanted his daughter to know what she'd be missing if she ran away from home."

He smiled at Dory, freezing the runaway at the mast.

"Unfortunately," said Sue Ellen, with a trace of bitterness in her voice, "that man doesn't exist anymore."

James gazed over the river as they continued upriver. At one time his father had known what was important in life, and then the whiskey had taken control. If you could remember their father before the whiskey hooked him, you would certainly harbor some bitterness. Sue Ellen had been betrayed at a much younger age.

Dory turned away from James and offered half her sandwich to his sister.

"No, thanks," said Sue Ellen. "I'm on a diet."

"You said that before. Is that some kind of a sickness?"

"Well, if it is," said James with a laugh, "half the population of Charleston suffers from it."

TWENTY

It was early December and the wind off the Atlantic was nippy. There had been rain the day before, but nothing slowed teams of men on both sides of the river working to install Christmas lights on the spans that had been swung into place. The bridge was beginning to take shape.

Word came from New England that Nicholas's father would arrive soon, looking for a place to build another mill, this one making hosiery. Greenville and Spartanburg had exploded with textile mills; even Florence and Rock Hill had one. It was Charleston's turn, and Yankee businessmen arrived on a regular basis to examine the prospects of making a buck in the Holy City.

James Stuart was aboard the floating concrete plant when the pneumatic caisson began to tilt. Word went out to halt the flow of concrete to the caisson. James stood there rubbing the pocket containing the engagement ring. He had to make up his mind. Should he ask Hartleigh to marry him or not? Christmas would be here soon, and there was no better time to propose.

He'd noticed how competitive the girl was. She'd won one rubber after another at bridge and had demanded that the girls pay room and board just like the boys. That'd taken nerve. Could her sister have done that? James didn't think so, nor did he think Mary Anne would have cared. Boys, girls, and cards were all viewed through a social prism by Mary Anne.

Of course, that wasn't fair to Mary Anne. She'd grown up when her family lacked for nothing. Still, James wondered how she would've handled her family's fall from grace.

"Must be a serious itch," said the reporter for the *News & Courier*, "the way you're rubbing that pocket."

James jerked his hand from the pocket. "Fleas. I need to fumigate *Rising Market*, but when I'm there, all I do is sleep."

Gesturing at the tilting caisson, the reporter asked, "What's happening over there, Captain Stuart?"

"The only reason for a caisson to tilt is if the sandhogs hit some particularly hard material: most likely a pack of oyster shells or a patch of sand."

The reporter looked from where they stood on the bow to the drum that revolved so the concrete wouldn't set. "What happens next?"

James dug a cheroot from his shirt pocket. "We wait until the sandhogs even out the bottom so we can continue to pour concrete and force the caisson into the river bottom."

"Because pouring more concrete on top of the sandhogs would make the caisson top heavy and tip over?"

James lit the cheroot, cupping his hand to protect the flame. "And water would rush into the chamber."

The reporter cleared his throat. "Captain Stuart, if you don't mind, I'd like you to read over my dispatch before I send it in."

Though he wore a slouch hat and sunglasses, James shaded his eyes to examine the position of the sun. "Well, it's going to be a long day, perhaps an even longer night."

It was well after midnight when James staggered into the house, clothing stained with perspiration, work boots clogged with dirt. Slouch hat in one hand, a bottle of bourbon in the other, he took note of the closed doors of the reception room and stumbled into the parlor, sprawling on the settee. His hat dropped to the floor, and a trail of mud now led from the front door into the parlor. That was how Alexander found him, drinking bourbon from the bottle and cursing their bad luck.

Quickly, Alexander was on his knees, unlacing the muddy boots. "We don't need Miss Elizabeth seeing all this."

Wearing her robe, Hartleigh appeared at the parlor door and flicked on the light. "Is what they said on the radio true?"

It took a moment for James's eyes to focus on her. Alexander glanced at the girl before beginning to unlace the second boot.

"They reported seven men dead on the second shift. Is this true?"

James looked off in the distance while Alexander removed the second boot. Once he had both boots, the black man tried to relieve James of his liquor bottle.

"No!" shouted James, jerking back on the bottle. His eyes were cold. Hard.

Alexander took the boots and left, closing the front door behind him. Outside, they heard him knocking the boots together.

"Remember where you are, James. No liquor allowed in this house."

He only stared into the distance.

Hartleigh gasped. Her hand rose to her mouth. "Artie Moultrie?"

"One of the seven," said James without any emotion. "Operations have been suspended until after the funerals."

Hartleigh felt as if she'd taken a blow in the stomach. She gripped the door jamb to remain on her feet. "And Susan?"

"Already been there. Funeral's day after tomorrow. They'll have visitation tomorrow night."

Hartleigh glanced at the bottle and turned to go. "I'll get a couple of glasses."

"Hartleigh?"

She returned her hand to the door jamb to steady herself. "Yes, James?"

"Forget the glasses, turn out the light, and come here."

The following morning, Sue Ellen woke to the sound of humming. Hartleigh, wearing her robe, sat in front of the dresser, brushing her hair. And humming. On a pallet on the floor slept Dory, who had again fallen asleep while reading. She was being paid a dollar for every book she read, and this really irritated Benjamin. He had to read all the same books for free.

"What time is it?" asked Sue Ellen from the double bed.

Her roommate swiveled around and smiled at her. "Time to fix breakfast for our young gentlemen."

"And that's reason to be cheerful? We do it every morning."

Before she could fall asleep, Sue Ellen remembered the news of the previous day. She rose up on an elbow. "After what happened, how in the world can you be so happy?"

Hartleigh's brush stopped in mid-stroke and her heart filled with despair. Not once since she'd woken up had she thought of the seven dead men. What was wrong with her?

She knew the answer. She was in love with James Stuart. She had always been in love with James, and if she hurried, she just might be able to sit next to him during breakfast. And hold hands under the table like other couples did.

In the kitchen, Pearl arched an eyebrow. "You all right?"

"Yes, yes," said Hartleigh, taking down cups from the cupboard. "Why wouldn't I be?"

"I've seen that look before."

Hartleigh could not face the black woman. Instead, she gripped the counter, "What look is that?"

"The one on your sister's face when Mary Anne stayed out all night and snuck in the house before your mama could catch her."

There was little conversation at the breakfast table, not even speculation about the stock market. Franklin Belle did not join his sister, who had moved back into the house. Edmund Hall spent the morning smoking cigarettes and pacing back and forth on the front porch, then snubbed out his final cigarette and left for the marina to take out his boat.

The weekly poker game had been canceled, an event the engineers had lobbied hard for: one night of whiskey, cigars, and cards. Actually, the girls had talked Elizabeth into holding such an event upon learning that *their* young men actually preferred a night on the town—without them! In retaliation, the girls gathered in one of the upstairs bedrooms and held a "smoking party." That is, until Elizabeth Randolph put an end to that. And since there was no work, many of them trooped off to memorial services.

As they cleared the table, Hartleigh inquired as to the whereabouts of Sue Ellen's brother.

"I imagine he's with Susan Moultrie."

Hartleigh's legs weakened. Dishes fell from her grasp and shattered on the floor. That brought her mother through the door.

"Everyone all right in here?"

She saw her daughter picking up pieces of crockery. Hartleigh was joined very quickly by Abigail Mullins, who helped pick up the remaining pieces.

"Hartleigh, you must be more careful."

"I'm...I'm sorry, Mother." Tears formed in her eyes. Tears she didn't dare wipe away.

"Remember," said Elizabeth to those in the dining room, "there may be funerals tomorrow, but we still have responsibilities to our guests." She smiled at Abigail. "And one special guest arriving later today."

Abigail returned the smile. Sue Ellen rolled her eyes, pushed her way through the swinging door, and delivered a stack of dirty dishes to Dory, who stood at the sink in the kitchen.

The runaway asked, "Someone else in trouble for a change?"

"No reason for you to worry on that account, honey," said Pearl from where she and Molly prepared food to be delivered to the bereaved families. "You'll always be my favorite when it comes to that."

Dory frowned and returned to the dishes.

Hartleigh never saw James that day, not even at the visitation for Artie, but Mrs. Moultrie spoke highly of him. "Why James was at our house most of the day, Miss Randolph, very attentive to my daughter-in-law. He and Susan go back a long, long way."

Hartleigh choked up, and everyone thought it had to do with viewing Artie in his casket. The casket was surprisingly elegant: mahogany with brass handles, and just the thing to start talk in a town that thrived on gossip.

Hartleigh didn't know the man, but she knew his widow, and several times Susan had to be led away to another room where she composed herself and returned to the visitation line.

Where was James? With the project closed down, could he really be that busy? Or was he at a blind tiger bragging about how he had seduced another Randolph girl—and planning to comfort the widow Moultrie later tonight?

"Where you going?" demanded Sue Ellen as Hartleigh turned away from St. Michael's. The day had dawned blustery and chilly. Everyone wore topcoats. Christmas was only a few weeks away.

"To St. Mary's," replied Hartleigh.

"But we're not Catholics."

"Susan is."

"Who's Susan?" asked Dory.

"I'll explain later."

"You know," said Dory, scanning the crowd going up the cathedral steps, "we haven't seen James lately."

Hartleigh stopped and turned on the girl. "Why should it be any concern of yours as to where he is?"

"Well, you have to admit, he is kind of cute, and if he was my boyfriend, I'd keep an eye on him."

Inside the church Sue Ellen saw her brother's arm around the waist of a sobbing Susan Moultrie. When the baby began to cry, Susan's mother rocked back and forth, trying to comfort the child.

Hartleigh strode down the aisle, and Sue Ellen looked left and right, smiling to those in the pews, most of whom she didn't know. She almost drifted into the casket before Hartleigh pulled her into a pew. Dark Sunday dresses, funeral veils, and men in black, hats in their hands, seemed to be the order of the day. Dory looked around, curious. Catholics looked like any other folks.

James heard the murmuring, turned around, and saw Hartleigh kneel, head bowed, and praying for forgiveness as she always did upon arriving at the Episcopal church. When he looked at his sister, Sue Ellen shrugged, knelt, and also asked for forgiveness. Dory hastily followed them to their knees.

At the gravesite, the wind remained blustery, and James stood, arm around Susan Moultrie, who wore his topcoat. The priest said the last rites and dirt was thrown on the casket once it had been lowered into the grave. Susan trembled. In her arms was the son Artie had always wanted, now three months old and about to face his first Christmas without a father.

Once the graveside service concluded, James excused himself and stepped over to Hartleigh and Sue Ellen. He embraced, first his sister, then her best friend. He nodded to Dory.

"Sorry," said James, taking Hartleigh into his arms, "but you know how loyal I am to my friends."

And as Sue Ellen watched in astonishment, Hartleigh drew James close, and just before they kissed, her best friend said, "As long as you're always loyal to me and our children, I have no problem with who else you're loyal to."

Now this, thought James, was the moment to ask this girl to marry him. James patted his pocket where the ring should be.

Not there.

He was wearing his Sunday suit. There would be no proposal, but there would be another kiss, this one in front of God and everybody.

Sue Ellen gasped.

Dory giggled.

Twenty-one

It didn't take long for news of the kiss, or kisses, to reach the Battery and even less time for Elizabeth Randolph to corner her daughter in one of the upstairs bedrooms once Hartleigh returned from the funeral.

"You just had to go and make a complete fool of yourself, didn't you? I guess all that can be said for the gesture is that you did it in front of a bunch of Catholics."

"The Chases are Catholic."

Elizabeth plowed on like she'd never heard her. "Here you are a descendant of the Randolphs of Virginia and the Belles of Charleston and you take up with some swashbuckler. I suppose you consider that rather daring."

"Mother, I'm in love with James."

"I warned you that he was a seducer of women and soon you'll be nothing more than another notch on his bedpost."

Hartleigh stared at her mother, speechless, then flushed and turned away.

Her mother's mouth fell open. "Oh, no, you haven't! Oh, no, not really. No! No! No! You can't have. What were you thinking? Why would you do this? Why would you do this to me?"

Hartleigh could not meet her mother's eyes.

"Why is this happening? What did I do to deserve this additional humiliation?"

Hartleigh turned around. "Mother, I'm in love with this man. And he loves me."

"Love? You know nothing of love. Do you think I loved your father when I married him? Marriage is where you discover love, and you honor your mother and father's choice. Once you're married, you can become as passionate about your mate as you wish to be."

"Is this the kind of marriage you think I should have?"

"Of course. Don't you believe I loved your father?"

"Well...after a fashion."

"Oh, Hartleigh, you read too many romances. Love is what you make of a marriage. Love becomes special when two people work through their difficulties." Elizabeth uttered a small sob and headed for the door. "Love is until death parts you."

At the door, she gathered herself and gripped the doorknob. "Well, you've finally concluded the ruin of this family. We cannot pay our way once the bridge is finished, and James Stuart will, if he has the common decency, marry you, while I'm left to live somewhere north of Broad."

"James is talking about starting an engineering business right here in Charleston. You know, with a couple of the other engineers."

"Oh, don't you believe that for a moment," said Elizabeth, facing her daughter again. "How many people would hire Southerners to build anything? Yankees still think we walk around shoeless down here."

"But I thought . . ."

"That's your problem, Hartleigh, you don't think. You could've married well, someone like Franklin Belle, and we wouldn't have ended up destitute. You had an obligation . . ."

There was a knock at the door, and Elizabeth jerked her hand from the knob and stared at the door.

"Mrs. Randolph," said Abigail Mullins from the other side, "Nicholas's father has arrived."

Raising her voice, Elizabeth said, "I'll . . . I'll be right there."

She returned to the dresser, bent over, and checked her hair. She did not check her makeup for her generation wore very little. She pinched her cheeks. Satisfied, she left the room and joined Abigail Mullins at the head of the stairs.

Hartleigh collapsed on the bed and simply lay there. What had she done? What had she done to her mother? She had betrayed her family and her mother. Tears formed in her eyes.

Rachel Belle knocked on the open door. "May I come in?"

When Hartleigh didn't object, Rachel entered the room and took a seat on the bed beside her. "Is it true—you and James?"

Hartleigh nodded.

"Oh, my."

Hartleigh sat up and touched at the corners of her eyes. She reached back to see if there had been any damage done to her hair. She must make this up to her mother. She must atone for her sin. Perhaps a visit to St. Michael's?

Hartleigh cleared her throat to clear her head. "Rachel, I'm not the same person I was when you moved back in."

"You know, that's probably true."

"And I have little time for foolishness."

Rachel did not know what Hartleigh meant, and in such cases, she always held her tongue.

"It occurred to me that I should marry your brother and become your confidante. I know how much you hate being depended on. At least it would give you someone to confide in."

Rachel shrugged. "If the girls need a leader, I'm fine with discharging that responsibility."

Looking at the white gloves Rachel always wore, Hartleigh asked, "Then why do your hands break out?"

"It's a medical condition. Runs in the family."

"Rachel, I have a mother who's a striver and you have a stepmother cut from the same cloth. Left to our own devices, you and I would probably marry boys who would take us away from all this. But we can't. Being a Charlestonian is a life sentence."

"Is that the attraction—that James will take you away? Then I warn you to look before you leap. The Stuarts were fun when we were children, but we're grown-ups now."

"I'm trying to be reasonable."

"This is you being reasonable?" asked Rachel with a flinty smile.

Hartleigh stood up and smoothed down her dress. She checked her makeup in the same mirror her mother had used, adding a bit of lipstick. "You're out of touch, Rachel. This is an age of getting things done, not resting on family laurels."

"Oh, Hartleigh," said her friend with a laugh, "a family of rogues, such as the Stuarts, will always be attractive to any girl, but you have a place in Charleston society. It's not something you can afford to take lightly, not in any day and age."

"And this from someone who's fallen for a boy from Dairyland, Wisconsin."

Rachel got to her feet, walked over to the dresser, and checked herself in the mirror. "We're just friends."

"As are Franklin and I, and it'll never go any farther."

"Why, what do you ever mean?"

"A few days ago, your step-mother called on my mother while I was at the grocery with Sue Ellen, who is very close to that little spy who recently joined our happy family."

"Dory?"

"Through our little spy, I learned that your stepmother believes its time for Franklin to marry and carry on the Belle name."

"But you and James have . . ."

Hartleigh smiled. "Nothing more than rumors stoked by an overactive imagination of one of the girls living here. Your brother deserves a virgin, and I'm sure he'll find one."

"Well, it certainly wasn't me encouraging Franklin, especially now that you and James—"

"Rachel, please don't gossip. If you do, people may learn that your grandmother, the one you quote so often, the very woman you were named for and look up to, was from Lowell, Massachusetts. You and Abigail Mullins are second cousins."

In the hallway, where a second phone had been installed, the phone began to ring. On her way to the stairs, Hartleigh picked up the receiver. "No," she said into the phone, "she will not call you back." And she depressed the bar and left the phone off the hook.

In the parlor, Abigail and Nicholas took a seat on the settee and held hands while Elizabeth sat in one of the Queen Anne chairs; Nicholas's father took the other. Nicholas, Senior, a successful shoe salesman, was quite different in appearance from his son. Where Nick was square-shouldered, square-headed, and blond, his father was slump-shouldered, thin, and bald.

"I'm sorry to arrive following such a tragedy," said Nicholas, Senior. "Sadly, I've seen all this before."

"Before?" asked his son.

He and his fiancée's hands slipped apart. For some reason, Abigail Mullins had begun wearing gloves. Everyone figured she was just trying to keep up with the belles.

Elizabeth smiled, seeing which way the conversation went and if she would have to guide it in a more cheerful direction.

Nicholas, Senior, took a pipe from an interior pocket and looked to Elizabeth. Once Elizabeth nodded, Senior worked at getting his pipe going.

He said, "Girls have gone crazy over the Mary Jane ankle strap button shoe. We can't keep up with the demand."

His remark caused Elizabeth to ponder Christmas. The festivities this year would be rather subdued because of the accident. She knew there would be a tree and table arrangements, a few presents, but more than that she did not know. There was little extra money. And what exactly were her obligations to the girls living here? Were they expecting gifts?

"When I was Nicholas's age," said Senior, once he had his pipe going, "I traveled through Canada selling shoes. I was in Quebec when a truss failed in the bridge being built across the St. Lawrence. Seventy-four workers were killed in that accident. Ten years later, I was training salesmen in Winnipeg when that same bridge was being renovated. Eleven more workers died."

Abigail's gloved hand rose to her throat. "I never knew."

"Hon," said her fiancé, patting her knee, "it happened in Canada. Americans are much better at building bridges than Canucks."

"Canucks?" asked Elizabeth.

"French-Canadians," said Nicholas, Senior, "like you Southerners call us 'Yankees.'"

Elizabeth fingered the fabric of her dress. "Well, I try not to."

Senior chuckled. "I've traveled the world selling shoes and the only people who take offense at being called a Yankee are Southerners traveling abroad."

"But why do men take such dangerous jobs?" asked Abigail.

Nicholas, Senior, deferred to his son.

"It's the pay," said Nick. "And those who do this kind of work know that our company has done everything in it's power to make the site safe. If someone dies, the worker knows we'll settle with his estate as John Patrick Grace and Turner Logan are doing with those widows of the sandhogs."

Abigail trembled. She'd barely known Susan Moultrie, but the girl was much too young to be a widow. And raising a baby with no father. How did women survive in such circumstances?

Nicholas was talking. Perhaps she should be listening.

". . . bridges without a certain amount of loss of life, and that's why we throw training dummies off the bridge and practice lifesaving techniques. Even Alexander has pulled workers from the water." Nick smiled. "I swear that Negro has the best job in the world, sailing up and down the Cooper and waiting for a signal from James Stuart."

Nick was selling hard. Up to a few months ago, he *had* been a desk engineer, computing stresses on sections of the bridge. But once the staggered ridge of pilings had begun to rise on the Cooper, John Patrick Grace had tapped Nicholas to be the public face of the bridge to anyone from up north.

Taking the pipe from his mouth, Nicholas, Senior, said, "Being paid to sail a boat." He grinned at Elizabeth. "No one told me such jobs existed while I was slogging through another Canadian winter."

Elizabeth returned the smile. Since meeting this man, she'd wondered when he'd last had a decent meal or a good night's sleep. Women might be able to live without men, but men living without women became drunk, diseased, and dirty.

"But workers still die," said Abigail, trying to keep the conversation on topic.

"Not engineers," said Nicholas, patting her knee.

"For the most part, engineers are office workers."

"Nick, how can you say that? James Stuart climbs all over that bridge—on both sides of the river!"

Nick glanced at their hostess. "James is the technical man for this project. It's his job to climb all over the project, and even go down in the pneumatic caissons."

Abigail ignored this. "I have brothers, and boys love to compete." She gestured at the closed doors of the former reception room across the hall. "You can't tell me those engineers don't wish to match whatever James Stuart does."

"Well, certainly not me."

"You're only saying that because of who's in this room."

"Abigail, please! I'm a desk engineer."

"Pardon me," asked Nicholas, Senior, cutting in, "but you've piqued my interest. Who is this James Stuart?"

Abigail and Nicholas looked at Elizabeth.

"A young man who fancies my daughter."

Senior nodded. "Boys flocked to our house and pulled the most outlandish stunts until my girls finally chose one." He puffed on his pipe before adding, "Tell your daughter to pick another. She must be obedient."

"Yes," said Elizabeth, smiling, "it's as easy as that."

"Mrs. Randolph," said Nicholas, Senior, rising to his feet, "I wired ahead and have reservations for dinner on Sullivan's Island. Would you care to join us?"

"Many thanks for the offer, but duty calls." She smiled. "Somewhere in this house."

In the hallway, the phone began to ring.

TWENTY-TWO

On the back porch Sue Ellen shivered, smoked a cigarette, and mentally counted the days until Christmas. She had to get some shopping done. And how would she handle Christmas? Last year, she'd been drunk out of her mind. Certainly she could improve on that.

Then there was the issue of her best friend and her brother. Was that true love? Or was Hartleigh nothing more than a replacement for Mary Anne?

Oh, who cared? Her brother should grab all the life he could. After all, look what had happened to Artie Moultrie.

Dory came out of the house and asked if she could bum a cigarette. The runaway wore Molly's coat.

"You're too young to smoke."

"Men don't say I'm too young for anything."

"Men have other plans for you."

"I'll say, and so did I, but they wouldn't hire me."

"Oh," said Sue Ellen, amused. She took a long

drag off her smoke, then exhaled and crushed the butt in a sand-filled coffee can nailed to a porch post. "Where did you apply?"

"Apply? You sure do use some highfalutin words."

"You'll have to know such words to travel the world."

Dory considered what Sue Ellen had said. "They wouldn't hire me 'cause I don't have no bosoms."

"Pardon?"

Dory presented her chest to Sue Ellen. "No bosoms. No—"

"I get the idea!"

Sue Ellen pulled her coat tight, then stared at the girl. "You applied for a job at a bordello?"

"If a bordello is the same thing as a whorehouse—yes. You've got bosoms. Doesn't it make life easier?"

Sue Ellen laughed. "Yes, I guess it does." She gripped her cigarettes in her coat pocket and considered lighting up another. "I guess when it comes to bosoms all girls are the same."

"No," said Dory, shaking her head. "Boys like the girls with the really big ones."

"Could we change the subject?"

"Sure. What did you want to talk about?"

"Anything but bosoms."

Dory examined Sue Ellen's chest. "Yeah, well, I can see how that might bother you."

Sue Ellen straightened up. "Now listen here, young lady."

Dory rolled her eyes.

"Now that's just being impertinent!"

"I get that a lot, but I still don't understand what it means."

"It means you're being rude, plain and simple.

You won't travel far if people learn you don't have any manners."

The breeze cut through the screened-in porch, and both women shivered. Sue Ellen thought smoking outside was idiotic.

"You sure do worry a lot about what people think."

"That's because I'm a lady."

"And what's that got you? Working in a bordello is easy compared to farming. You just lie there."

"Dory, this must stop!"

"What'd I do wrong? I used your word for whorehouse."

Sue Ellen sighed. "Dory, the world's not that simple. There are consequences." Oh, my, but she sounded like her mother.

"What consequences?"

"Well, let's start with the bordello."

"I thought you didn't want to talk about that."

"Only to make a point. You can get sick in those places."

"Sick of men? I'm already sick of them. They're a real bother." She grinned. "One of your words again. And some of the girls in this house are really bothered by your brother."

"Girls are drawn to James. Not only is he handsome in a rugged sort of way, but girls think they can change him."

"What's wrong with him?"

"He works all the time. Don't get me wrong. He'll do right by you, but he's not going to be there all the time." As her good friend Hartleigh will learn when the stars fall from her eyes.

Dory put a hip into the porch railing. "That's okay with me. James Stuart might work all the time, but he'd be coming home to my house."

"He's twice your age, Dory."

"Well, once my bosoms come in—"

"Please! No more talk about bosoms." Sue Ellen wrapped her arms across her chest. "You should aspire to be a lady. Then you'll be someone."

The runaway gestured toward the interior of the house. "Like your friends? Don't get me wrong. I'm glad you took me in, but working here is pretty close to living on the farm."

"This is not a good example. The Randolphs have financial difficulties."

"Then where's it better?"

"At my house. Daddy goes to work every day and when he comes home servants have cleaned the house, prepared his meal, and done his laundry." *And if he's not drunk, he'll notice.*

"And your mother, what does she do?"

"Well"—*if she's not tight*—"she makes sure the servants do their jobs and there's the charity work for the church and the annual Community Chest drive. She's a lady."

"Sounds good to me. Where do I sign up?"

Sue Ellen laughed as she took out her cigarettes. "That's the tricky part. Men won't do for you unless they think you're worthy."

"How do you fool them?"

"Well, you sure as hell don't go to work in a bordello."

"What do you do?"

"Are you serious about this?"

"Yes, ma'am. I want to go places and see things, and men have all the money."

Sue Ellen lit another cigarette. After letting out a

smoked-filled breath, she said, "Since men do have all the money, it's your job to make sure the men in your life regard you highly. If you do this properly, men will share their money with you."

Dory nodded. "I'm ready for that."

"All right. Now tell me, when you first meet someone what do you first notice?"

Dory thought about this. "What they're wearing?"

"More elementary than that: whether the person is a boy or a girl. Young or old. And most important: is this person someone you must respect. So, when people first meet you they see—"

"A girl. A kid."

Sue Ellen nodded. "What they don't know is whether you must be taken seriously or not."

Rachel Belle opened the door, strode out on the porch, and lit a cigarette. She stood there, smoking in anger and staring over the backyard. When she finished, she dropped the butt to the floor and ground it out under her heel.

Rachel was involved in the politics of the Junior League and the women's auxiliary of the Huguenot church; her latest cause was Charleston's Orphan House. Her generation wanted all orphans placed in foster homes where they could interact with the greater society. And as Rachel buzz-sawed her way through life, she found it useful to categorize people. As far as she was concerned, Sue Ellen was a slut and Hartleigh just didn't get it. But just moments ago, upstairs, Hartleigh had implied . . .

Rachel turned to go back inside and noticed Sue Ellen and Dory. "What're you two doing out here? A bit chilly for my taste."

"Sue Ellen's teaching me how to be a lady."

Rachel looked at Sue Ellen and laughed, then left them on the back porch.

"She's really mean."

"Let's review what you've learned."

"What?"

"Apply what I've just taught you to our visitor."

"If being a lady means being like Rachel Belle, I don't want to be one."

"Concentrate!"

The word snapped across Dory like a lash. Anger filled the runaway's face.

"Dory, someone just joined us on the porch. Use what I've taught you."

The runaway let out an angry breath. "Okay. The person who joined us on the porch was a young woman...who was no lady."

"But, despite your own opinion, is Rachel Belle someone you must take seriously or not?"

"I said I didn't care for her."

"Answer the question!" snapped Sue Ellen.

Dory became crestfallen. "Why are you being so mean?"

"You asked me to teach you how to be a lady."

"And I tole you—"

"It's 'told,' not 'tole.' The last letter is a 'd.'"

Dory appeared close to tears.

"Dory, I have lots of boyfriends; Rachel Belle does not."

This appeared to ease the girl's pain. Still, Sue Ellen did not relent. "Rachel Belle is respected by all Charleston. I am not. The point is: You make of life what you wish, such as when you abandoned your family to come to Charleston."

"Do you really have lots of boyfriends?"

"I didn't at first. Now boys line up to take me out." Uh-huh. They may not wish to marry me, but they damn well want to be with me. "Very few could stomach Rachel Belle."

"I'd rather be like you."

"Yes, well, you can't loosen up until you've tightened up."

"Pardon?"

Pearl stuck her head out the back door. "Dory, we need you in the kitchen."

"Pearl, may I have Dory for five more minutes?"

Pearl didn't like it, but she agreed.

"Don't worry," said Sue Ellen, smiling. "I'll take up any slack."

"Okay," said Pearl, not completely convinced.

"Come on, Dory."

And Sue Ellen led the girl into the house and down the hall to the front door. On the way, they ran into Rachel Belle.

"Now where are you two going?"

"I'm going to teach Dory a thing or two about men."

Rachel laughed. "Well, you're certainly qualified for that."

As they passed the parlor, Prescott Mitchell called out: "Dory, how about four hot chocolates?" Prescott was sitting with the engineer from Carnegie-Mellon and the blonde and brunette from down the street. Music from the radio played in the background.

Sue Ellen said, "She's with me, Prescott."

Rachel had followed them down the hallway. Now, she rounded the corner, turning into the parlor. "Prescott, we're not your mother no matter how badly you might need one. Get the hot chocolate yourself."

Prescott scrambled to his feet, hurried out of the parlor, and headed for the kitchen.

Sue Ellen winked at Dory. In a low voice, she said, "I'll bet you'd like to be able to do that."

Dory nodded.

"What's that odor?" demanded Rachel, wrinkling her nose.

On his way down the hall, Prescott threw over his shoulder, "Edmund's fishing clothes."

"I'll have to speak to him about that. My goodness, but this place falls apart whenever I leave for the least bit of time."

Rachel stomped off down the hall in the direction of the kitchen, only to stop, think of something, and return to the phone.

The first call she made was to her father; a second call requested the family driver to bring the car down the street; then Rachel went upstairs where she stood for the longest in the upstairs bath, staring at her hands once she'd pulled off the gloves.

On the front porch, young men leaped to their feet upon seeing Sue Ellen emerge from the house.

"Sue Ellen, baby, where have you been?"

"Hon, I've been waiting all day."

Another said the two of them were to catch the ferry and go dancing on Sullivan's Island; a fourth said he had finally gotten reservations for dinner at a Shem Creek fish camp.

"A moment, boys. This calls for reinforcements." Sue Ellen opened the door, stuck her head inside, and shouted, "Anyone interested in dinner and dancing across the river?"

The blonde and brunette shrieked, leaped to their

feet, and raced out of the Randolphs' parlor.

"I'm in!" shouted the blonde, pulling on her coat.

"Me too," said the brunette, taking hers down from a rack near the front door. She handed it to one of the young men and he helped her into it. Both girls wore the latest fashion: the little black dress.

At this call for action, Hartleigh had reflexively come downstairs, then watched as her friends went out the door. A year ago, she would've been one of those girls, perhaps only because she was Mary Anne's sister, but she would've piled in a car with all the others and been off for a night of fun and frolic.

As she passed the parlor, Hartleigh saw the engineer from Carnegie-Mellon sitting on the settee. "Anything I can get for you?" she asked.

"A girl?"

Hartleigh smiled, entered the parlor, and took a seat in the Queen Anne chair. "Will I do?"

"More than adequate," he said with a warm smile.

"You know, I don't think I know your name."

Again that smile. "Nobody does."

"Well, we'll just have to rectify that."

In the hallway, Dory listened intently, so she was almost bowled over when Rachel Belle came down the stairs and rushed out the front door.

When the Buick arrived, Rachel found her stepmother, Georgiana, sitting in the rear. The only mother Rachel had ever known, Georgiana's family hailed from Georgetown when Georgetown had been something to write home about.

The driver held open the door, but Rachel balked before getting in. "I'm sorry, Mama. I didn't know you needed the car."

Georgiana patted the seat next to her. "Nonsense, my dear, I'm sure I'm going your way."

"I'm going to father's office."

"Did you call ahead?"

"Before I called for the car." Reluctantly, Rachel slid into the seat next to her stepmother.

"Haven't seen you for a few days. We've missed you."

"I've been tied up."

Georgiana patted Rachel's leg. "Well, your father misses you, as do I. I saw the Craven boy just the other day."

"I'm not going to marry Billy Ray."

Her stepmother studied the Randolph house. "Well, as long as you don't let a Yankee turn your head. You know how that would grieve your father."

Rachel said nothing, only took her compact from her purse and began touching up her makeup.

Her stepmother said, "You know how I don't like you doing that."

"Mother, everyone wears makeup these days."

"I've made peace with that, my dear, but must you apply makeup in public?"

When her stepdaughter didn't reply, Georgiana said, "I'm meeting your father for a late lunch."

Without drawing her attention from the compact, Rachel asked, "Do you have an appointment?"

"Don't be impertinent, my dear." Georgiana glanced again at the Randolphs' as the car pulled away. "No telling what sort of habits you girls are learning by living there."

"Don't blame Mrs. Randolph. Blame me."

"Why, whatever do you mean?"

"Mrs. Randolph believes she can make her house most comfortable by allowing me to run it."

"Why, I do declare! Why not her daughter?"

"It's beyond Hartleigh's capacity."

"Then you've become a straw boss for Elizabeth Randolph?"

"I guess you could say that."

"Outrageous! You're a Belle of Charleston."

"And by birth, too."

At her father's architecture firm, both women were ushered into Franklin Belle's office. Franklin, Senior, was in conference with his partners when the two women arrived.

Greetings were extended by two of the partners as they left the room, but the third partner tarried. "Rachel, my wife and I were disappointed that you broke off your engagement to our son."

"Well, sir," said Rachel, taking a seat, "I certainly hope you were equally disappointed when you learned that your son had a girlfriend living west of the Ashley."

The room went silent, then, "Rachel, this is not what I was told. I will look into this matter further."

"Well, sir," cut in Georgiana, "the Belle family has no wish to intrude into the affairs of your family, but I hope this puts an end to the rumor that my stepdaughter broke off the engagement so she could do something frivolous, such as spending the next couple of years dancing with Yankees. I believe you know the Belles' feelings toward anyone from up north. They're responsible for the deaths of a good number of Belles during the recent unpleasantness."

Once the door closed behind the last partner, Rachel asked, "Daddy, was my grandmother, Rachel Belle, a Yankee from Lowell, Massachusetts?"

Twenty-three

"Maybe this isn't such a good idea after all," said James, tightening his grip around Hartleigh's waist.

It was close to Christmas and they were strolling along the river. Minutes after they'd arrived, Hartleigh was freezing to death.

"Come on, James," Hartleigh managed to get out before her teeth began to chatter. "Don't you want me to show an interest in your work?"

Though she wore gloves and boots, Hartleigh could not feel her fingers or her toes. The wind off the harbor chilled her to the bone, and this man, if he ever did marry her, would quickly learn it would be impossible to get her out in this sort of weather again.

James glanced toward the causeway that climbed the rows of temporary scaffolding and headed for the shipping channel. James wanted to tell her that it was much colder than he'd expected and that they could wait until another day, but he had finally gotten up the nerve to pop the question and didn't want to waste the opportunity. It had not worked out with Mary Anne, and James was determined not to botch it again.

Still, he was nervous and fell back on something inane. "You know, I'm gone a lot."

"Well, yes, my dear, but did you ever consider children?" Hartleigh said this as demurely as possible with the wind trying to lift her dress and petticoat. Maybe there was something to wearing trousers. Her hose did nothing for her, and she had on two pair!

You'd have to be a fool to be out in this weather. Luckily, there had been no rain. Honestly, if James had asked her to go strolling along the river with the possibility of rain in the forecast that would have ended their friendship.

They strolled through the jumble of machinery, the piles of steel—oh, my, but that had to be cold; she wouldn't dare touch it—and piles of sand. She had heard that fathers who slipped the guard a few bucks were allowed to back up their cars to these piles, and now plenty of children in Charleston had their first sandbox.

Would James do that for their children? Would there be any children? Would he ever ask her to marry him? Hartleigh flexed her fingers and her toes. How desirable could a woman be who was missing her fingers and her toes?

James appeared to be struck dumb by the mention of children. Hartleigh wasn't surprised. Her mother had often said that men rarely thought through the responsibilities of marriage. Did James really believe, if they should marry, that she would remain behind in Charleston? With her mother?

"Of course there would be children." Again his nervousness surfaced and James laughed. "We could fill up that big old house of yours with kids."

Hartleigh glared at him with eyes colder than any wind off the river.

James shrugged. "Or maybe one or two."

She pushed on, dragging James with her and shivering at the sight of the causeway rising over Town Creek and Drum Island. She'd read somewhere that air turns colder the higher you go. She shivered at the thought.

Hartleigh had given up trying to understand James's fascination with this bridge. Oh, she had no doubt that James cared for her, but it did irritate her that she would always place second in his life and that he would spend more time on his projects than with her. Married women rarely mentioned this aspect of marriage, but it was as simple as husbands going off to work and their wives remaining at home, hiding their disappointment.

James seemed to be at a loss for words, glancing here, glancing there, so she tugged him along. She had to keep moving or she'd freeze to death. Thank the Lord, she'd not worn heels.

"I know you have men working two ten…two ten-hour shifts," stuttered Hartleigh, "but at this point…at this point in the construction, are you…ahead or behind schedule?"

And off James went, happily droning on about the progress being made with the bridge. They were actually somewhat ahead of schedule.

How did you tell the love of your life that you hated cold weather? You wear boots and gloves and the fool thinks you're warm as toast. Evidently there was nothing you could . . . .

James stumbled, and Hartleigh, who had not heard a single word he'd said, pulled him to his feet. She thought James stuffed something into his pocket, but by then she had released his hand and had begun to swing her arms around to keep warm.

She looked up and down the empty shoreline. Who would be out here in this weather? Her engineer boyfriend, of course.

"I didn't mean to be pushy," said James. "We don't have to rush. I know how your mother feels."

What did her mother have to do with this? It wasn't her mother's Sunday to be off, and now, as she openly shivered, Hartleigh wished it hadn't been hers. Love was supposed to keep you warm; well, not on a day like this.

Enough was enough! Hartleigh grabbed her boyfriend's arm and tugged him toward the street, skirting the piles of gravel and sand and stacks of steel girders. Just being in a car would eliminate the wind. Again, she shivered.

"We can take as long as you wish," said James. "I do have a bridge to finish."

Evidently, she'd missed nothing. They were still on the subject of the bridge.

Hartleigh pulled to a stop when Prescott and Sue Ellen appeared from behind a pile of gravel. What in the world were they doing out here? Hartleigh shivered and could not stop.

Sue Ellen grinned at her brother. "What'd she say?"

James glanced at Hartleigh. "She didn't give me an answer." For the first time, James appeared to realize that it was cold out here. "We need to get you girls out of this weather."

Sue Ellen looked at Hartleigh, perplexed.

"I have a cab waiting," said Prescott, a cigarette dangling from the corner of his mouth. He clapped his hands together and rubbed them, then took Sue Ellen's arm and headed for the cab. Both were passed by Hartleigh, and James was left far behind.

James asked to be dropped off at his boat, and Prescott said he had to see a man about a dog and disappeared into the rear of the house. Even the thought chilled Hartleigh. She didn't see how men could bathe in a building without any heat, though she had occasionally seen smoke rising from the old kitchen chimney.

Sue Ellen and Hartleigh warmed themselves in front of the fire. And called for hot chocolate. A bridge game was breaking up: Christian and Rachel against Franklin and the brunette from down the street. Franklin and the brunette had whipped the other team soundly, but it didn't appear to bother Christian and Rachel. Their minds were elsewhere.

"Afternoon, Hartleigh," said Franklin, nodding to them. "Sue Ellen." He flashed a warm smile at Hartleigh.

The brunette saw this and asked Franklin if he was going to help put away the table and chairs. In the hall, the phone rang and the brunette stalked out of the parlor and picked up the phone.

"No," she said. "He's not here. Call his house."

While she was gone, the table was broken down and the folding chairs closed up and moved away. Christian was on his knees, running through radio stations, looking for something slow to dance to. Rachel stood beside him, one hand on his shoulder. Franklin rolled up the area rug, and Dory appeared with hot chocolate, but only Hartleigh and Sue Ellen took mugs, quickly sipping from them.

"Can you believe that?" asked the brunette. "A girl calling a boy. How bold!"

She pulled Franklin into her. "Now don't tell me you can't dance, Franklin. I attended dances at the Citadel, and in your youth, you could certainly cut a rug." She snuggled into his arms, something else Christian and Rachel never noticed.

Rachel's grandmother had always said: One woman, one man, and your work has just begun when you find that one man. Rachel Belle thought she had found her man.

In a hoarse whisper, Sue Ellen leaned over to her friend. "James was trying to propose to you."

"Propose?" Hartleigh stopped sipping from her hot chocolate.

"Of course."

"Then he must've lost his nerve," she said, her teeth chattering. "All he talked about was the bridge." She shivered. "It was freezing out there." Hartleigh sipped again from her cup and stood with her back to the fire.

During Hartleigh's childhood, the parlor had served as a cozy center where the family played cards, checkers, dominoes, and acted out charades and sang in sing-a-longs. The girls always had a new play that Hartleigh had written and their younger brother became the male lead, mouthing lines he didn't quite understand.

The first radio had arrived in this room. Her mother

had called it "a terrible waste of money," but when Hartleigh and Mary Anne were kept home during the Spanish Flu epidemic, they were astonished to learn how much time their mother spent listening to the machine that had replaced their old Victrola.

"Wait a minute," said Sue Ellen, putting her cup on the mantelpiece. "James didn't ask you to marry him?"

The brunette raised her head off Franklin's shoulder and stared at them.

Hartleigh faced the fire and lowered her voice. "Sue Ellen, I was there. I should know if some fellow asked me to marry him."

"He's not some fellow. He's my brother."

"I'm sorry. I didn't mean it that way. You know I have the greatest respect for your brother."

"Greatest respect?" Sue Ellen shook her head. "Oh, brother."

"You know what I mean."

"What I do know is that my brother took his favorite girl to what he thought was the most romantic spot in Charleston and you didn't even give him the courtesy of an answer." And warmed by the fire, or her anger, Sue Ellen stormed out of the parlor, leaving behind her hot chocolate.

Franklin and the brunette stopped dancing and watched her go. Rachel and Christian remained oblivious, though the song had ended and the announcer was reading copy about a new set of tires.

TWENTY-FOUR

One day in the spring, Sue Ellen and John Jacob sat in rockers on the front porch watching a sudden downpour move across the harbor, then march through the Battery. On the street people ran for cover and children on bikes raced for home. The downpour made it impossible to see the harbor. There was no wind, no lightning, only a line of rain that swept inland from the ocean. Water coursed through gutters, flowers bent under the sudden onslaught, and inside the house, Pearl called to Molly to come help her snatch clothing off the clothesline.

"John Jacob," asked Sue Ellen, "being with the YMCA, you've had a good deal of experience with people and their drinking habits, haven't you?"

"Indeed I have. I was one of them in my youth."

"Really?" She looked at him.

"I'm from the school of thought that believes you must be a sinner before you can achieve sainthood. I'm always suspicious of those who preach from inexperience, though I must admit that Billy Sunday did bring a lot of people to Christ."

"So you drank."

"And I've heard all the jokes about folks with the last name 'Boozer.'"

Sue Ellen went quiet long enough for him to ask, "What's on your mind, Sue Ellen?"

It was another long moment before she said, "I'm trying to understand my parents' drinking."

"Let me guess. There's no history of drinking to excess in your family."

Sue Ellen stopped rocking. Outside the wrap-around porch, the rain continued to come down, and a couple of young men raced up the steps and took shelter on the porch. They smiled and nodded, then moved to the other side of the porch to shake off the rain and light up cigarettes.

Sue Ellen continued, and she didn't have to lower her voice because of the downpour. "I've talked with my grandparents on both sides of the family and everyone is just mystified at how much my mother and father drink."

"Times have changed."

"Prohibition was supposed to end all that."

"Ah, yes," said John Jacob, watching the two strangers.

The young men nodded to John Jacob, snubbed out their cigarettes, and flipped them into the front yard. After that, they took seats around the corner of the wraparound porch.

John Jacob returned his attention to Sue Ellen. "I was a member of the Anti-Saloon League. We thought we'd done a wonderful thing by having the government ban the sale, manufacture, and transportation of alcohol. And it could've worked, but the Wets control the law enforcement process, so there's little money for enforcement but plenty for graft."

"You really believe that?"

"Then why haven't all the blind tigers been shut down?" John Jacob leaned toward her. "Better question: if the pay is so ridiculously low, why do men line up to secure one of those appointments as a revenuer?"

"You're saying that the government agents are corrupt?"

"There's plenty of money to go round, so revenuers wink at the speaks and your mother can drink in public. Nowadays, there's more of a stigma attached to women smoking in public."

"You're saying my parents' generation is the first to embrace public drinking?"

"Well, think of it this way, men have always drunk in public, and gotten drunk. The cocktail hour has been around longer than Prohibition, blind tigers even longer, so we can't blame alcohol for all this drinking."

"But isn't it progress if women can drink like men?"

"If you want to call it that."

To further complicate matters, whenever Sue Ellen went to a speakeasy, she had loads of fun. Of course, there were times when she woke up the following morning and couldn't remember what she'd been up to. And she'd noticed there were more and more College of Charleston girls bellying up to bars at their local speak. But that was only natural. Ladies' bars, rooms established across the hallway from the men's bars, weren't nearly as much fun as the men's side. And John Jacob was wrong about Prohibition. She'd seen plenty of barrels of hooch destroyed by the cops. Scenes like that were regular features on *Metrotone News*.

Edmund Hall came out of the house with a glass of iced tea and a copy of *Scientific American*. Not wishing to be a third wheel, John Jacob excused himself to work on his Sunday school lesson, but before he did, he made a hidden gesture at the other side of the porch before going in the house. Edmund nodded, took his seat, and dropped his magazine on the deck beside his iced tea. He and Sue Ellen both sat there and watched the rain come down.

It wasn't the first time these two had paired up. Besides the occasional double date, Edmund and Sue Ellen often sat on the porch, he smoking, she downing another aspirin. This afternoon Edmund had iced tea while Sue Ellen had her flask. But when she took the metal bottle from her purse, Edmund touched her hand.

Sue Ellen looked at him.

"Try this." And he passed over his iced tea.

"Edmund, I don't need someone to take care of me."

"I'm not taking care of you. I'm taking care of us."

Sue Ellen considered this, put away the flask, and sipped from the glass as the rain stopped just as quickly as it had begun.

Edmund was the one engineer who didn't talk about the bridge all the time. Sue Ellen swore if she were struck blind, she'd still be able to keep up with the progress of the bridge. At the moment, Charleston was all atwitter as cranes moved the cantilevered trusses into position on both sides of the river; her fellow Charlestonians couldn't wait until the two spans converged. A celebration was being planned; folks coming from all over.

"It's gone," commented Edmund as the sun came out and the Battery began to glisten. In the distance, trolley cars rang their bells.

Edmund was also the girls' favorite because he could usually be found lying in bed, reading, or sitting on the front porch, rocking, and easily become a fourth for bridge. That is, if you caught him before he went fishing. It would appear that any girl interested in Edmund Hall would have to have an abnormal interest in fishing.

Inside the house, the phone rang, and it continued to ring until someone picked it up.

"Edmund, may I ask you a personal question?"

"I guess so. We've gotten to know each other pretty well doing all this rocking."

Sue Ellen could never tell whether Edmund was having fun at her expense, but since he only said such things when the two of them were together, she let it pass.

Sue Ellen sipped from the iced tea again. "Since I've met you, I don't think I've seen you take a drink."

"I used to drink, but not anymore."

"Do you mind telling me why?"

"It interferes with my work and I can't concentrate."

More silence as they watched the traffic splash through puddles on South Battery; farther out, Murray Boulevard. Inside the house someone finally answered the phone.

"Your family drinks, don't they?"

Sue Ellen colored, but who was she to protest?

"They do," she said rather coolly.

"I killed my brother while I was drunk. Let's hope something terrible like that never happens in your family."

"I'm . . . I'm so sorry. How . . . how did you kill your brother?"

"I don't remember."

"You don't remember?"

Edmund stopped rocking and turned to her. "So, you wonder, how do I know that I killed him?"

Sue Ellen could only nod.

"The police said he fell out of my car while we were traveling at a high rate of speed. Willie was always doing one damn fool thing or another. He was the kind of person who stands on the running board or jumps in or out while the car's still in motion. My mother said it was all my fault since I was the eldest and knew Willie could be such a joker."

Sue Ellen didn't dare speak.

"It was a convertible, and all they know is that I was speeding, and that's what I was ticketed for. Well, that and driving while drunk. The judge suspended my license for a year. That was the year I learned how to study."

They were sitting in silence, their rockers not moving when Prescott Mitchell came through the door, phone in hand and at the end of its tether.

"Okay," he said into the phone, "I can see that it's stopped." Prescott paused. "Sure. I'll bring her along." He placed the receiver on the base. "Sue Ellen, some of us are meeting at Christian's for cocktails. Would you like to go?"

Sue Ellen glanced at Edmund, who continued to stare across the street. The two young men came around the corner of the porch, saw Prescott standing in the doorway, and went down the front steps to the sidewalk. There they stood around as if trying to make up their minds what to do next.

"Why not?" asked Sue Ellen, leaving her rocker. "Let me get a wrap."

Prescott opened the door with his free hand, then turned to Edmund, who had stood up when Sue Ellen left her chair. "You want to come along? I'm picking up Rachel, but we have plenty of room."

Edmund took a last drag off his cigarette before putting it out in the sand bucket. "Wish I could, but I'm expecting a call."

"Well, you know where we'll be." Prescott glanced at the sidewalk where the two young men had been, then lowered his voice and leaned out of the door. "Rachel Belle knows more good-looking women than you can shake a stick at, and at smaller get-togethers you don't have to compete with all the other engineers."

At breakfast the following morning, Thomas Stevenson dropped by as he sometimes did for breakfast. A fellow Citadel grad, Thomas had graduated in the same class as Franklin Belle.

This pleased Elizabeth Randolph no end. The more young men who took their meals here crowded out James Stuart, or so she thought until she found James taking early breakfast at the kitchen table with her daughter acting as his personal chef.

In the dining room, Rachel tried to make conversation at a table where everyone seemed to be in their cups, their coffee cups, that is. "Don't forget Saturday night's birthday party for Christian." She beamed at her boyfriend.

Her boyfriend flushed and stared into his plate.

"It'll begin right after supper."

Sue Ellen came into the room, took a seat, and simply sat there, hand around a coffee cup. The others ignored her. Sue Ellen could be a real bear in the morning.

Again Rachel tried. "We're having our annual bake sale at the Huguenot church Saturday." Big smile. "There will be some really delicious baked goods there." Pause. "But don't wait until the last minute. The best of the lot sells out before noon."

The women nodded, then the table returned to its slumber.

This really irritated Rachel. She had been raised to believe that anyone in her social strata should surround herself with others of like mind, or those who could carry on an intelligent conversation, but there were simply too many out-of-towners at this table. Of course, she didn't mean Christian. He was probably exhausted from working long hours, plus the ferryboat ride to and from his job.

Rachel tried a third time, falling back on the old standby: the bridge. "Anyone know when the two spans will be joined?"

"End of June," said Thomas Stevenson.

Christian laughed. "He's only saying that because he picked the end of June."

"Picked the end of June?" asked Abigail Mullins, nervous whenever the conversation turned to the bridge. In the hallway, the phone rang. Everyone ignored it.

"Yes. There's a pool."

"A pool?" asked Abigail.

"For betting when the two spans will be joined," said Prescott. "Winner gets to walk across the completed bridge first."

With a warm smile, Rachel asked Abigail, "Not much gambling in New England, is there?"

"Needless to say," concluded Christian, "the end of June is much too soon, though we're well ahead of schedule."

Thomas smiled from his side of the table. "Well, we'll just have to see about that."

Christian made a point of eating at least two meals a day at this house. Lunch was out of the question since he worked in East Cooper, though Rachel did pack his lunch. She would write notes on his waxed paper saying: "Miss you already" or "See you at dinner" or "Be careful."

Damned if Charleston wasn't the best place in the world to court a dame. It had parks, plantations, and old churchyards, along with the Battery where you could stroll to the sounds of a string quintet or a brass band in the gazebo. No place like it.

Abigail turned to her fiancé. "Nick, don't tell me you've selected a week in this pool."

The men, including Nicholas, returned their attention to their breakfast.

"When?" demanded his fiancée.

"When do you think?" asked Prescott, grinning from the other side of the table.

"Aw, come on, guys," said Christian, quite sensitive to the fact that he was courting the most attractive but most difficult woman in Charleston. "Don't tease Abigail. Just be happy that maneuvers have been postponed until after opening ceremonies and we'll all be here to celebrate."

Many of the engineers were ROTC grads and continued to hold their commissions. Of all the engineers, Nicholas looked forward to their Monday night drills. In uniform, they were all fellow soldiers.

"I know which week," said Rachel, smiling.

"What do you mean?" asked Abigail. For some reason she could not fathom, Rachel Belle had become even more difficult to deal with.

"You've seen the pool?" asked Prescott.

"I don't have to see the pool to know what week any Yankee would pick."

Everyone looked around the table, then in unison, "The Fourth of July!"

Rachel nodded. "No self-respecting Reb would pick that week."

More laughter. These Rebs and Yanks were getting to know each other, and the other "side" didn't look all that different—the belles so charming, the engineers so capable.

"Nick, really," said Abigail, "you shouldn't have."

With the final sections of the superstructure going up, the bridge had become quite real, and Abigail was one of the few people in Charleston who no longer enjoyed strolling along the shoreline.

"There's no harm in it, Abigail. Like Rachel said, the Fourth of July week was open, and I took it, more in support of the Union than anything else."

Christian thumped his silverware on the table. "The Union now and forever!"

"The South will rise again!" shouted Franklin.

"Take it outside," chimed in everyone else.

In truth, all this manufactured animosity between the North and South had become rather tedious. Christian and Prescott had been the most vocal in arguing over the causes of the war, but Prescott had lost his debating opponent once Rachel began to express an interest in this Yankee from Wisconsin.

Dory backed through the swinging door with a pot of coffee and a tray of biscuits. Several of the men whistled at her flapper dress and bobbed hair.

"Well, well," said Prescott, nodding in approval, "our country cousin has finally come to town."

Dory flushed and looked at Sue Ellen. Sue Ellen didn't appear to notice. Dory moved around the table, refilling coffee and offering biscuits, then returned to the kitchen.

Elizabeth Randolph and Nicholas Eaton, Senior, entered the dining room to check on everyone. They were off to church and would not eat until after communion. Down the hall the phone continued to ring until Elizabeth picked it up on her way out of the house. She jotted a note on the pad before going out the door.

Edmund Hall arrived, nodding to the folks around the table and taking a seat next to Sue Ellen. There was always an open seat next to Sue Ellen.

"Did you enjoy last night?" he asked, unfolding his napkin.

Sue Ellen couldn't remember last night, and this included whether she'd allowed Prescott to get to second base, or even farther.

"You know," continued Edmund, "I waited all afternoon for that phone call, but it never came."

Rachel, in an attempt to keep the conversation rolling asked, "Just who were you expecting to call, Edmund?"

"Er...dear," said Christian, "Edmund might've been expecting a call from home."

Someone down the table snorted, then laughed, certainly one of the guys.

Rachel realized her faux pas, if a Belle of Charleston could actually commit a faux pas. "I apologize, Edmund. It was none of my business."

Abigail Mullins said, "I thought you'd noticed by now, Rachel, but Edmund doesn't drink."

Rachel's eyes flashed, but she quickly recovered. She smiled at Edmund. "You're always welcome at our parties. We have plenty of ginger ale." Looking at Abigail, she added, "Being a teetotaler is never enough reason not to be invited to one of our parties."

"Yes," said Prescott, chuckling, "though the day Sue Ellen stops drinking, we're going to miss that girl who shows up whenever Sue Ellen's tight."

TWENTY-FIVE

The guard slept soundly in his shack, feet propped up and mouth wide open—from a bottle provided by Edmund Hall earlier in the evening. Edmund left Sue Ellen outside the guardhouse and stepped inside to shake the man. It was early Sunday morning and Charleston slumbered.

The guard coughed, shifted in his chair, but never opened his eyes. Satisfied, Edmund rejoined Sue Ellen outside the shack.

"We're on."

"You don't drink," said Sue Ellen. "You don't want me to drink, but you gave him a bottle of booze."

"Jim Beam, right from your father's warehouse— the best liquor that guard will have until Prohibition ends."

"Prohibition was an amendment to the Constitution."

"And it will end that way, too." He pulled her away from the guard shack.

"I don't know. It was tough enough to push the original amendment through."

"It won't be as hard to repeal. Everyone is sick and tired of all this government corruption."

"What corruption?"

"Corrupt revenuers, corrupt judges, and corrupt cops. Do you want our children to grow up in a world where there are two different systems: one for us and one for the rich?"

"Our children?"

He glanced at her. "I'm not as pure as you think, Sue Ellen. I can be seduced by a pretty girl as easily as the next guy."

Sue Ellen was still trying to figure out what Edmund meant as he pulled her around the piles of sand, gravel, timber, and steel beams. The causeway climbed the staggered-height piers where the two sections would soon be joined. Crews pouring concrete followed the completed sections of the bridge. When finished, the crews would have been pouring concrete for over a year.

Edmund and Sue Ellen had stayed up all night, drinking coffee and dancing until the last station signed off; then they rocked for a long time on the front porch. Hartleigh and Dory, exhausted from a long day in the kitchen, had fallen into a deep sleep. Sue Ellen would not be missed until, well, right about now.

The wind off the harbor was brisk, but warm and humid; the sun had yet to break over East Cooper. Stars shone more brightly this far from the city, and since you could see little in such darkness, the usual crowds of onlookers and picnickers had yet to arrive. Sue Ellen watched Edmund toss coal into the furnace of a miniature train used to haul building supplies to the uppermost point of the unfinished bridge. A grimy off-white dust covered the rail cars inside and out.

"I've never stayed up all night unless I was tight."

Edmund laughed. Both of them were bleary eyed. "Before then, you always passed out."

"Edmund, don't be mean!"

Still bent over and feeding the fire, Edmund looked at her. "You can't drink like the others, Sue Ellen. You're much too thin."

"I didn't come here to be insulted."

Edmund straightened up. "I thought that was the fashion, you know, a boyish figure, and you've got that in spades."

Sue Ellen didn't know whether to slap him or kiss him. "Edmund, you can't allow a few drinks to come between us."

"It *has* come between us, and it's not just a few."

He threw a blanket over a chair placed in the first empty car behind the coal car. Sweeping out his arm, Edmund said, "Your steed awaits you, Miss."

Sue Ellen allowed him to assist her into her seat, which, curiously, faced the shoreline, not the river.

"I thought I'd be looking at the river, not a pile of blankets." She was referring to the stack of blankets on the floor of the miniature railway car.

"Oh, you won't be disappointed."

Edmund disappeared behind a pile of steel beams and returned with another blanket, this one nailed to a square-wooden frame he jammed into the railroad car behind her. "This serves as a windshield."

"Like on a car?"

"Yes. Something to keep the ashes off."

He covered her with another blanket, then pulled on gloves, goggles, and a slicker like he was going for a ride in one of the first Model Ts. Raising his voice over the noise of the engine, he leaned over and shouted, "Don't leave this car and never stand up."

The look on Sue Ellen's face turned apprehensive.

He clapped her on the shoulder. "Don't worry, babe. The train makes this journey several times a day so there's nothing to fear—unless you leave the car or stand up." He gave her a peck on the cheek. "You're about to be the first girl to travel to the top of the Cooper River Bridge."

"Unless my brother has brought Hartleigh up here."

That stopped Edmund. "You really think your brother has taken Hartleigh up there?"

"Why not? He acts like he owns this bridge."

"Yeah," said Edmund, returning to the engine, "but to work on, not to play on."

By the time Sue Ellen was able to relax on the noisy, shaky journey, the sun had begun to rise over East Cooper. Looking toward downtown, Sue Ellen gasped as Rainbow Row burst into color—it would've made Dorothy Porcher Legge proud; church spires twinkled in the sunlight. The city looked fresh and new from where the train climbed the roadway.

"Oh, this is wonderful! Absolutely beautiful."

At the farthest point, Edmund stopped the train and assisted her out of the small, open railcar. He took the blanket, then her hand as she crossed the concrete deck to the edge of the bridge.

Sue Ellen trembled as she peered down. Now that was a long way. What was it? A hundred and fifty feet?

A huge crane blocked the view of the other half of the bridge originating in East Cooper. A strong breeze pushed her into Edmund.

"Wow!" he said, taking her into his arms. "This is better than waiting for the ghost of Stede Bonnet to return to White Point Garden!"

"Don't be mean, Edmund! This is scary."

"I'm no meaner than the girls who have no time for me."

Sue Ellen gave him a playful thump on the chest. "Now, that is mean."

"And you're sober."

"Edmund, are you trying to convert me?"

"I simply wanted to share this view with a good friend and you and I, living in that house, have spent more time together than I have with any dame."

"I like you, too. You don't talk about the bridge all the time."

"Well," he said, taking her shoulders and turning her upriver, "a picture is worth a thousand words."

Sue Ellen saw the Cooper disappear upstream, way upstream, even beyond the naval shipyard. She'd never seen the river reach this far inland, not even from the Ferris wheel on the Isle of Palms.

Taking her shoulders, Edmund turned her toward Charleston as the morning mist lifted. As she watched, the darkness fell back west of the Ashley, and then revealed the coast in all its glory.

"Oh, my!"

Her mouth was still open when Edmund kissed her. Sue Ellen liked kissing, and since she wasn't drunk, this was one kiss she'd remember. She closed her eyes, surrendering to Edmund and his touch. She did not notice the cinders blow from his slicker onto her jacket, but she did feel his hand slide up under her dress.

A few weeks later, James finished checking one of the bearing shoes, that piece of the bridge where the cantilevered truss and road deck connected on one of the anchor piers. As traffic crossed the bridge, these massive hinges would allow the superstructure to rotate slightly, minimizing stress to the truss.

James walked to the edge of the pier, reaching around and gripping the top of one of the horizontal steel beams. A couple of steelworkers reached down, took his hands, and pulled James up to the concrete roadbed.

One of the workmen gestured at a young man in a white business suit. The two halves had been joined, and the city was in a celebratory mood. No matter how hard you tried, you could not keep the civilians off the bridge.

But this civilian James recognized as one who spent a good deal of time with his sister. "Prescott, what you doing up here?"

The engineer from Georgia Tech appeared to be evaluating the single steel beam connecting the two sides of the bridge.

"Prescott!"

The engineer faced him. "Oh, sorry, didn't see you standing there." Wind off the Cooper caused Prescott to hold his derby with both hands. Depending on where you stood, you could hear the wind whistling through the steel beams.

"What can I do for you?" asked James.

"What if I wanted to ask for your sister's hand in marriage?"

"I'd turn you down."

"I could ask your father."

"Uh-huh. Just make sure you take along a pistol. We Stuarts are known for our hot-bloodedness."

"Hence, the allure of your sister."

Prescott stepped to the edge where the single beam joined the two sides and peered down. Lord, but he wouldn't want to fall down there, particularly with all the boats moored around an anchor pier. A few weeks ago, one of the workmen had fallen to his death from this bridge.

"Prescott, my sister may appear to be a party girl, but down deep inside she's not."

The Georgia Tech engineer continued to stare below. "First time I've been up here," he said, more to himself. "Exhilarating."

James removed his hat and sunglasses and wiped his forehead with the handkerchief hanging around his neck. It was July in Charleston and hot as blazes, but the end was near. A month from now they would be dedicating this bridge.

Prescott stared downstream toward the harbor, then over the roof of the city, finally looking upriver. He glanced at East Cooper but saw little as the other side was blocked by a matching crane working in their direction. Between the two sides of the bridge was an open expanse of space connected by two single eighteen-inch steel beams. On that beam, a solitary workman crossed to their side, finally looked up, then nodded and made his way past them.

"So Thomas Stevenson won the pool," said Prescott, observing the warren of beams overhead.

"The last week in June," confirmed James.

"You two were in cahoots."

"Uh-huh. And when was the last time you remember me doing anything for a Citadel grad?"

"Who had the following week?"

"Nicholas Eaton."

"Oh, that is rich."

James wiped his face again. "As is the fact you had a hand in building a bridge that'll bring even more Yankees to Charleston."

"At least this time they'll bring money, not guns." Prescott walked over and stuck out his hand. "Well, the job's completed, and I'll have to admit it's been a helluva a first job."

"So," said James, shaking hands, "you're off to close the bars in yet another town needing a bridge?"

"Not without your sister. She is the ultimate good-time girl."

"Sue Ellen wants children, Prescott."

That stopped him. "Are you sure?"

"Why do you think she dotes on Dory?"

Again Prescott looked upriver. "Hmm. Maybe that's why Edmund brought her up here."

"What? Who brought Sue Ellen up here?"

"Early one Sunday morning last month. I'm surprised you didn't hear about it."

"But...how?"

Prescott gestured at the miniature train on the track behind them. "Edmund returned to the house covered with soot, and even though he wore a slicker, hat, and goggles, everyone knew."

Prescott did not add that Sue Ellen was also a mess, but he did not care to consider what that might mean.

James's hands clenched at his sides. "Totally irresponsible."

"I was annoyed that I didn't think of it first."

"Then I'd be jacking you up."

"Yeah," said Prescott, rather wistfully, "but consider the prize." What this man didn't understand was that his sister belonged to him. Prescott had put his stamp on her more than once, though he did have misgivings about marrying a girl who never seemed to remember their coupling.

"It was probably the only move Edmund had left. He reads all the time, fishes on his day off, and never parties. Well, my turn now."

And Prescott did a little dance to the edge of the bridge before walking out on the beam connecting the two sides. He turned around, slapped his hat on his head, waved again, and then misjudging his first step, plunged headfirst into the Cooper.

TWENTY-SIX

James was sitting in the emergency room of Roper Hospital when Sue Ellen and Hartleigh came through the double doors. Elbows on his knees, brim of his slouch hat held by both hands, James leaned forward and stared at the floor until he heard the sound of heels on the highly shined wooden floor.

He got to his feet. "Sue Ellen, I need to talk with you."

"Is it true?" asked Hartleigh.

"The truth is what I want," said James, speaking to his sister.

"Prescott really fell off the bridge?" asked Sue Ellen.

"I was told you'd been up there."

"Where?" asked Hartleigh.

"What?" asked Sue Ellen.

"To the top of the bridge."

Hartleigh's hand rose to her throat. "He fell all the way...?"

"Is it true?" asked James, looking at his sister.

"Is what true?" An innocent look appeared on his sister's face.

"What's the prognosis?" asked Hartleigh.

"Bad move," said James, shaking his head. "What will people think?"

"What will people think? What does it matter what people think?" Hartleigh's voice began to rise. "The house has become a morgue. Everyone mopes around. First Artie, then that sandhog that died of the bends, the worker electrocuted, and now Prescott. How much longer before the bridge is finished?"

"You're not my father," said Sue Ellen.

"But everyone knows you're looking for one."

"Don't analyze me, James. Girls can do things, too."

"Not you. Your family's reputation precedes you."

Hartleigh could only watch as the conversation bounced back and forth. What in the world were these two talking about?

Hands on her hips, Sue Ellen said, "You have no business telling me what to do."

"Someone should. Prescott's interested because he thinks you're some cuckoo dame."

Sue Ellen drew herself up. "You'd speak to your own sister in this manner?"

"Don't go all righteous on me. I used to double date with you."

"What in the world are you two talking about?" asked Hartleigh.

James turned to his sister. "Prescott expressed his intentions."

"Really?" Sue Ellen couldn't help but smile.

Looking back at his sister, he said. "He wants me

to convince our parents that you two are a good fit."

Hartleigh turned to Sue Ellen. "Prescott has spoken to you about this, not your father?"

The surgeon came through the swinging doors. He looked from one person to the other. "Any family members?"

"On their way from Missouri."

"Well," said the doctor with a sigh, "it's not like Mister Mitchell is going anywhere."

"I'm James Stuart. I represent the Cooper River Bridge Company." He pointed at Sue Ellen. "This is my sister, Prescott's intended, and Hartleigh Randolph who's . . ."

"Will he live?" asked Hartleigh, hand at her throat.

"Not as well as he could have."

"What . . . what do you mean?" asked Sue Ellen.

"Mister Mitchell will never walk again. He'll be in a wheelchair for the rest of his life."

This couldn't be true, thought Sue Ellen. Prescott was the life of the party, the wisecracker, the catalyst—the perfect guest to make a party start hopping.

Sue Ellen shuddered. Prescott's life was over before it had ever begun.

"You're the man who supervises work on the bridge?" asked the surgeon of James.

"One of them."

"I'm surprised I haven't tended to you. You have a reputation for climbing all over those monkey bars, even going down into the pneumatic caissons."

James glanced at his sister.

Sue Ellen began to tremble. She knew nothing of her brother working below the river's surface. Men had been crippled for doing just that. Artie Moultrie and six others sandhogs had died.

The surgeon noticed Sue Ellen turn pale. "Miss Stuart, are you all right?"

Sue Ellen's knees buckled and her eyes rolled back in her head. The doctor and her brother grabbed her before she collapsed to the floor.

The admitting doctor was an elderly fellow who had treated female hysteria.

"She doesn't look hysterical," argued her brother. "I thought hysterical women screamed and hollered, you know, had fits."

Sue Ellen lay in the bed, staring at the wall, tears running down her cheeks. Over and over, she muttered, "No, no, no . . ."

"Young man," asked the doctor, "are you a physician?"

"A civil engineer, but as a representative of her family, could I request that you wait an hour before treating her? She's a pretty tough cookie."

The doctor glanced at the girl in the bed. "I'll need someone to sit with her, and I can't spare a nurse with the number of cases coming into the emergency room from the bridge."

"That won't be any problem. Her best friend is down the hall using the telephone."

Hartleigh explained to Pearl that Sue Ellen had fainted. "The doctor said they'd keep her overnight."

"Is Miss Sue Ellen in the family way?"

Hartleigh did not know how to respond. She, herself, had lain awake at night worrying about that very subject until the flood began. Then she'd gone about her chores humming. Odd, wasn't it, she'd begun that month humming, then become desperately worried, and finally humming again.

"Your mama ain't gonna let no gal in the family way live in this here house."

Hartleigh had never considered that. If she were in the family way, James and she would marry and live together—with their child—happily ever after. But how could Sue Ellen marry Prescott, a man destined to spend the rest of his life in a wheelchair?

"And you sure don't want Miss Sue Ellen going home. That's the wrong house to be raising a baby in."

All this was true, thought Hartleigh. Oh, my goodness! Where would Sue Ellen live? On her brother's boat? But she'd always thought she and James would—

"You find out, Miss Hartleigh, 'cause somebody's got some planning to be done."

Hartleigh stood there, phone to her ear until the operator came on the line and asked if she cared to make another call.

"No. No thank you."

She hung up and turned into the face of James Stuart. Hartleigh jumped.

"Everything all right? You were on that phone an awfully long time."

"Yes, yes. I was just telling Pearl—"

James reached for the phone. "I need to call my mother and tell her what's happened. Sue Ellen requires a nurse or babysitter around the clock."

Hartleigh put her hand on his hand. James had a strong, tanned hand. A capable hand. "I'll go see your mother."

"Didn't you hear me—someone must sit with Sue Ellen right now."

Hartleigh removed his hand from the phone. "I'll have Dory sent over. Alexander can bring her."

"I'm not sure I want you seeing my mother."

"I'll take someone along. You tend to the bridge. You're very close to finishing."

She took the phone off the hook, and before he walked away, she said, "James, you're going to have some very serious choices to make in the near future. You don't really believe you can walk out on all the relationships you have in Charleston, do you?"

In the hospital room, Hartleigh found Sue Ellen had cried herself to sleep, so, once Dory arrived, Hartleigh returned home with Alexander to find only Edmund there. Strangely, Edmund was more concerned with Sue Ellen than with Prescott. Well, Edmund had gone on all those double dates with them.

"Edmund, are you aware that it's quite inappropriate for you to visit a young woman in the hospital without a chaperone."

A look of despair crossed the young man's face.

Hartleigh took his hand and smiled. "What you do is go visit Prescott, then, because you're in the building, ask to see Sue Ellen. Now, let's walk over to the Stuarts and bring them up to date."

An encounter that put even more people in the hospital.

TWENTY-SEVEN

In a conversation held in the parlor earlier that week, Nicholas Eaton had tried to allay his fiancée's fears about bridge building. "Abigail, being an engineer is not hazardous work."

"And how many more must die before you recognize my concerns? You attend Monday night guard duty, leaving me home alone. And two weeks of maneuvers every summer."

"Maneuvers are not an issue. You return to New England for the summer. And you're not alone Monday nights. You have the other girls."

"If I've told you once, I've told you a dozen times, these belles are the biggest phonies on earth."

With the mention of the word "belle," Nicholas couldn't help the image of Rachel Belle flashing through his head. The girl was too beautiful by half.

"Nick, are you listening to me?"

"I was just thinking . . ."

"Of who? What's her name?"

"Her?" He frowned. "Why her?"

"Why would you not be listening?"

"Abigail, I have no idea what you're talking about."

"Are you going to sit there and lie to me?"

"Abby, I'm not lying."

"You don't think I see the way you look at her?"

"Her—who?" he asked again.

"Rachel Belle."

"What in the world do you mean?"

From there the conversation disintegrated in to "He said, she said," then onto "She believed, he believed."

And the day Prescott Mitchell fell off the bridge, Abigail returned her engagement ring, packed her trunk and suitcases, and took the first train north.

At Union Station, corner of Columbus and East Bay, Laurens Rutledge was accompanied by her parents to see her husband off for his new job in New York. Once Lawrence was onboard, Laurens' mother started in on her daughter about returning home with the baby. They passed Rachel, Elizabeth, and Abigail on the platform with only the slightest degree of acknowledgment.

Nicholas chose not to see his former fiancée off. This did not upset Abigail, but the presence of Rachel Belle unnerved her.

"We're certainly going to miss you," said Rachel, smiling. "Nobody knows how to clean a house like you do."

"The one thing I'm sorry about is that this leaves Nicholas open to your charms." Abigail glanced at Elizabeth Randolph. "All the belles' charms, is what I meant to say."

Continuing to smile, Rachel said, "I'll make sure Nicholas writes his father every week."

"I'm sure you will."

Rachel took her hand. "My dear Abigail, you can't understand how much closer you and I have become during your stay in Charleston. One day, you may even invite me to Lowell."

Abigail glanced at their hands. Both women still wore gloves.

Elizabeth tried to move the conversation in a different direction, apologizing for Nicholas not seeing Abigail off.

"This is not your fault, Mrs. Randolph." Abigail pulled her gloved hand from Rachel's. "I just never thought a nice boy from Lowell could take on such a dangerous occupation, and now he's talking about building dams for TVA."

"TVA?" asked both Elizabeth and Rachel.

"The government is considering building a series of dams along the Tennessee River to electrify the river valley. Nicholas wants to build those dams. I may never get him out of the South."

Rachel didn't know where the Tennessee River Valley was, nor did she care. It obviously had nothing to do with Charleston.

"But why would the government put money into such a project and not build a bridge over the Cooper River?" asked Elizabeth.

As the conductor hollered "All aboard" and the whistle shrieked, Abigail leaned over and raised her voice, "Because Tennessee had a difficult time making up its mind whether to secede from the Union or not. But you people in South Carolina, you actually started the war."

Edmund accompanied Hartleigh down the street to the Stuarts'. On the porch, he rang the doorbell, stepped back, and stood beside her. When there was no answer, Edmund rang the bell again. Usually a maid or butler would answer the door, but Hartleigh remembered her conversation with Molly and Pearl and the difficulty the Stuarts had in keeping help.

Jeb Stuart jerked open the door. "Yes? What is it you want?"

Edmund introduced them. "You, of course, know your neighbor from down the street, Hartleigh Randolph."

"Oh, yes, the house that takes in boarders."

"Mister Stuart, may I see your wife?" asked Hartleigh.

"What for?"

Evidently, thought Edmund, though a native Charlestonian, Jeb Stuart did not remember *his* manners.

"It's a personal matter," said Hartleigh with a smile.

Jeb evaluated Edmund. "And just who the hell are you?"

"Sir, watch your language. There's a lady present."

Jeb stepped onto the porch. "Why, you little pip-squeak. This is my property and I'll speak any way that I wish."

"And I remind you that you are keeping a lady waiting."

Jeb glanced at Hartleigh. "No lady I know accepts boarders into her house."

Hartleigh touched Edmund's arm. "Edmund, please . . ."

Jeb grinned. "Listen to your mama, little boy."

Edmund bristled.

Hartleigh pulled him away. "Come on, Edmund. There's more than one way to skin this cat."

Edmund wasn't so sure, but he trailed Hartleigh down the front steps, out the gate, and down the sidewalk to her house.

At home, Hartleigh tried the phone, but the operator said, "I may be wrong, Miss Randolph, but I believe the Stuarts' phone is off the hook. That happens occasionally."

Hartleigh thanked her and hung up. How could she get through? "Wait here, Edmund." She headed down the hall.

Edmund trailed after her. "But what about Sue Ellen?"

"First things first."

"Sue Ellen is first on my list, not what her father thinks."

Hartleigh stopped at the doorway to the kitchen. "Could you give me one more chance?"

"I'm worried about Sue Ellen. And Prescott."

"I understand," said Hartleigh with a quiet smile.

"It's not what you think—Sue Ellen's for Prescott. I know you don't think much of me because I don't fit into your social scene, but I do care about the girl."

"And I'll make sure Sue Ellen hears that when we see her."

"You'll tell her?"

Hartleigh moved her hand across her chest. "Cross my heart and hope to die."

With that reassurance, Edmund Hall followed Hartleigh Randolph around like a lapdog, including when Rachel Belle and her stepmother, Georgiana, and Hartleigh bullied their way past Jeb Stuart and into his house. A few minutes later, every one of them, plus Mrs. Stuart, piled into the Stuarts' Cadillac and headed for the hospital. With all the women in the car, there wasn't room for a single, unrelated young male, so Edmund was left to deal with a drunken Jeb Stuart. The result put Jeb in a room just down the hall from his daughter, and Edmund Hall in the Charleston city jail.

TWENTY-EIGHT

When James returned to his sister's room, Sue Ellen was awake. She had stopped muttering to herself, but she had not stopped crying.

"Don't get her riled up," cautioned Dory.

James smiled. "Yes, ma'am."

Dory raised a finger. "Don't you mock me, James Stuart." And she wandered off to explore the hospital. Dory had never been in one before.

Once she left, James took a seat next to the bed.

His sister rolled over and faced him. She wiped her tears away. "James, were you there when Prescott fell?"

"Yes. Alexander fished him out of the water." James quickly asked, "Sue Ellen, do you remember last year when you began dragging me to all those dances?" He didn't want another onset of the vapors over his going down in the pneumatic caisson.

Her head rose off her pillow. "You volunteered to go. It was even your idea to bring Hartleigh and

Edmund along." She blotted away the tears, then lay her head on the pillow again.

"I went dancing to make sure people understood that I held no grudge, and this resulted in you having too many boyfriends."

She smiled. "A girl can never have too many boyfriends." She put a hand under her head to raise it up. "You didn't care to go? You certainly looked like you were enjoying yourself."

"That was Hartleigh. She made everything run smoothly."

"Don't talk like an engineer. It's off-putting."

"If I can't find a husband for you, I'm not fulfilling my responsibilities as your brother."

Now his sister sat up, scooted back against the pillow, and crossed her arms. "Well, don't overexert yourself for my sake. I'm doing just fine."

James reached over and touched her, but Sue Ellen leaned away, so he sat back in his chair. "You've been spoiled by having too many young men at your beck and call."

"At least you didn't put it in engineering terms."

"It's called the Law of Unintended Results."

"Now that's a relief," she said with a sour look. "For a moment, I thought you were some alien from the Buck Rogers comic strip."

"Someday there'll only be one you'll be devoted to and that guy must believe everything you've done up to this point has been frivolous and inconsequential; nothing serious."

Sue Ellen's head snapped around. "What's this? Marriage advice from my big brother? Then I have some advice for you: marry Hartleigh. Since the Randolphs took in boarders, Hartleigh's become almost as boring as you. Maybe you can liven her up by turning her into your next project."

"The point I was making had to do with you, not me."

"Oh, James," she laughed, "you'll make absolutely no headway with me. There are too many cute boys in this town."

"You'd marry a Yankee?"

"Prescott is no Yankee, and neither is Edmund."

"You know what I mean: an out-of-towner."

"I'd consider it."

"And move away?"

Reflecting on the battle fatigue she'd experienced on the home front, she said, "I guess I'll have to."

"That doesn't seem to be the correct reason to marry."

"Hey," she said with a grin, "not all of us can be rich."

James shifted around in his chair. "I really don't understand how that rumor got started."

"The boat, you ninny. You have the most beautiful yacht in the harbor."

"Good enough reason to sell it," said James, rather glumly. "I don't like all the attention."

"Oh, James, don't take everything so seriously."

"I seem to have been born that way."

"Were not!" His sister sat up. "The brother I knew was all kinds of fun."

"Sue Ellen, sooner or later you must grow up."

She stared at him for a very long moment. "James, why are you talking to me like this?"

"Because you went up on the bridge with Edmund Hall."

"What business is it of yours where I go?"

"Because you're getting a reputation."

"Is this your way of asking if I'm a good girl or not?" She shifted around in the bed and looked straight ahead.

"I do need to know whether I should fight for you or not."

"You mean, defend my honor? Well," said his sister, lying through her teeth, "on that score you have nothing to worry about."

"I certainly hope not. It would get our father killed. He's not all that good a shot."

"Oh, please! These days men do not go out in the woods and duel over women."

Her brother said nothing, only leaned back in his chair.

"Oh, don't tell me . . ."

"Don't worry. It was up north, and I walked a lot of punishment tours when word got out."

His sister's hand was at her mouth. "You didn't kill anyone, did you?"

Still, her brother said nothing, but he did smile.

"Who was the girl?"

Her brother stopped smiling.

"James, I can't be responsible for what people think of me any more than you can be responsible for what people think of you."

"Sorry, but you're a girl and . . ."

A knock at the door, and Hartleigh Randolph, Sue Ellen's mother, and Rachel's stepmother entered the room. When James saw Alexander standing in the hallway behind them, he gave his mother a peck on the cheek, and joined the Negro in the hall.

But before leaving, he said, "Thank you for coming along, Mrs. Belle."

"Happy to." And to his surprise, Georgiana followed him into the hallway and took him aside. "James, I need to ask a favor."

"Ma'am?"

Alexander moved out of earshot, down the hall.

"James, I don't consider myself a meddlesome stepmother, but now that this bridge is finished, I'm concerned that I have two children who are almost three years older and neither of them is married."

James said nothing and his face gave off no clue as to what he might be thinking.

"You, Franklin, and Rachel have been close all your life, and I wanted to know if there's anything of which I should be aware."

James had to decipher the remark. Once he did, he quickly said, "You have nothing to worry about on your son's behalf, Mrs. Belle, and, well, Rachel is Rachel. She's going to pick who she's going to pick, and when she wants to pick him."

"And the environment of a boarding house has nothing to do with this? Franklin may not live there, but he certainly spends a great deal of his time there."

"All a boarding house does is to give your daughter more beaus to pick from. As for Franklin, he loves to be around women, but being with one girl is a bit overwhelming."

Georgiana nodded. "I knew I shouldn't have encouraged him to draw. His father says I've spoiled them both, but I wanted to be a good mother. I know, I know, I should've selected a boy for Rachel and had my husband approach the boy's parents. That's what was done for my generation."

She shook her head. "I don't know what's wrong with this modern generation, but I don't like it. I really don't like it at all." She took his arm again. "James, could you do me a favor? Get Franklin to ask Hartleigh out and perhaps you could ask Rachel out."

"Oh, I don't know about that . . ."

"I know you have a lot on your mind finishing up the bridge—oh, I want you to know that the bridge with its double arches turned out beautifully, but since you're so close to my children, perhaps all of you could go out together." Her hand made a come-along motion. "Oh, what is it the young people call it?"

"A double date?"

"Yes, yes, that's it, go on a double date, and I would be eternally grateful."

And she patted his arm and disappeared into his sister's room, closing the door behind her. James felt his pocket. The ring was still there. What was it that he'd told Franklin: that Hartleigh Randolph might not be available forever.

Alexander strolled over. "It may not be the right time to tell you, but the talk you asked me to listen for—it's started."

James continued to stare at the door and rub his pocket.

"James, did you hear me?"

"Sorry," he said, turning from the door. "What'd you say?"

"White folks touting individual stocks."

Now, he had James's complete attention. "When did you hear this?"

"It started a couple of weeks ago."

"You're sure?"

Alexander nodded. "Those folks are sure enough

excited. They're full of all kinds of tips."

"Okay. I'll sell our positions."

"Er...James, what if we get out too soon?"

The white man grinned and clapped the black man on the shoulder. "What's your portfolio worth these days?"

"Almost fifty thousand dollars, according to the newspaper."

"So, is this a desire to round up or just old-fashioned greed?"

Alexander ignored his question and asked one of his own. "Can I keep the children's college fund in the market?"

"Absolutely not. Those are the first stocks you should sell."

"Well, I'll let you know."

After a phone call to his broker, James found his father's room down the hall. "You took on a kid and lived to tell the tale?"

"That kid sucker punched me!"

"Now calm down, Jeb," said his wife, who sat next to her husband's bed. She had gray hair, dressed liked a matron, and wore no makeup as that would make her look cheap. "You heard the doctor. Complete rest."

"That boy's another Yankee come down here to steal our women!" His father was red-faced.

"Edmund Hall is from Raleigh."

"You know what I mean."

"James, don't argue with your father."

"You took on a former Golden Gloves light-heavyweight contender. You're fortunate Edmund didn't kill you."

"Next time we meet it'll be on a field of honor."

"Then make sure your affairs are in order, because as the respondent, Edmund will have his choice of weapons, and in our guard unit, he's rated marksman."

Jeb waved off Edmund's credentials. "And the best this fellow could do was to hit me when I wasn't looking."

"James, you're upsetting your father, and you're embarrassing me by hanging around those people in that boarding house."

James reached back and pushed shut the door. Thinking the door had closed because he heard the click, James interrupted his mother's rant about the coarseness that had become the hallmark of the Randolph family.

"Why, we had to ask Elizabeth to leave our garden club." A rebuke almost as serious as a daughter not being presented at cotillion.

"Mother, you need to watch what you say. Once this project is finished, I intend to ask for Hartleigh's hand."

"Impossible! What will people think?"

Unbeknownst to James, Sue Ellen had been pushed through the door behind him, and pushing the wheelchair was none other than Hartleigh Randolph. His mother's eyes widened in horror, and James turned around to see what had startled her.

Hartleigh smiled generously. "You don't have to wait until the bridge is finished to propose to me, James."

"Well," said Sue Ellen, "I'm glad that's settled. Now let's see if we can work on a double wedding. You're still responsible for finding a decent husband for me, big brother."

And that set her father off on a rant that drove everyone from the room, including his daughter.

"Watch out, Daddy, or I'll marry the man who beat you up."

Back at the house, everyone worked to get the next meal on the table, and Rachel, checking behind everyone, found Nicholas Eaton in the dining room, drinking sweet tea. He hastily got to his feet and formally seated Rachel, then returned to his seat.

"I'm sorry things didn't work out between you and Abigail."

"James Stuart is to blame for all my misery."

"Pardon?" asked Rachel. "You're not blaming James for what happened to Prescott, are you?"

"James lured me to Charleston to build a bridge for less than six million dollars."

"Well, wherever you'd gone, Abigail would've been just as disappointed."

Nicholas shook his head. "There are just too many good-looking women in this town."

Rachel smiled. "Blame that on the College of Charleston."

Nicholas went on as if not hearing her. "Luring me to the land of sweet tea, beautiful dames, and warm weather—how can I ever return to New England?"

"Nicholas, are you sure that's sweet tea that you're drinking?"

TWENTY-NINE

After James and Hartleigh smuggled Sue Ellen out of the hospital in a wheelchair, they piled in a car and drove to the jail where Sue Ellen demanded to see Edmund.

"He's my fiancé."

The chief of police glanced at her gloveless hands. "Yes, Miss, but where's your ring?" The chief was a broad-chested man with a ruddy complexion.

"He intends to give it to me later."

"It's none of my business, Miss Stuart, but you'd best be careful with those types of fellows and the promises they make."

"You're right. It's none of—"

James cut her off. "Chief, Edmund Hall works for me on the bridge."

"Oh, I know all about the bridge personnel, Captain Stuart. We have plenty of them in here, and the city council failed to appropriate enough money for all those lawbreakers."

"I'm not saying my engineers haven't crossed a line or two, but as far as I know, no one's been brought up on charges."

"The victim in this case is your father."

"And my father threw the first punch."

"You were there?"

"I didn't have to be. Edmund Hall is a former Golden Gloves light-heavyweight contender. Why would he need to throw the first punch?"

"That true?" The chief was a big boxing fan and knew that a large card of matches had been laid on for the grand opening of the bridge. He came out from behind his desk. "Just a moment, I need to check on something."

"You girls stay here," ordered James, and he followed the chief out of his office.

The two young women remained there because Sue Ellen could not convince Hartleigh to follow the men out of the office, down the hall, and up the stairs.

Policemen in the hallway gaped at them. Hartleigh didn't notice. She was starry-eyed. She was to be married once the bridge was completed. She would have children, but most of all, she would have her own home, though perhaps not the one she desired. Well, a girl couldn't have everything.

James followed the chief upstairs to the lockup where several men lay on the floor, and Edmund Hall was being held from behind so he could be struck by a jailer raising a billy club. Before the jailer could bring the billy club forward, James stepped inside the cell and grabbed the club from behind.

"Let's not do that."

The jailer tried to jerk free, and turned on James, who offered no target by moving when the jailer moved. The trusty holding Edmund tried to hold Edmund with one hand, and at the same time, reach over to give his partner a hand. When he did, James let go of the club and the jailer's hand came forward and the billy club cracked the trusty across the forearm.

The trusty screamed, Edmund slipped from the man's grasp, and James, still behind the jailer, clapped him on both ears before the jailer could re-cock his arm. The jailer yelped, dropped the billy club, and Edmund charged, knocking him into the chief, who stood in the cell door. Both the chief and the jailer went down in a heap. James stepped over the two men and hurried down the cell block with Edmund right behind him.

"You know," said Edmund, "I could've dealt with those two."

"Don't worry about those two. You have bigger problems—me!"

Hurrying for the stairs, he asked, "And what's your beef?"

"You took my sister up on the bridge."

Edmund paused long enough at the top of the stairs that James glanced over his shoulder. "You took advantage of her innocence." At the bottom of the stairs, James added, "When a guy encourages a girl to do something like that, it means he never had any sisters."

Edmund said nothing as he came down the stairs. It was true. He had no sisters. But Sue Ellen Stuart was no innocent.

"What I'm saying is you should ask me what my

sister has permission to do or not to do."

Sue Ellen rushed into Edmund's arms when the young man from Raleigh strode into the chief's office. "I was so worried about you, darling."

Before Sue Ellen could give Edmund a proper kiss, her brother ordered her back into the wheelchair.

"James, please, a moment."

"You've already had that—on the bridge. Now, in the chair!"

At the mention of the bridge, Sue Ellen glanced at Edmund, then meekly returned to the wheelchair.

Hartleigh heard feet thundering down the stairs. "Clear the way, James!"

The two young men preceded the wheelchair out of the chief's office and past the desk sergeant, who looked up to see them hustling across the assembly area and toward the door.

"Hey, you, stop there!"

The sergeant came down from his perch only to find the front door of the station blocked by a wheelchair. By the time the cops had cleared the door, Hartleigh and Sue Ellen had turned the corner and were sitting in the backseat of a taxi.

"James, must we go in so early?" asked his sister. "Haven't you had enough fun for one night?"

"I have," said Hartleigh. "Driver, take us to South Battery!"

And off sped the cab while the two men raced down the street and ducked into the first speakeasy they came across.

Once they made themselves comfortable, James and Edmund stuck their feet out, slouched in their chairs, and sipped their drinks.

Staring at his boots, James said, "It's difficult to apologize for a parent, but I apologize for whatever my father did."

"Don't worry. I've done plenty of stupid stuff when drunk."

"And that's why you don't drink?"

Edmund eyed him, wondering what his sister might've told him. "I learned that I couldn't think straight while drinking and had a horrible freshman year." Edmund shrugged. "Typical boy off the farm being dazzled by big-city lights."

"Tell me about it. I fell for a girl and couldn't get back on post. Several times."

"The post meaning West Point?"

James nodded. "I was crazy for that girl, and she was a long way away." Mary Anne Randolph was who James was thinking about, and in the course of doing so, he considered what Sue Ellen had said. Did Hartleigh and he make a pair? He rubbed at the ring in his pocket.

"I could go for your sister," said Edmund, "given any small amount of encouragement."

"Sue Ellen's got to figure out how she's going to make a marriage work with a husband in a wheelchair."

"At least I gave it my best shot," said Edmund, distracted.

"Edmund, I don't even want to know what that means."

The NC State engineer pulled in his feet, sat up, and leaned on the table. "James, nothing happened. You have my word on that."

"I hope not. You're the former Golden Gloves boxer and would have thoroughly trounced me."

Edmund looked James right in the eye and lied. "I took your sister to the one place where I could most impress her, and while we were up there, I kissed her. You don't really believe anything else happened at one hundred fifty feet over the Cooper, do you?"

"I want to believe you, Edmund, but there are rumors of what is being called the hundred-and-fifty-foot club."

"What's that?" asked Edmund, leaning back in his chair and cultivating an air of nonchalance. "A club for picnickers?"

"No," said James, "that's not what they do at all."

THIRTY

A little more than a month before the dedication, the bridge company completed a booth on the East Cooper side to collect tolls from those coming from or going to Charleston. This meant the end was near for the Randolphs on South Battery, and on the day of the completed toll booth, Elizabeth was polishing silver in the dining room instead of serving afternoon tea.

She sighed. The work never ended, and if she wished her home to be held to a higher standard than an ordinary boarding house, she had to pitch in and help.

The doorbell rang, and Dory brought news that her attorney wished to speak with her.

"You do know where those cards go, don't you?" asked Elizabeth, not looking up from the pitcher she was polishing. "The silver tray on the table near the door."

"Yes, ma'am, but he's here."

Elizabeth looked up. "To leave his card?"

"No, ma'am," said Dory, placing the card on the table. "Mister Ravenel asked to see you."

Elizabeth glanced at the card. "Right now?"

"Yes, ma'am."

"Well, that's not proper, and I certainly hope we've taught you better."

"Yes, ma'am. You want me to send him away?"

"No," said Elizabeth, putting down the pitcher and her Selvyt polishing cloth. "The answer to rudeness is never more rudeness. Please tell Mister Ravenel that I'll be right out, and offer him a glass of iced tea." She glanced through the open dining room window. "It's awfully hot out there."

Elizabeth waited until Dory had served the iced tea, then strolled into the parlor. Before she did, she closed the pocket doors to the room where the engineers slept.

A dormitory. That's what her home had become, with people coming and going without preamble or announcement. And that's why her attorney believed he could show up on her doorstep.

The phone rang, and she answered it. She made a note on the pad before going into the parlor. "Yes. I'll tell her you called."

The attorney stood when Elizabeth entered the parlor and he thanked her for seeing him on such short notice. Ravenel appeared agitated; nervous, apprehensive.

At least, thought Elizabeth, the man's mother had raised him properly. This was not the correct way to pay a call, and in his heart of hearts, attorney Ravenel knew it.

After she was dismissed, Dory took the phone off the hook and stepped down the hall where she could overhear their conversation.

In the parlor, Elizabeth took a seat on the settee and hoped she did not reek of silver polish.

The attorney was a balding, overweight man with tufts of white hair at his ears. He had very dark, bushy eyebrows. "I have an offer on your house."

"But, Mister Ravenel, as I told you before, I have no desire to sell my home. My grandfather built this house as a wedding gift for my grandmother after the original structure caught fire at the beginning of the war."

"But this offer is quite different. The buyer has no interest in occupying the premises."

"Not occupying...Is this another rich Yankee? I can't abide that! The Beales and the Yanceys might've sold out, but I don't care to be included in that group." *Oh, yes, Elizabeth. Stick to your guns, and when the bridge is completed you will find yourself, and your daughter, out on the street. But you'll be able to hold your head high as you march down those steps one last time.*

Ravenel brought out a handkerchief and mopped his forehead. "I'm not making myself clear. You may continue to live here until Hartleigh marries."

"Hartleigh marries. Why should that make any difference?"

"Well, she is of age, and I'm sure there are quite a few young men who have shown an interest, especially with all these new boys in town. The buyer assumes you'll move in with your son-in-law wherever he decides to live."

Ravenel sipped from his iced tea. Elizabeth's glass remained on a glass coaster on the coffee table. Sweating.

This was the quandary with which she struggled: bills paid, head held high, but residing in an entirely different type of neighborhood north of Broad. How could she ever tolerate that?

"Why, if I set such a precedent, there would soon be empty houses up and down the Battery."

Ravenel gulped down more tea, then stuffed his handkerchief in his pocket and got to his feet. "Then I'll take my leave. I'm sorry to have bothered you, but I did think this was the best offer by far."

They were all good offers; anything that allowed her to walk away from her home with dignity—after endorsing over a check to the bank. No one would ever hound her for money again, and no one would know where she had gone. Or care.

Elizabeth looked up from the settee. "Mister Ravenel, may I inquire as to the offer, that is, if you don't mind me asking?"

"Not at all." Ravenel glanced at the hallway and returned to his seat where he whispered, "One million."

"One...million dollars?" Elizabeth made no attempt to lower her voice.

In the hallway, Dory's mouth fell open. To her, it sounded like all the money in the world.

One million dollars! thought Elizabeth. My Lord! And she instantly chastised herself for taking the Lord's name in vain.

But the Lord should forgive her. This was a way out of her financial difficulties.

"Yes," continued Ravenel, "but there's another condition, one which I did not mention since we didn't get that far. There will be no counteroffers. There will be no haggling." Ravenel glanced at the doorway of the parlor. "One million dollars, Elizabeth, take it or leave it."

"So," she said, trying to keep her voice even, "I walk away from my home?"

"With quite a bit of money, yes."

Elizabeth nodded. The engineers had helped make ends meet, but she knew nothing about running a boarding house—there were costs she'd failed to anticipate. She and Hartleigh were already behind, or "in the hole," as Hartleigh had so delicately put it. And here, in one fell swoop, she would no longer lie awake at night wondering where the next dollar would come from.

But she would no longer live in the house where her children had been born; the house to which her late husband had brought her after their honeymoon. With all the memories flashing through her mind, it was hard to judge if this was a good thing or not? Her eyes moistened.

Ravenel chuckled. "You accept this offer and you'll be ahead of the game. You could use the excess to invest in the stock market or in land in East Cooper. Remember what happened to land prices once the bridge over the Ashley was completed."

Elizabeth wasn't so sure. She remembered her conversation with Abigail Mullins, that the North would continue to punish the South, and would do so by picking on South Carolina.

No, she would not invest across the Cooper, but the stock market sounded tempting. Everywhere she went people talked about the market, and they made it seem like anyone could play.

"As you know, one of the richest men in Charleston lives under your roof."

"Who?"

"Why, James Stuart, of course. I'm sure he'd be pleased to give you some picks." Ravenel glanced at the hallway again. "If he does give you a tip or two, don't hesitate to call." The attorney laughed. "You let me know what stocks James Stuart is invested in and you'll never pay another attorney's fee."

"But he's nothing more than an engineer."

"Really? Then how did he pay for that yacht? Actually, I thought Captain Stuart and your daughter—" meaning Hartleigh.

"Oh, no. Nothing ever came of that," said Elizabeth, thinking of Mary Anne.

Ravenel rose to his feet. "Twenty-four hours, Elizabeth. I'm allowed to give you twenty-four hours to consider the offer."

Her head jerked up. "Twenty-four hours?"

"You must give me your answer by . . ." He glanced at his watch. "By this time tomorrow. Well, I'll show myself out."

Leaving the house, the attorney ran into a plain-looking young woman with the most marvelous smile.

"Mrs. Randolph," called Ravenel, ushering the young woman through the front door, "you have another visitor."

Elizabeth found Polly Blount of Missouri standing on her front porch; a cab parked at the curb, its driver leaning against the vehicle and smoking a cigarette.

The two women embraced as the attorney went down the front steps. Finishing the steps, Ravenel turned back to the house. "Don't forget, Mrs. Randolph. I shall call again tomorrow afternoon at this same time."

Elizabeth nodded to Ravenel, then said to Polly, "What a marvelous surprise."

"I've—I've come to see Prescott."

"Of course. Do you know of the accident?"

"Yes. I was hoping I might stay here again. I really don't know anyone else in Charleston."

"Why, of course. Please come in."

"Thank you." Polly waved at the cab.

The driver flicked away his cigarette, rolled off the side of the cab, and began to pull luggage from the trunk.

"You can have your former room back," said Elizabeth, ushering the girl down the hall. "Someone just moved out."

The driver came up the steps with several suitcases and dragging a steamer trunk.

Polly knew the procedure and preceded the cabbie to the second floor. "Man on the floor! Man on the floor!"

The blonde from down the street stuck her head out of one of the bedroom doors. Someone always did whenever there was a man on the floor. The phone rang and the blonde hurried to answer it. She wore a robe and flashed a big smile. In her hand was a powder puff used to darken her shiny rayon stockings.

"How have you been?" she asked into the phone. "Oh, yes, I remember you."

Once the luggage was in the proper room and the cabbie had been paid and tipped, the two women returned to the parlor. Along the way, they passed the blonde on the upstairs phone.

"Oh, I'd like that. No, no, that's not too late."

In the parlor, Polly took a seat on the settee and

patted down her dress. "I've already been to the hospital. When Prescott is released he'll need a place to stay."

"Certainly, but you weren't thinking—"

"Oh, no! It'll take a few days, but I'm sure I'll find something."

"For who?"

"Oh, no!" Polly's face colored. "I wouldn't live with him, though I have considered marrying Prescott so we can live under the same roof."

"Really?" Elizabeth found herself fascinated by how low this girl would stoop. "You have special training as a nurse?"

"I soon will. After the Great War, the hospital maintained its training facility. I know it's not very becoming to be a nurse, but hard times demand sacrifice."

Hartleigh entered the parlor and rushed over to Polly, who rose to meet her. "Oh, I heard you were here!"

The two young women embraced and kissed each other on the cheek. After complimenting each other on how well each other looked, Polly returned to the settee and Hartleigh took a seat in the other Queen Anne chair.

Elizabeth brought her daughter up to date.

"So Prescott intends to remain in Charleston?" asked Hartleigh.

Polly nodded. "This is where the job is."

The Randolph women didn't look reassured.

Polly explained. "Prescott broke his back, not his neck."

"Oh!"

"Oh!"

"I know this is all rather strange, but Prescott needs me."

The Randolph women glanced at each other.

Hartleigh asked, "So what can we do for you?"

"Well, your mother has agreed that I can live here."

"Rent free," affirmed Hartleigh, nodding.

"Hartleigh!"

"Mother, we must."

"And we must pay the bills." Elizabeth smiled. "I'm sure Polly understands."

"Mother, Polly's in town on a mission of mercy."

"Missions of mercy require money, too."

"My father will pay all expenses," said Polly.

Both Randolph women stared at her.

"At first Daddy was skeptical."

"I can imagine," commented Elizabeth.

Hartleigh glanced at her mother, wondering which one of them would have to tell this girl the truth about the man she loved.

Without noticing their concern, Polly rattled on. "Daddy finally realized it was fate. Prescott and I were meant to be together."

The Randolph ladies' heads bobbed in agreement, a reflex action to hide their despire. "Of course, of course."

"But there is a silver lining."

"What's that?" asked the Randolphs, puzzled.

"Prescott could've been killed."

"Oh, yes!"

"How true!"

For a moment, Polly said nothing, just picked at her dress, then: "They say James Stuart was there."

Now it was Elizabeth's turn to glance at her daughter.

"Yes," said Hartleigh, looking at the floor. "He was."

"I was very concerned when I heard about that."

The room went quiet until Hartleigh whispered, "I'm sorry to have to tell you this, Polly, but Prescott went to see James to ask for Sue Ellen's hand."

"Well," said Polly, with an iciness in her voice neither woman had ever heard before, "that explains that."

Hartleigh's head came up. "Explains what?"

"They must've had a terrible row."

"Are you saying James is somehow at fault?"

"Oh, no! I don't know about that."

"Then what?"

Polly fiddled with her dress. "James does have a reputation for being quite able."

Hartleigh leaped to her feet. "That's the most outrageous thing I've ever heard."

"Girls, girls," said Elizabeth. "This borders on gossip and I won't have gossip spread in my house."

"You will pay the full amount for your room and board," said Hartleigh. "Now I will show you to your room."

Polly got to her feet. "I've already been assigned a room by your mother." And the girl from northern Missouri lifted her skirt and strode out of the parlor.

Elizabeth tried to correct her daughter, but Hartleigh was gone, disappearing down the hall and into the rear of the house. Again, the doorbell rang, and this time Dory opened the door to a shoe salesman who followed the runaway into the parlor.

"Sorry to barge in on you like this, Elizabeth," said Nicholas Eaton, Senior, "but I don't like what I'm hearing about my son."

THIRTY-ONE

As Elizabeth greeted Nicholas, Senior, again, she had the urge to rush into the kitchen and whip up a good meal for this man. He was as thin and pale as ever.

"Alas, Mister Eaton, but Nick no longer lives here."

"Beg pardon?" He took a seat in the Queen Anne chair. "And please call me 'Nicholas.' You did when I previously visited."

"Well," said Elizabeth, putting her hands together in her lap, "perhaps you should defer your cordiality until you hear what I have to say. I fear your son tired of living here and found quarters elsewhere."

"Did this have anything to do with the dissolution of his engagement with Abigail Mullins?"

"You'll have to ask your son that, but he did move out the following day."

Senior glanced around the room. "I cannot see the slightest reason why a young man would not want to live here. Why, his dead mother would have completely agreed with the high moral standards to which you hold your guests."

Elizabeth basked in the man's compliment. Now, if she could only reciprocate by moving him into the dining room. There were quite a few leftovers from lunch.

The senior Nicholas pulled out his pipe. "I've probably spent too much time on the road since their mother died."

"You must provide for them."

"Yes," he said, filling the pipe, "but evidently you must be there for motherless children. Unfortunately, I sent them away to boarding school."

"Nicholas?"

He looked up from tamping his pipe. "Yes?"

"When was the last time you've eaten?"

Senior had to think. "There was a meal on the train today, or did I remain in my cabin and catch up on paperwork?"

Elizabeth picked up a silver bell and rang it. "Well, I'm going to do something about that. You are a guest in my home and if I did not feed you, Southern women everywhere would be shamed."

Instead of arguing, Nicholas played along. It was a different world south of the Mason-Dixon Line and it was better to go along to get along.

Dory and Hartleigh arrived. Elizabeth introduced both girls and Dory took the meal order and headed for the kitchen.

Senior had gotten to his feet. "Afternoon, Miss Randolph," he said to Hartleigh.

"Good to see you again, sir. Your son will certainly be surprised."

"Do you know where—"

"Nicholas," said Elizabeth, cutting in, "please don't embarrass my daughter by asking the whereabouts of some young man, even if the young man in question is your son. She might actually know of his whereabouts, and in her current mood, say so."

"Of course."

Hartleigh stared at the floor.

"My daughter will send a servant to locate Captain Stuart, and I can guarantee that she will fulfill that mission with the proper amount of zeal."

Hartleigh's head snapped up and words poured from her mouth. "James is at the bridge. They're joining the two halves together today. When I'm finished, I'm going down to watch them." She paused. "I'll be taking Dory along. She rarely gets to see the bridge, and Alexander has agreed to take us out on *Rising Market*."

"Thank you, my dear. Now please have Pearl send Benjamin to find his father and check on that sandwich for Mister Eaton."

Once Hartleigh had left, Nicholas, Senior, said, "Well, I must say, your daughter looks radiant."

"She's in love."

"Ah, yes, a woman in love. Thankfully, my daughters are married so I'm not as much at risk as you are. I take it you were able to point out the virtues of other men than this James Stuart?"

Elizabeth shook her head. "Sad to say that though many a young man has shown interest—even your son accompanied my daughter to a few dances— James Stuart put those stars in her eyes. It's for this reason that I continue to find myself being a strict enforcer of the rules of decorum."

Nicholas settled back into his seat and put his pipe in an ashtray. "Well, you can depend on me to make sure that others hear of your rules. On more than one occasion I have mentioned you in my travels, how I have found this perfect lady who lives in Charleston, South Carolina."

Benjamin and Alexander found James on the causeway over Drum Island where the temporary scaffolding had been removed. Both sections of the bridge were completed with the exception of pouring the concrete road: two lanes, each ten feet wide. All that would be left to do would be to bring down the riveting cages and dismantle the two cranes.

As they walked through the dust kicked up at the former intersection of America and Lee streets, James listened closely to what Benjamin had to say.

He gave him a dollar and turned to the boy's father. "Where?"

"Mimi's. He says her cook makes the best shrimp and grits in Charleston, so he may still be there. He's paid up for a week."

At the curb, James was taken aback by seeing the family car parked at the curb. Behind the wheel sat Hartleigh.

He hurried over to the Cadillac. "Everything all right?"

"It is now, darling," she said rather breathlessly as she hung out the window on the passenger side.

"Then what are you doing here?"

"Oh, I thought you might need a ride. I'm the one who sent Benjamin to fetch you."

"Well," said Benjamin rather sourly, "you could've given me a ride. Trolleys cost money."

"Boy," cautioned his father, "you'd better watch your tongue. That's a lady you're talking to."

"Hop in the backseat, Benjamin," said James, walking around to the driver's side. "We'll take you home. I'll meet you at the marina, Alexander."

Before he climbed into the car, James glanced around. There didn't appear to be anyone watching, so sliding into the car, he continued toward Hartleigh whose cheek was being offered. James gave her a peck on the cheek. In the rear of the car Benjamin giggled.

James turned the starter and shifted into gear. "We'll drop you at the house."

"No need." Hartleigh smiled warmly. "I'm caught up with my chores."

James made a U-turn in the traffic. The side streets between Meeting Street and the Cooper River were becoming thick with traffic as cleanup took precedent over the building of the bridge. Every hour, a bus disgorged workers, tourists, and the curious.

"Finding Nicholas could take some time," said James.

Hartleigh slipped her hand into his after James had shifted into third. "I have the whole afternoon free. I don't work again until breakfast."

"I wish you didn't work at all."

"Well," said Hartleigh with a sly smile, "there's only one way to solve that problem."

A few minutes later, James pulled up in front of the Randolphs'. "Get the door, Benjamin. By the way, Hartleigh, how did you come by this car?"

"Your father leaves the key over the visor. Didn't you know that?"

"I do now."

Hartleigh picked at James's sleeve. "You know, it's not a crime to spend time with your girlfriend during the day. I am your girl, aren't I, James?"

"Of course."

She continued to pick at his sleeve. There was a stain there she did not recognize. It didn't appear to be blood, but she would be very pleased when this project was completed. *Oh, my, but I'm becoming a regular Abigail Mullins.*

"I thought you might take off the remainder of the day so I packed a picnic lunch. You haven't eaten, have you?"

James glanced at the basket on the backseat. The lid was up, which meant Benjamin had been into the contents. Behind her, the boy opened the passenger-side door.

"No, I haven't."

"You're missing too many meals, James."

"Hartleigh, I work during the day."

She straightened up and her hand came off his arm. "Well, once we're married, I hope you'll come home for supper. There will be others' feelings to consider."

"I realize that your mother will be living with—"

"I meant the children!" And Hartleigh scrambled out of the car, hurried up the sidewalk, and rushed into the house.

James rubbed the pocket with the engagement ring. *Not the right time to ask a girl to marry you. Or reveal where you're headed.*

THIRTY-TWO

At Mimi's, James told Benjamin to stay put.

"Aren't you going to leave me the keys so I can listen to the radio?"

"Busy yourself with the picnic basket. I'm not giving you the keys."

Inside the building a large white man recognized the engineer. They shook hands, and James described Nicholas Eaton.

The large white man pointed up the stairs. "He's with Shelia. Asks for her every time. Three-oh-three."

Houses of ill repute posted bonds the first day of every month, as did blind tigers and the local gambling dens, and automatically forfeited them. It was as John Jacob had told Sue Ellen, there was enough money to go around for everyone.

James knocked on the door, then walked in on the happy couple. Nick and the whore sat at a table overlooking the Ashley. In front of them were steaming plates of shrimp and grits, homemade biscuits, and mugs of hot coffee. The girl pulled up a sheet that had fallen down around her waist and covered her breasts.

"What's this?" asked Nicholas.

Seconds later, James was eating shrimp and grits while Nicholas stood under a cold shower. The whore with the bedsheet wrapped around her pressed Nick's shirt with an iron, and a bootblack called up from the street shined Nicholas's shoes.

From the bathroom, Nick hollered, "He wasn't supposed to arrive until next week."

"Does that mean you're returning to the house?"

Nicholas didn't hear him. "What?"

"Nothing."

James wiped his mouth and stood up as Nicholas came out of the shower. "It beats me why you go to such lengths to keep your father from learning that you patronize bordellos."

"Oh, yeah," said Nicholas, giving the whore a peck on the cheek before slipping into the pressed shirt, "let me know when hypocrisy stops playing a major role in the Stuart family."

Seeing that his son appeared to be quite fit, Nicholas told him to remain on the porch while he hurried down the steps and hailed James Stuart.

"Captain Stuart, if I may."

James stopped on the sidewalk in front of his family's house. Inside, a curtain was pulled back.

James waited for the older man to catch up. "Yes, sir?" Eight years out of the Point he still had to remind himself not to come to attention.

Nicholas, Senior, had to stop to catch his breath. "I'm...Nicholas Eaton's father."

"I know who you are."

Senior looked James over, taking in the dirty boots, jeans, and red shirt. His slouch hat was sweat-stained, and his shirt pockets held a pair of sunglasses.

"I was here when you dropped off Miss Randolph."

James said nothing, but his gaze became more intense.

"You don't understand the anguish you've caused this family, and yet you insist on toying with Miss Randolph's heart—"

"Toying?"

"You Southerners are keen on honor, sir, but if so, where's Miss Randolph's engagement ring?"

"Not that it's any of your business, but Hartleigh and I were waiting for her mother to catch up." Without thinking, James rubbed the pocket of his pants. The ring was still there.

"You really believe Mrs. Randolph will agree to such a union?"

"We hope so."

"Meanwhile, you break the heart of a woman who had to endure your courtship of her twin, Mary Anne."

"Just what business of this is yours?"

Nick stood at the porch railing, gripping it. He couldn't hear what was being said, but he didn't think his father was thanking James for bringing him home.

A police car raced around the corner and screeched to a halt. As James, Nick, and the senior Eaton watched, two officers got out of the car, and after hitching up their utility belts, joined them on the sidewalk.

Jeb Stuart rushed out of his house, down the stairs, and through his front gate. "That's the man who stole my car!"

The cops glanced at the Cadillac, then evaluated Nicholas, Senior.

"Well," asked one of them, "what have you got to say for yourself, mister?"

"Me?" asked Senior. "I've never stolen anything in my life."

On the porch, Hartleigh and her mother joined Nick.

"Not him!" said Jeb, jabbing his finger at James. "Him!"

"But this is your son, isn't it, Mister Stuart?"

"Yes, and I want him arrested. He and his harlot took—"

James punched his father in the face. Jeb stumbled back and sat down on the sidewalk. On the porch the Randolph women gasped and reached for each other's hands. This was that famous Stuart temper. Up to a couple of years ago, the Stuarts had owned warehouses full of liquor; that is, until Jeb began to sample his own product, so, it wasn't long before Jeb was no longer a major bootlegger but the town drunk. Still, the Stuart temper, and family money, kept the authorities at bay.

"Jiminy, Captain Stuart, you sucker punched him."

"He's been warned."

Jeb dabbled at his nose with a handkerchief, then glared up at his son. "Sir, my second will call on you."

"Tell your second to wait until I finish the bridge. I don't have time for your foolishness."

The two cops helped the senior Stuart to his feet.

Once he was upright, Jeb threw off their hands. "Arrest him!"

"You're still pressing charges?"

"You're damned right!"

Nicholas, Senior, realized everything Elizabeth Randolph had told him about James Stuart was true. He glanced over his shoulder and saw Elizabeth shepherding her daughter into the house. A shame the girl had to see this, but maybe it would put an end to her infatuation with this man.

"Mister Stuart," asked one of the cops, "have you forbidden your son to use your vehicle?" The officer knew he had to tread carefully when dealing with those living south of Broad.

"You either arrest him, Officer, or I'll meet him on the field of honor."

"He's drunk," offered James.

"No, no, there'll be no dueling."

"What I'm trying to understand," said the first cop, "is whether you forbade your son the use of your car or not."

"Then arrest him for striking me. You're a witness. Both of you." Jeb gestured at Senior. "As is this man."

James reached over and jerked the Colt from the policeman's holster. Before the other cop could pull his weapon, James put two bullets in the headlamps of the Cadillac, then twirled the pistol on his finger and jammed the weapon back into the cop's holster.

"Meet me on a field of honor, my ass."

"Well," said one of the cops, "I guess for sure you're going to the station now."

THIRTY-THREE

Rachel Belle pulled back sheers that provided a degree of privacy yet allowed a breeze into the house. She saw the commotion down on the sidewalk.

"What in the world is going on down there?"

Laurens joined Rachel at the window. She studied the men on the sidewalk as she rocked her baby.

"Isn't that James's father?"

Dory came over to the window. "Then James better watch out. His father is a bad man."

"Please show a little restraint in your remarks," cautioned Rachel.

The three young women had gathered in the bedroom to rotate the baby among them. The child was colicky and difficult to get down for a nap.

"It's the truth," said Dory.

"That's your opinion," said Rachel.

"No, ma'am, I've had a run-in with him before."

"Please," said Laurens, "let's not turn this into more gossip about the Stuarts."

Sue Ellen came through the bedroom door for her turn with the baby. "More gossip about my family? What do you mean?"

Below them, James planted a fist in his father's face, and Jeb fell back and sat down on the sidewalk.

"Oh!"

"Oh!"

"Wow!"

A tingle ran through Laurens and Rachel. Each had been attracted to James when they had been much younger. Now they felt a little warm.

"What in the world are you looking at?" asked Sue Ellen, joining them at the window.

Her voice trailed off as her friends stepped back, giving her a full view of the street. Then came the two shots from the policeman's pistol and all four girls screamed. The baby began to cry. They ignored him. They were watching as James was led over to a police car. Nicholas, Senior, and Jeb Stuart, holding the handkerchief to his nose, got into the Stuart family Cadillac and went after them. Nick came into view, running across the front yard and climbing into the backseat of the Cadillac.

Rachel started for the door. "I'm going down there."

"I'm going to the jail," said Sue Ellen.

"That's what I meant. We can't allow one of the boys to be carted off to jail. They dispense too much rough justice in that building down on Magazine Street."

At Rachel's remark, Laurens stopped moving toward the door. She stood there, clutching her child.

In the upstairs hallway Rachel used the phone installed so the women would not have to come downstairs to answer it. The phone rang before she could put her hand on it.

Rachel picked up the receiver. "No. She's not here." She depressed the bar, clicking it several times. "Goodness, but I don't think anyone leaves cards anymore."

At her brother's work, she learned that Franklin had already left for the day. She called home. Not there either, but the maid said that her stepmother wished to speak with her.

Rachel hung up.

Laurens came into the hallway, rocking her baby, but could suggest no one. Lawrence was in New York City. "And my father's crippled with arthritis."

All headed downstairs, and on the ground floor they ran into Elizabeth and Hartleigh.

Rachel explained James's predicament.

Feeling guilty from trying to lure James away from work, Hartleigh burst into tears. "What are we going to do? What are we going to do?"

"Well," said Elizabeth, "none of you are leaving this house."

At the raising of the voices, Pearl and her sister appeared in the hallway. Dory had stopped midway down the stairs. Now she took a seat. The phone on the table rang. They all ignored it.

"Pearl," said Sue Ellen, putting on her hat, "would you please send Benjamin to find his father."

"He's at the marina."

"Good, then have him—"

"You cannot send a Negro down to that jail," said Rachel.

Elizabeth raised her voice. "You're not listening to me. None of you are to leave this house."

"Listen, ladies," said Rachel to those gathered in the hallway, "everyone goes to the toilet before we leave, and don't forget your parasol and gloves when we reconvene on the front porch."

"Preposterous!" shouted Elizabeth. Looking for a weak link, she zeroed in on the woman with the baby. "Laurens, I cannot believe you'd take a child to a city jail. Wait until your mother hears of this."

"What about Christian?" asked Hartleigh, wiping tears away.

Rachel shook her head as Sue Ellen picked up the phone and cleared the line. "Christian's on the other side of the river."

But Sue Ellen was able to reach Edmund, whose office was only a few blocks away. He said he would head over to the jail.

Once Sue Ellen hung up, Elizabeth said, "Well, that takes care of that."

Rachel took the phone. "I'll call a taxi."

"Over my dead body," objected Elizabeth.

"Please, Mrs. Randolph—"

"And who do you think the driver is going to believe: me or some boy-crazy girl?"

That gave Rachel pause and she asked the operator to put through a call to the Chase Bakery. Susan Moultrie said she would meet them at the jail.

"And you harbor no ill will against James?" asked Rachel. "I must know before we assemble at the jail."

The baker's daughter replied in the negative.

After hanging up, Rachel said, "Susan will have to bring the baby along. They're really busy."

Hearing this, Laurens returned upstairs to fetch her diaper bag. Dory scooted over on the stairs and watched her go.

"You girls have lost your minds."

"Please, Mrs. Randolph," said Rachel, "I'm trying to think."

"That's what you aren't doing—thinking."

Hartleigh stood at the entrance to the parlor, holding onto the jamb. What could they do? What could they do?

Rachel asked the operator to dial another number.

"No one is to leave this house!" shouted Elizabeth.

"Mother, someone has to do something."

"Then call the sheriff."

Sue Ellen shook her head. "No law enforcement officer would dare trespass in another's jurisdiction."

"I'm calling your parents the moment you leave."

"Mother, stop being irrational. James is in real danger."

Elizabeth turned on her daughter. "I'm being irrational? There's a reason why women aren't police officers, and you actually want to go down there." She shook her head. "You're ladies. You cannot involve yourself with the most common of people."

"This is Rachel Belle," said Rachel into the phone. "May I speak to your daughter?"

While they waited, Elizabeth fumed, and Hartleigh found herself pacing up and down the hall. She saw Laurens coming down with her baby. "You don't have to go, Laurens."

"Of course I do, especially after what I've said about James."

Hartleigh turned to Rachel. "We'll need more cars."

"Hartleigh, you're not to involve yourself in this affair!"

"He's the man I love, and I'm not going to stand around while a bunch of goons beat him to a pulp."

Elizabeth stalked off, only to return. "What will people think? What will people think?"

Over the telephone, Rachel explained James's dilemma. "We need at least two cars."

A name was suggested from the other end of the line.

"I'll call her. Thanks. Yes. In front the Randolphs'."

"I should call the police myself. And once you leave this house I may do just that."

Sue Ellen uttered a sick little laugh. "Good luck, Mrs. Randolph, but if they have my brother down there, none of them will want to miss the fun." And Sue Ellen disappeared into the downstairs bathroom.

When Rachel looked at Laurens, the young mother said, "I went when I was upstairs."

"I tell you this," said Elizabeth, "anyone goes down to that jail will vacate these premises before nightfall."

"Mother, be reasonable."

"No, no, no! You don't understand what you're putting me through." Elizabeth gestured at Rachel, who spoke on the phone with another party. "Why, the parents of the very girls Rachel's calling haven't spoken to me since we took in our first boarders."

Rachel concluded her instructions and hung up. When she turned to Elizabeth, Hartleigh said, "I've got this, Rachel."

"Then we'll meet you at the curb."

"And that's where you'll find your belongings when you return: at the curb."

"Mother, please calm down."

Elizabeth walked down the hallway where the Negroes peered around a corner. "Molly, Pearl, please come here!"

"Mother, don't act this way."

"I can. I sold the house. You'll come home to nothing."

Hartleigh was thunderstruck. "You can't be serious."

Returning from the restroom, Sue Ellen heard the news.

Before she entered the downstairs bathroom, Rachel said, "Hartleigh, we don't need you for this."

"But James does."

"I can't believe you'd abandon me like this," moaned her mother. She wrapped her arms around herself. "You're the most ungrateful child a mother could ever have raised."

"Mother, please stop."

"You think people won't remember your throwing yourself at this boy? You don't think they'll talk. This family will be, if we aren't already, the laughingstock of Charleston. How could I ever live here?"

Hartleigh saw Molly and Pearl moving toward her. The appearance of the two Negroes jarred Hartleigh into a new reality, and she looked around and upstairs as if seeing everything for the first time. This was no longer her home, nor did she care to live here. In the future James would determine where they lived.

Hartleigh's voice turned as cold as her mother's was hot. "Aren't you forgetting something?"

"What?" asked her mother, face twisted into helpless rage.

"You're supposed to be supervising Molly and Pearl so they can leave my bags at the curb when I return from the jail."

THIRTY-FOUR

At the jail, the police chief welcomed James with enthusiasm.

"Captain Stuart, good to have you with us again. I do believe there are several fellows upstairs who've been looking forward to a return match."

"As have I." James was not handcuffed because of his standing in the community.

His father and the two Eatons came through the door, escorted by the desk sergeant.

Holding a handkerchief to his nose, Jeb Stuart gestured at his son. "He sucker punched me, Chief, and since he refuses to meet me on the field of honor, I am compelled to press charges."

The chief looked at his officers.

"It's true, Chief," said one of the cops.

The other officer nodded. "And Captain Stuart discharged a weapon within the city limits of Charleston."

The chief was incredulous. "Now we're charging

people for discharging weapons within the city limits. You'll have to do better than that or all of Charleston will soon be upstairs."

"I saw the whole thing," said Nicholas, Senior. "I'm a witness to Captain Stuart striking his father."

"And you are?"

Senior told the chief who he was and what he had seen.

"James was provoked," said Nick.

Senior shot his son a severe look. He did not appreciate being contradicted by his son, especially in public. "I was there."

"You don't know what you saw."

"Then you are without the least bit of common sense, despite any kind of degree you've earned."

"Folks," said the police chief, clapping his hands together, "this case will be settled in a court of law, not in my office."

"I'll post the bail," said Edmund Hall, the last to arrive.

The chief eyed this newcomer. "Don't I know you?"

Edmund gestured at James. "I'm engaged to his sister."

This was news to James, and his father.

"What the devil are you talking about? I have not agreed to betroth my daughter." Jeb eyed Edmund. "You're not one of those damned Yankees come down here to build the bridge, are you?"

"I'm from Raleigh, Mister Stuart, and I'm going to marry your daughter."

"Over my dead body."

"Edmund is a crack shot, Father," said James, smiling, "and I can't stop you from meeting *him* on a field of honor. Me...I simply wouldn't show up."

Jeb drew himself up. "Then you, sir, are a coward."

"Hey," said the chief of police, "I do the threatening around here." To the officers who had arrested James, he said, "Take Captain Stuart upstairs."

"You can't do that!" shouted Edmund. "James should be allowed to call his attorney."

"I know his attorney. It's John Patrick Grace." The chief looked at his sergeant. "Where do people get these crazy ideas?"

"It's those movies," suggested the desk sergeant. "Talkies will be the ruin of civilization."

To Edmund, the chief said, "Can you imagine how much time it would take if we served up justice on a platter?" He studied the engineer. "I know this bird from somewhere. Keep them both on ice until I figure out from where."

Edmund seized Eaton's arm before being led away. "Don't let them do this, Nick. Last time I got out of here by the skin of my teeth."

"Now I remember!" thundered the chief. "And put them in different cells."

Nick turned on his father. "James wouldn't strike anyone unless it was a point of honor."

"You're one to talk about honor. You led Abigail on."

"Is that what this is all about?"

"You broke that girl's heart."

"I'll break your nose." And Nick punched his father in the face.

The chief laughed. "Boy, is it fun watching you south of Broad people mix it up." He threw an arm out, pointing to the hallway. "Take this young pup upstairs with the rest of them."

At the nearest speakeasy, Jeb Stuart and Nicholas Eaton drowned their sorrows in drink. Senior had pieces of a napkin stuck in his nostrils and found it difficult to swallow.

Jeb touched his injured nose. "Gave that boy every opportunity and this is how he repays me."

Nicholas, Senior, placed his glass to his nose. That helped. At least it'd stopped bleeding. "You won't get any argument from me. MIT is an expensive school."

Since the federal government had paid for his son's education, Jeb didn't think this was the time or place to have a full-blown discussion on the price of tuition.

"Not to offend," said Nicholas, "but the impression I get is that your son is some sort of talented rogue."

"That he is, Mister Eaton, that he is, and on occasion, he makes his mother and me proud."

"'Nicholas' please."

"Then Nicholas it is," said Jeb, raising his glass.

The glasses clinked together.

"What shall we do about our sons?"

Jeb pulled a timepiece from a vest pocket. "Oh, give them another half hour. They should be finished with them by then."

"Finished with them?" Nicholas put down his glass.

"This isn't the first time James has tangled with the locals. The chief of police and his boys have some evening up to do."

It took about two seconds for Senior to understand what Jeb meant . . . which meant his son knew exactly what he was doing by punching him in the nose. What in the world would generate such loyalty to a couple of boys from the Carolinas?

Senior slid off his stool. "If you don't mind, sir, there's something I need to take care of."

Jeb gestured over his shoulder. "John's behind that curtain."

"Yes, yes," said Nicholas, nodding. "That'll certainly do as well as any other reason."

The blonde and the brunette drove like crazy—terrifying Laurens, who clutched her baby with one arm, the other outstretched to brace herself for the impending disaster—and arrived minutes after Jeb Stuart and Nicholas, Senior, had sauntered off to the speakeasy.

"Where's the chief?" demanded Rachel.

She did not wait for the desk sergeant to step down from his perch but pushed her way through two officers emerging from the rear of the building. The officers made way. This gave the other women access to the rear of the building.

"Miss! Miss!" shouted the desk sergeant, running after them. "Do you have an appointment?"

Rachel was followed through the door by Sue Ellen, Hartleigh, Laurens with her baby, the brunette who lived down the street, and Susan Moultrie with her child. The two officers who had stepped aside tried to stop the second wave. This second wave included the blonde and the mother of the children James and Franklin had walked to school, then came Pearl, Molly, Benjamin, and Chloe.

"What's going on here?" asked the chief as women began to pour into his office. The big man scrambled to his feet.

"Chief," said Rachel, after introducing herself, "we need your help."

The chief had no idea what this woman wanted, but she was a Belle of Charleston. "Whatever I can do, ladies." He wasn't sure if his office could hold all these women but somehow it did.

Last one into the room was the desk sergeant, squeezing his way along the wall and trying not to bump into anyone. "Sorry, Chief, but I couldn't stop them."

The chief smiled all around. "Nothing to worry about, Sergeant." Still, for the life of him he could not understand why all these women were here— even a colored gal with her children.

Once the room fell quiet, the chief asked, "Now what can I do for you ladies."

"You have James Stuart in here."

The chief nodded. "And also Edmund Hall and Nicholas Eaton."

"That's why we're here."

Overhead, there was a thump, followed by several shouts and a scream.

The chief glanced in the direction of the stairs. "Ladies, if you will excuse me, I need to see about this."

When everyone looked toward the stairs, they saw policemen running past the door with billy clubs in their hands.

"Chief," said Rachel, "before you go, please consider this."

Squeezing through the crowd, the chief asked, "Yes?" He stopped at the door.

"Twenty minutes ago we were busy with our lives."

"And I'm pleased you took the time to come down and air your complaints, but first, there's something I must attend to."

"Think about it, Chief," repeated Rachel, "only twenty minutes ago we were going about the business of our lives."

"I don't understand. Why you are telling me this?"

"Because all of us, including the Negroes, are registered voters. Actually, many of us worked in the last voter registration drive among women of both races."

And for this reason, it wasn't long before Edmund, Nick, and James were reunited with their women. The chief knew that John Patrick Grace had been voted out of office by ignoring the women's vote in the last mayoral election.

Hartleigh threw herself into James's arms. He had a bruise over one eye, but otherwise appeared to be intact. Sue Ellen had the same reaction when she saw Edmund Hall, who sported a cut to the back of his head. A bandage had been hastily applied before Edmund had been brought into the chief's office. Nicholas wandered in, dazed, that is, until Rachel kissed him.

Nick smiled at his father, who had reappeared at the station with pleas for his son's release. "Father, this is Rachel Belle, Abigail's competition."

Rachel slapped Nick on the shoulder. "Watch what you say, Nick. I'm an engaged woman." She pulled a glove off and held out her hand for all to see. "Christian asked me last night and we went straight to see my father. Daddy's still trying to get a grasp on having a son-in-law from Dairyland, Wisconsin."

Everyone had to see the ring, even the chief, the desk sergeant, and Nicholas, Senior, who said he did not want his son charged. It had all been an unfortunate misunderstanding. Some of the biggest smiles were worn by Molly and Pearl, who, unbeknownst to anyone, were about to turn in their resignations.

"No charges should be filed against my boy either." Jeb shrugged. "He has a good heart."

Nicholas, Senior, evaluated the man's son. "I'd agree with you, Jeb, but only if James stops upsetting the Randolphs."

James opened his mouth to protest but was drowned out by all the women speaking up for him, touting "all the wonderful things" James had done for their families.

Susan Moultrie cleared her throat, and Rachel Belle told everyone to give her the floor.

"You know who I am," said Susan, bouncing her baby boy in her arms to keep him distracted. "My husband was one of the sandhogs who died last Christmas."

There were sounds of condolences on everyone's lips.

"If anyone should harbor any ill will against James, it should be me, but I don't feel that way and neither does my family. James Stuart is welcome in our home anytime."

Hartleigh gave Susan a sideways hug.

"Do you love this girl, Captain Stuart?" asked Nicholas.

"Yes, sir, I do."

"Then what are you waiting for?" asked Senior. "Make her an honest woman."

James looked around. The room had fallen silent. He looked at Hartleigh, a girl he believed to be more beautiful and capable than any girl in Charleston. His father grinned at his discomfort.

"Well, James," asked Rachel, "are you going to carry that engagement ring around in your pocket forever?"

He turned to her. "You know about the ring?"

"Everyone knows about the ring."

"Proposal, proposal!" shouted the crowd.

The chief could only smile. It would appear that the inmates had finally taken over the asylum.

A great cheer went up when James went down on one knee and fumbled in his pocket for the ring.

After the incident at the city jail, everyone returned home to find Elizabeth Randolph supervising the loading of two steamer trunks, three suitcases, and an overnight bag into a cab parked at the curb.

"Mother," asked Hartleigh, almost in tears, "you're actually throwing me out?"

Susan Moultrie had parted ways with them, as had Laurens, who asked to be dropped off at her mother's house. Hartleigh, James, Rachel, Sue Ellen, Edmund, and Nick met Elizabeth on the front porch.

"You win, my dear, I'm leaving. Skedaddling."

"Mother, all I ever wanted was for you and me"—she glanced at James—"and my husband to live here together." She wanted to show her mother her ring but didn't think this was the time or the place.

Elizabeth gave James an icy glare. "I'll never live in Charleston again. I'm no longer accepted, so, like some rich Yankee, I'm off to see the world." She gestured at the trunks and suitcases being loaded at the curb. "This is all I need from Charleston."

The runaway appeared on the porch dressed to the nines and carrying her own suitcase.

"Dory has agreed to travel with me. And though

I'm leaving, I know I upheld the highest standards of Charleston society under the most bitter of circumstances."

On the most momentous day of her life, for a second time, Hartleigh burst into tears: once out of joy, the other out of despair.

She clutched at her mother. "Oh, please don't go! Please don't do this! I wouldn't know what to do without you."

Elizabeth returned the hug, and then held her daughter out where she could see her. "You've done pretty well the last couple of years, while I've sat in my bedroom and felt sorry for myself."

Hartleigh wiped the tears away. "Mother, you've made significant contributions to our boarding house."

"And always reluctantly, as it created even more of a chasm between me and the people with whom I grew up." Elizabeth looked down the street in the direction of High Battery.

Her mood became more upbeat when she turned back to her daughter. "Don't worry about me, child. I'll be back from time to time to check on you, but I doubt you'll be living here, so make sure the neighbors have your new address."

"Mother, you're breaking my heart."

"Not like Charleston broke mine." Again, Elizabeth hugged her daughter. "You have all your friends. Besides, the terms of the sale allow you to remain in this house until you marry." She smiled wickedly at James. "So pick well when you choose."

"Actually," said James, returning her smile, "the terms of the sale are that Hartleigh can live here as long as she cares to."

It was a moment before realization dawned on Elizabeth. "You purchased my house! You really are a snake." Sneering at him, she added, "What other choice does my daughter have but to marry you to keep the home she loves?"

"The deed is in Hartleigh's name, Mrs. Randolph, not mine. Hartleigh can marry anyone she cares to."

"Until you and John Patrick Grace figure a way to finagle it away from her."

And Elizabeth Randolph marched down the steps, out to the taxi parked at the curb, and out of their lives.

Hartleigh followed her to the edge of the porch. "Mother, please don't go! I'll give you the house. I'll . . ." She looked at James.

"Transfer the deed into your name."

"Yes, yes. I'll transfer the deed into your name!"

When her mother did not stop, Sue Ellen leaned over and whispered, "Go after her."

Rachel agreed, nodding. "She's the most difficult woman I have ever dealt with, but she's still your mother."

Hartleigh turned to James. "You'd live here with her?"

"With her, without her. Wherever you wish; this house, another house. I just want to live with you."

Hartleigh looked at the curb where Nicholas, Senior, was ushering her mother into the rear of the cab. Senior followed Elizabeth and Dory inside, and from the car, everyone heard Elizabeth say, "That is all well and good, Nicholas, but first we'll have to fatten you up a bit." And Elizabeth Randolph leaned over to where she could make eye contact and smiled at her daughter.

On the porch, Hartleigh turned to her fiancé. "James, I need to ask you a question about my sister."

"You were right, my dear. I was afraid to be around you because you reminded me of Mary Anne."

"And now?"

"I'm afraid not to be around you."

Hartleigh took his shirt in both hands and pulled him close. "What changed your mind?" she asked with a lazy smile.

He, too, smiled as he took her into his arms. "The night Artie Moultrie died I began to take stock of Mary Anne's dreary little twin and her many attributes."

"I'm not sure that's the correct answer, but once we're married we can work on it."

EPILOGUE

The great Cooper River Bridge opened on August 8, a little more than three months before the great stock market crash of 1929. The celebration would last from Thursday through Sunday, and when three couples married at the foot of the new bridge, they soon found they could not leave town. Nor did they wish to. There was just too much going on: parades, automobile and motorboat races; fireworks exploded over the city and the celebratory parade not only crossed the new bridge—where several vehicles stalled at its height—but continued up the Coastal Highway through Georgetown, ending the parade in Conway.

Immediately, Charlestonians began calling the Coastal Highway, the Washington Highway, and dances were held at the pavilions on the Isle of Palms and Sullivan's Island. The city even used the opportunity to open a new grass-field airport out near the old phosphate plant.

And in the midst of this celebration, Rachel found Hartleigh sitting at a table on the second-story front porch overlooking the Battery. Her friend wore a robe and slippers and studied a pad, the eraser of her pencil tapping against her teeth. Hartleigh's hair needed a good combing. In contrast, Rachel had dressed for the day, her hair perfectly coiffeured.

"Good morning."

Hartleigh gestured at the silver pot with her pencil. "Have some coffee." There was also toast.

Rachel poured a cup, then refreshed Hartleigh's. Once seated, she mixed the proper proportions of cream and sugar in her cup. "What are you working on?"

"A list of dos and don'ts for the household staff."

"Didn't your mother have a similar list?"

Hartleigh looked up from the pad. "Yes. I guess she did." And the pad went sailing over the railing into the front yard.

Rachel laughed. "Your mother had some good qualities, too. After all, she did keep this house running when I left after bopping Christian over the head for coming upstairs."

"And you almost lost Christian when James evicted him."

"Honey, that's why I moved back home. I didn't want anything standing in the way of Christian leaving his card, if he cared to call."

Hartleigh stared at her. "I swear but you are the most devious woman I know."

"My grandmother always said: 'Husbands bring home the bacon, but wives figure how far it will go, and where.'"

"This, the grandmother who turned out to be a Yankee?"

Rachel flashed a knowing smile. "Might've been, might not have been." She held up her hands. "Look, no gloves." Rachel lowered her hands. "You'll be responsible for how your family is regarded in Charleston. You didn't exactly marry the most sociable of men."

Hartleigh held up a hand of her own, the one with the rings. "Know why James had this in his pocket? It was meant for my sister."

"Has that man no fear or is he just plain stupid? Imagine, sharing information like that with a new bride." She sipped from her cup.

"We agreed not to have any secrets."

"Very un-Southern of you, if you ask me."

They sipped coffee and watched the cars go by. In the harbor, boats left the marina and headed for the new bridge.

"This is what this porch was meant for," said Rachel, sighing. "You could watch the sun come up in the morning."

"We did."

"Oh, that's the reason for your disheveled appearance?"

Hartleigh tightened her robe and brushed back her hair. She glanced at the door leading to her bedroom. "Truth is, I might be called back into service shortly."

"I think Christian is trying to set some sort of record. Did you hear Sue Ellen last night?"

"I was asleep."

"Talk turkey, Hartleigh. We newlyweds must stick together."

"Sorry, but I won't speak ill of my new sister-in-law. Did I tell you that I received a letter from my mother? She's living in Boston and has enrolled Dory in a finishing school."

"That farmer's daughter attending a finishing school? I wouldn't be that child for all the money in the world."

"Mama said she'll establish a scholarship in the name of Mary Anne if Dory successfully graduates."

"Perhaps your mother is ready to forgive and forget."

"I don't know. The letter was addressed to me under my maiden name."

"Maybe she doesn't know about the wedding."

"It was on *Metrotone News*. I've gotten letters from all over because I was part of a triple wedding."

"So that's what all that mail is stacked up at my house. This must be the strangest honeymoon in recorded history."

"You know, Rachel, I can't leave until everyone moves out and the new staff is properly trained, but you and Sue Ellen can leave anytime."

"Wouldn't miss this for the world. Three couples honeymooning on the Battery in the same house. That'll get tongues wagging. Besides, Christian wants to go with Edmund to a few of the boxing matches."

"If James hadn't sold *Rising Market*, we could've all sailed off into the sunset."

"Who bought *Rising Market*? I never heard."

"Alexander."

Rachel laughed. "So, James and Alexander rode the stock market to riches."

"Enough to pay for this house, but I fear we, like many Southerners, are now land-poor."

Rachel looked over Battery Park. "Well, there are worse places to be stuck." After sipping from her cup, she took cigarettes and a lighter from her purse and lit her first cigarette of the day.

Letting out a smoke-filled breath, she said, "Daddy couldn't stand hearing about James's good fortune in the stock market. He finally went down to E.A. Pierce and opened an account. No one could talk him out of it. Not Mother, not me, and certainly not Franklin. Daddy's already made several thousand dollars and never lets us forget it."

"James got out of the market."

"To purchase this house."

"No. Way before that."

"But he could've stayed in and made more . . ." Rachel looked up Murray Boulevard as if seeing Battery Park for the first time. "Good lord, wait until this gets around the neighborhood."

"I think it already has. Our calendar is filling up pretty fast."

"Oh, no," said Rachel, holding a hand to her forehead. "I need to go home and count my invitations. In the past, fathers have given homes to daughters who wished to live south of Broad, but for a groom to . . ."

Her voice trailed off as they stared over Charleston harbor; Hartleigh's heart filled with love, Rachel shell-shocked.

There was a shout from the street, and the blonde and the brunette strolled by on the arms of Nicholas Eaton and Franklin Belle. All of them waved, and Franklin saluted them with his walking stick; then the four young people joined the throngs stretching their legs on the rock wall of the Battery. Over twenty thousand people were in town, and every one of them seemed to own a Brownie camera.

The harbor was filled with all sorts of watercraft, including *Rising Market*. Molly, Pearl, and the children waved as they sailed past. A photographer appeared from out of nowhere and snapped a picture of the two women sitting on the porch.

"Everyone thought my brother would get around to asking for your hand," said Rachel, "but he never did. Then James returns to Charleston and your goose is cooked."

Hartleigh nibbled at a piece of toast. "I don't know. There were fits and starts along the way."

"The point I'm making is that my family worries too much about what people think. The Stuarts don't. They go after what they want, and they usually get it."

For some reason the comment made Hartleigh feel warm all over. And safe.

"So why shouldn't that apply to Sue Ellen? Did anyone see this coming, you know, her interest in Edmund Hall? I know there were the double dates with your brother, but still . . ."

Hartleigh had to agree. "Sue Ellen's my sister-in-law, and I love her to death, but I don't see how a flapper marrying a teetotaler is going to work."

"Sue Ellen forgets when she drinks too much."

"Really?"

"Honestly, Hartleigh, now that you're rid of this boarding house, you need to pay more attention to what's going on in the world around you."

"Mother thought we'd never fit in again."

"Oh, honey, a triple wedding on the day they opened the bridge, and we all married men who built that bridge. Who wouldn't want to include us in their circle?"

Hartleigh gestured at the photographs being

snapped from the street below. "They were out in front of the house yesterday, even one from the *Savannah Morning News*. Now why would anyone care about a family in Charleston if they lived in Savannah?"

"Because we're celebrities. Peggy Mitchell, who scandalized Atlanta by being the first woman to write a newspaper column, says people can't get enough gossip."

"About celebrities?"

"Of which you and I are minor players on the stage of life."

"I don't think I care for that."

"Then keep your head down."

Rachel took a final drag on her cigarette and snubbed it out. "In a few weeks, Christian wants to take me up to Wisconsin to meet all the relatives. I'll probably be the only brunette in the room. Anyway, I thought I might learn a thing or two from you before I go."

"Learn from me?"

"Like how to get things done without appearing to be bossy."

Hartleigh chuckled. "If Abigail Mullins was an example, it would appear that Yankee women are treated as equals by their men."

"What a horrible thought," said Rachel, pushing the ashtray away.

"Yes," said Hartleigh. "Everyone knows men were put on earth to serve women."

Rachel looked at her, quizzically.

Hartleigh smiled. "I had a grandmother, too."

Sue Ellen came out of Hartleigh and James's bedroom, closing the door behind her. "Oh, there you are. I see my brother's still asleep." She sat down and reached for the coffee. "I hope you didn't mind me coming through this way."

"Not this time, I don't."

Sue Ellen pulled back the hand reaching for the coffee, but when both of her friends smiled, she picked up the pot and poured a cup of coffee.

After that, she lit a cigarette, leaned back in her chair, and stretched. "This is the life."

"Until you have babies," said Rachel. "Then where are the men?"

"They can learn," suggested Hartleigh.

"Really? I can't see James Stuart changing a diaper."

Sue Ellen nodded in agreement. "Not my brother."

"Then I'll have to work on that."

Sue Ellen sat up, wrapped her arms around her knees, and lowered her voice. "I overheard them talking last night. They don't know that I know."

"Know what?" asked Rachel.

"Who is this?" asked Hartleigh. "Our husbands?"

"Yes. They have another pool going."

"A pool? What for? The bridge is finished."

"No, no, this pool is made up of contributions by our husbands, you know, like a bet."

"Betting on what?" asked Rachel.

"On which one of us has the first baby."

Rachel and Hartleigh could not believe what they were hearing. They glanced at each other.

"Say that again?" asked Rachel.

"You heard me," said Sue Ellen. "The first one of us who gives birth is the winner of all the money in the pool."

"Those scoundrels!" Rachel shifted around in her chair. "No wonder they've been so attentive."

"I thought they were carried away by our wedding vows."

"Evidently not," replied Sue Ellen to Hartleigh.

"What do you expect?" asked Rachel, practically sneering. "They're men."

The table went quiet as the women considered the many shortcomings of men: Sue Ellen puffing away on her cigarette, Rachel sipping from her coffee cup, and Hartleigh staring into her lap.

Finally, Hartleigh looked up and asked. "Just how much money is in this pool?"

About the Author

Steve Brown is the author of the Belle family saga, which begins when Catherine and Nelie Belle arrive in Charles Towne just in time for Nelie to be kidnapped by Blackbeard and carried off to the Outer Banks. A century and a half later, and before the outbreak of the Civil War, the sixth generation of the family owns a huge rice plantation up the Cooper River; Franklin Belle goes off to West Point, his brother, Lewis, to the Citadel. Fifty years following that, three old maids, descendants of Catherine Belle, take in an orphan, a victim of the moonshine feuds in the Carolina foothills. Almost fifteen years later, the events related in this story occur, and during the sixties, Ginny Belle, thirteenth-generation Charlestonian, spends her summers on Pawleys Island where she and her girlfriends go to meet boys and dance.

The Pirate and the Belle
The Belles of Charleston
The Old Maids' Club
Charleston's Lonely Heart Hotel
Carolina Girls

BIBLIOGRAPHY

The Buildings of Charleston
Jonathan H. Poston

Charleston! Charleston!
The History of a Southern City
Walter J. Fraser, Jr.

Charleston: A Historic Walking Tour
Mary Preston Foster

The Illustrated Encyclopedia of Costume and Fashion
Jack Cassin-Scott

The Early Architecture of Charleston
Albert Simons and Samuel Lapham, Jr.

The Great Bridge
David McCullough

The Great Cooper River Bridge
Jason Annan and Pamela Gabriel

Great Bridge Builders and the Spanning of America
Henry Petroski

Isle of Palms
Wendy Nilsen Pollitzer

Last Call: The Rise and Fall of Prohibition
Daniel Okrent

A Review of the Cooper River Bridge
John P. Grace

A Short History of Charleston
Robert Rosen

South Carolina: A History
Walter Edgar

The South Carolina Encyclopedia
Edited by Walter Edgar